The Genius of the World

6/23/00

For Gene,
Thanks so much for your support.

The GENIUS of the WORLD

Alice Lichtenstein

ZOLAND BOOKS
Cambridge, Massachusetts

First edition published in 2000 by
Zoland Books, Inc.
384 Huron Avenue
Cambridge, Massachusetts 02138

PUBLISHER'S NOTE
This book is a work of fiction. Names, characters, places, and incidents are either the product of the author's imagination or are used fictitiously. Any resemblance to actual events or persons, living or dead, is entirely coincidental.

Some of the material regarding the discovery of the nuclear spin of sodium is based on material in John S. Rigden's *Rabi: Scientist and Citizen* (Basic Books, Alfred P. Sloan Foundation Series, 1987).

FIRST EDITION

Book design by Boskydell Studio
Printed in the United States of America

06 05 04 03 02 01 00 8 7 6 5 4 3 2 1

This book is printed on acid-free paper, and its binding materials have been chosen for strength and durability.

Library of Congress Cataloging-in-Publication Data

Lichtenstein, Alice, 1958–
The genius of the world : a novel / Alice Lichtenstein. — 1st ed.
p. cm.
ISBN 1-58195-018-7
1. Grandfathers — Fiction. 2. Scientists — Fiction. 3. Buddhists — Fiction. 4. Death — Fiction. I. Title.

PS3562.I315 G46 2000
813'.6 — dc21 99-089713

In Memoriam
Tilopa (1954–1976)

And for my family

ACKNOWLEDGMENTS

I am grateful to the MacDowell Colony and the New York Foundation of the Arts for their generous support of this work.

Many angels have helped me in the writing of this book. Melanie Rae Thon, Carolyn Wolf Gould, Marta Nichols, Liz Huntington and Charlotte Zöe Walker all read early drafts of the manuscript and made invaluable suggestions. I am indebted to Robb Forman Dew, Barbara Epstein, and Miriam Altshuler for their deep generosity in responding to the work of a first novelist. I also thank Derek Walcott, Laura Miller, Kate Finin-Farber, Michael Bordinger, Maura Ellyn, Anne Pollack, Cathy Schen, Andrea Modica, Reuven Ferziger, Tony Eprile, Agnes Jaffe, the Bercovitz family, Dr.'s O. and K. for their friendship and support. And Alicia Olmo, for peace of mind. Finally, my deepest thanks to Jim Bercovitz, husband, critic, dear friend — the one who is always there.

CONTENTS

FOUR
Devotion

ONE

The Genius of the World

PHOEBE, 1976

This is my theory: everyone everywhere is lying almost all the time. I am anyway.

Example. Wrote to Ira today. Told him I was happy. Told him I was beginning to see the Buddha nature, the good, in everyone and this was making me feel good.

Bullshit. I'm not seeing the Buddha nature. I'm seeing everyone's alive and oblivious to the privilege. I see that they're alive and he's going to die. I can't forgive all these blind people; can't forgive Ira for going about so calmly as if it's all a lie.

I DON'T WANT YOU TO DIE. That's what I should've written.

No one here to talk to. No one. Joanne tries, but I can't stand her tucked up in her desk chair like a cat, elbows on the desk and those reading glasses with the narrow rectangles reducing me in their lenses. Extending her forearms, she clasps her hands, leans her elbows on her propped thighs and peers at me over the rims. I swear it's some shrink trick she learned from her father. So obvious, so fake. She's only nineteen.

"How *is* your brother?" she asks in that whispery, throaty voice she's been cultivating all semester ("People tell me I sound like Greta Garbo," she says. In your dreams).

That's my cue to cry, I know. To eject myself into her waiting arms, pay her her due. I stay put. *None of your damn business.* Feeling so evil, so angry I could sink a dagger. *Buddha nature, huh.*

And she sits there still blinking, still compassionate in that clinical way of hers. Still gazing, waiting for me to break. Which I won't.

Finally she pulls her arms in, settles back in her chair. "If you need anything, you know I'm here."

I hold my silence as she swivels back to her desk, back to her open textbook. We're both taking Bio 1. Final's tomorrow morning.

I hate her perfect handwriting, her perfect notes, her line of admirers salivating down the corridors, panting in her wake.

How can she help me?

This morning my father called from San Francisco to tell me they've found a new tumor in Ira's brain.

After my father told me the news, a period of silence elapsed when all I could hear was light static falling across the wires. Last night I dreamt I was wheeling Ira down shiny corridors, metal doors opening one after another, just as we reached them, just as it seemed we were about to crash.

Should I fly out there? I asked.

Not necessary, my father told me in a smoothed-over voice. He, Michael Stein, would stay at the hospital until the tests were completed. That could be a few days or maybe longer. Would I be all right until then?

I sat on the bed. I could almost see my father hunched over the pay phone in the hospital, his address book open on the ledge in front of him. You can always count on my father to be efficient like this, to make all the difficult calls. He had flown to California for a business trip, not specifically to see Ira, and then this crisis had happened.

Are you all right, honey?

Of course, I snapped. I'm not the one with cancer.

I remember when my brother first announced his new name. My father was listening on the phone, his lips a small volcano of concern. He was agreeing to something with the deep drawling syllable he used when listening to a business client. It was a syllable that didn't actually confer agreement so much as the fact that he was listening. A tinge of skepticism in that purr.

Suddenly, he was motioning. "Pencil," he hissed. "Paper." He sounded irritated. "Say again," my father said into the receiver. "Spell it."

And so we hung on each letter of the new name, not knowing at all what we were piecing together until we heard him say, "Milarepa. I don't know if I can always remember it, but I'll try."

Ira was seventeen then. Sixteen when he left home for Berkeley. Occasionally, we'd get a postcard, the tourist kind, picturing the Golden Gate, stretched disappointingly orange across the bay, or the impossible S-curves of Lombard Street. His messages in flailing scrawl told us he was going to free school, selling *Berkeley Barbs* on the corner of Euclid and Hearst and living with a woman named Rita, ten years older than he.

Then, out of the blue, he'd found a guru named Rinpoche. He was leaving school; he was leaving Rita.

"As far as I'm concerned, he'll always be Ira," my father announced when he'd hung up the phone.

I felt sorry for him. As you would for a captain sinking bravely with his ship. I was more practical than my father. I knew Ira better. "I'm calling him what he wants to be called." I wasn't going to be jettisoned easily.

When I saw Ira last summer at his ashram, he'd changed completely from the brother I knew. Before, he seemed to blaze along a trajectory, paying no heed to the trail of fire behind, those falling sparks that would scorch the known landscape to make way for another. Acid-tongued, brilliant, he preached Revolution.

Now he spends hours each day in meditation. When he isn't meditating, he's busy doing chores: polishing the altar brass, sweeping the temple room, writing prayer sticks. I followed him around like a dog. I felt completely lost in the place unless I was with him. Even with him I felt lost.

I kept wanting to ask, What are you feeling? What made you change?

Instead, I sat beside him for hours until my legs grew numb and my head hurt. We sat in front of the moon mandala, a yellow circle of felt glued onto a black square of felt. Ira told me that if you're enlightened you see the Buddha in the center of the moon. I saw only black dots.

At ten o'clock, the snack bar's almost empty. The boy studying behind the counter doesn't look up when I place three brownies and a slice of apple pie on my tray. He doesn't notice when one brownie, then another, disappears into my knapsack. A voice in my head sings a thin song which I try to ignore: *Why're you doing this? Who are you?* And the response: *Don't know. Just feels with everything wound up so tight, only stealing and eating can get me to the place where everything's blank.*

Thank God the booth in the far corner is empty. I slide my tray across the Formica table. Then, settling myself onto the bench, I unwrap the brownies, chewing them down so quickly I can't taste them. For a second I think, *Save the pie for later.* Pseudonormal thought. But I devour the pie, too.

Back on line, I see someone's put out butterscotch brownies and blueberry pie. The boy behind the counter's disappeared, so I put two brownies in my sack and pay only for the blueberry pie.

All my life Dad's told me college is a "four-year interim devoted to the mind." He says he never worked harder or learned more than he did as an undergraduate. This scares me because he works all the time anyway. How could he have worked any harder? How could I ever work as hard as he?

I hate college. Boys hurling footballs down the halls. Girls talking about how to lose their virginity. I stay in my room, hermit, until one night, the boy next door knocks on my door and asks me point-blank if I know everyone in the dorm hates me.

I didn't. I'm devastated.

Legs. Shit. Why can't I ever find privacy? I've come to think of this as *my* bathroom, four stories underground, tucked away in the back corner of the library floor, past shelves and shelves of old, unread books, books that terrify me. All this stuff I'll never know, never understand, millions and millions of words, dead now between the rotting leather covers.

I can see Grandpa Abbey, flexing his tented fingers, beetling his brows: *What did you learn this semester?*

Grandpa Abbey, who doesn't suffer fools gladly, who says that women are incapable of great science, who is paying for my education though *I* am a fool.

Nothing, I would like to tell him.

Once I loved books. Now they make me feel like I'm standing in a vast cemetery, dead, dead, dead, and futile. No one will read these books a mile under. Trapped in cages. Dimly lit. Not a step stool in sight.

But back here safe, unused (I thought), empty (I thought), a bathroom, a woman's bathroom, the serif letters pasted onto a pane of smoky glass. Ancient decals rimmed in black and gold. WOMEN. Fooling no one, I thought. No one used this bathroom. Except me, I thought. This is where I come to void everything. My cubicle of peace and torture, *my chamber.*

The legs, of course, have feet. Hiking boots, corduroy cuffs. A knapsack sagging against the center wall. A student. Like me. Desperate. Like me.

The toilet flushes in a roar as I duck into the empty stall. Watching from the crack, I see a woman, not a girl, a graduate student, perhaps, thin as a stick, her corduroys sagging in the rear.

The woman bends to the mirror and coughs. *Gathering courage to face those books, to go back to her cage.* I watch as she grasps the doorknob with all her might, gives a real pull, aggressive and sure, and I envy her.

Then I'm alone. Working with the deftness of a surgeon, I press my middle and index fingers deep into my throat, deeper, until I gag and my stomach lurches responsively, as I've trained it to do. First comes bile, burning, sour, then a great clot of sweetish food. It's started, the river flowing backwards, engines reversed, working against gravity. Then the great blankness, no thought, no light, a dead place in which I'm numb to all. Numb to the horrific grossness of the act, numb to taste, to sight, to smell. A moment's peace, exactly like death.

Ira told me a *bardo* is the gap between things, between events like being born and dying, like dying and being reborn.

This then is my bardo, the gap in which I disappear. For seconds. Or whole years.

The roar of the water churning and dismissing, dissolving and disappearing as I stare at my shame roiled in the waters of the toilet bowl, then washed clean away as I'm cleansed for those moments anyway. *I'm sick. Crazy, insane.* I pluck a square of toilet tissue, pat the seat dry.

Stepping from the stall, I face myself in the mirror. A pale, miserable face. Don't like to look too closely or too often. I'm not mesmerized by my face as some are mesmerized by theirs. I would prefer to think I didn't have one, can't be seen. A bland little face, as misleading as the title down the spine of a book, not a good basis for judging the contents.

The floor seems deserted again. As far as I can tell, the corduroy woman has left or has been absorbed completely into those dark stacks. It would be nice just to curl up somewhere, tuck myself in a corner and sleep, but I have to study.

The picture of the cerebral cortex looks to me like an overgrown cauliflower or a boxer's glove, the temporal lobe, a folded-in thumb. Ira's brain looks like this and mine, too. Only his is filled with tumors fitted snug as orange pith against its sweet globes.

For the exam, I'll be expected to name the parts of the brain and how each part functions. I'll be expected to describe the structure of the axons and how the synapses cascade one to the other sparking thought.

I try to concentrate on the text, on those strange antlike words, but since this morning, since my father called, I cannot think at all.

IRA 1958–1961

"Ira," his father says, closing the picture book. "Isn't it time for bed now?"

Every night his father asks him the same question, asks him patiently, but it is as if a lead sinker were attached to the end of that question, the kind his father showed him how to tie on the end of the fishing string. The lead sinker drops the question, plop, into the mud. This is not a question at all. His father is saying, "Ira you must go to bed. You must go now."

"Don't ask him, tell him," his mother says, removing her glasses, rubbing the sides of her head with the sides of her thumbs.

His mother has caught on. She understands.

"I don't *want* to tell him, Eileen. I *want* to ask him. My father always *told* me and I couldn't stand it. He's my son, too."

His mother puts her glasses on again to see, perhaps, if she understands what he is talking about.

"He's *our* son," she says as though her lips were sewn together like the line down his pants.

Ira can't stand this. He'd like to tell them he's *not* their son, he'd like to say he's . . . what? Whose son is he? He'd like to say he isn't anybody's son. He'd like to say he just lives here for a while. He'd like to say he can take care of himself, but he can't.

"Ira, are we going up to bed?"

His father's face, up close, his chin filled with tiny, tiny black dots like the dots that make up dusk if you sit completely still, his small black eyes and puffy cheeks, his moist lips, grooved like the sides of worms.

Ira shakes his head. "We" are not. He is not and his father is not going to bed.

"Ira, I think it is time for you to go to bed. I think you are overtired."

That fools him for a minute. As though overtired were a disease like when he had the red spots on his arms and legs and his mother said, "I think you have the chicken pox," and she was right.

"Yes, he *is* overtired," his mother says, standing now, moving closer to him, herding him subtly towards the stairs and once they reach the stairs he knows that they will have the advantage, they can push him up, up, up, the way they've done before, his body arched so far back they are practically carrying him, if they let him go, he would fall and crack his head. The stairs only go up.

No, he shouts, the sound scaring him for only a second because he's getting good at this, it comes so easy now, he just gets enough air and opens his chest. "No!"

"Yes." His father's voice grim, grinding, like he had a mouth full of stones.

"No."

"Yes."

"No."

"Yes."

With every *no* his voice grows louder. He can feel it rush out of him, filling every corner of the room, blasting into the hallway, the stairwell, he can fill the entire house. *"No."*

His mother's hand swings back, but his father's is at her wrist, gripping hard.

"Don't hit him," he says.

"Why not? He's impossible."

"I don't want you to hit him." His father's shout is much deeper than his own. His father's shout falls as deep as China. Maybe deeper. In China, the people look up at the sky and think his father's shout is thunder.

His father is not a bad man. His father's confused. He looks very sad right now. His father does not like to shout. Ira feels sad. He makes them angry, he makes them shout at each other and at him. He can't help it. No matter how hard he tells himself he should listen to this man, this man is *his father,* it does not feel right. It does not feel right at all.

At times, though, it is right. The time when his father showed him how to tie the knot that kept the sinker on the end of the line and even though his father knew Ira couldn't tie it himself he pretended like he could and that he was proud of Ira, he liked him. He liked the smell of his father's pants that day, too. His father wore his blue jeans, worn smooth at the knee, not the suit pants, itchy, complicated. The jeans smelled like dirt, the dirt in the backyard, where they dug for worms, the jeans smelled like worm dirt and worm guts.

And the jeans had hard bumps on them, unexpected, like scabs. You could fold those places, scratch them, pinch them and it didn't matter. Those scabs were solder, his father told him. Solder was liquid metal. His father had metal scabs on his jeans from when he welded pipes in the basement. His father could join metal to metal with hot solder, a single drop would burn your finger away.

That day they fished together, dropping the line off the end of the pier and not saying anything at all, just waiting quietly for a tug, even a slight jerk; his father snapped his finger on the line to show him what it would be like, and smelling, they did a lot of smelling that day, of the salt rising from the warm dock, the seaweed, the barnacles like tiny dead volcanoes, the worms in the bucket, the dying fish in the men's milky buckets, their own sweat that began to smell like the sea.

They didn't catch anything that day, but it didn't matter. They liked each other that day.

For some time now his mother's belly has been growing larger and larger like someone's been dumping buckets of water into a big balloon. He watches her go into the bathroom, waits for her to close the door, then he's up against it, listening for the tinkle of pee pee and the flush. There is no flush and he thinks, That's what happens if you don't pee, you fill up and up and up like a water balloon about to bust. Why won't his mom pee when she's always telling him to run and pee now so we can go?

He's thought about bellies for a long time and he's decided that the belly's a big bag of blood and pee. He can feel it sloshing in there if he rocks side to side and listens hard, he's almost sure he can. If you could look inside you would see cigarette butts floating on the surface and the chewed up bites of what you just ate . . .

"Come over here," she says. She is lying on the brown sofa in the living room. She sleeps there every day just about, all afternoon and into the evening. "I want you to put your hand right here." She pats a spot on her big belly, but he stands, frozen. She pats herself again. "Come on, it's a surprise."

She reaches for his hand, even though he tries to wriggle it from her grasp, and squashes it flat on the place she was patting. He can feel the curve of the skin, so tight it surprises him, and hard, like red rubber balls the children bounce at recess. So tight and hard he wonders if it's his mother's belly after all.

"Don't do that," she cries, but he can tell it didn't hurt. "Just lay your hand there and you'll have a surprise." He doesn't want a surprise, he wants to get his hand away, but his mother's holding it down, flattening it with the palm of her hand, and then, the skin jumps, and jumps again, like something's beating hard from inside. He draws his hand back.

"That's a kick," his mother says. "The baby's kicking. He wants to get out."

The older boys teasing him, *Got Prince Philip in a can? Then let him out.*

Why if the baby's kicking, maybe he needs to get out, maybe the baby can't breathe.

"How can he breathe in there?"

"He breathes through me," she says. "We share the same lungs. You and I did once, too."

He thinks about that. About him and his mother joined at the lungs, breathing the same air, thinking the same thoughts.

She is closing her eyes, smiling. One hand rests on top of his head, the other on the top of her belly. "That's the baby," she murmurs, drifting into sleep like a swimmer on her back. He feels a pang. She is talking about the baby, not about him.

Gwendolyn takes care of him now. He loves Gwendolyn. Gwendolyn's skin is the color of ripe fig, so mysterious he likes to rub his finger back and forth on her arm and she doesn't care. "It don't come off," she says, laughing at him. Her lips are red, shiny, teeth white as bits of shell. He shakes his head. He knows the color is hers, he is looking at something different, the way the skin seems to pour under his finger, smoother than his mother's skin, smooth like the skin of a fig and sweet smelling like a fig, too. He sinks his teeth in, not hard, but she shakes her wrist away. "What do you think I am? Candy?"

He nods his head. You're candy, he says, candy. And she slips her hand in her big, black purse, too big for her, because she's only a thin young girl, who traveled with them from Ohio, cried when his mother offered to take her, *Couldn't take this place any longer,* she said. His mother agreeing, both of them dragging on their cigarettes and exhaling a wide veil of smoke like they were flapping a picnic blanket between them, *Me neither, Gwendolyn, if I see another bridge table, I'll shoot myself.* He overheard them talking about the new town. His mother had lived there when she was a girl. It was a cultured place, she said. It had a university. There would be opportunities for Gwendolyn. She should think about college . . .

Gwendolyn's hand comes out of her bag and she has a fireball, still in the cellophane. *Looking for something?* He grins, pops the big ball in his mouth, moves it side to side. The big ball makes him feel important, almost a man. He knows that men, not his father, who doesn't smoke or even chew gum, often have their cheeks puffed up with something, often spit, aiming at invisible bull's-eyes all over the ground. Not his father, who thinks spitting is vulgar, who never cared for smoking, but the other men, the men at the gas station, wearing suits covered with grime, the men he sees strolling down the sidewalks in the park.

Gwendolyn turns back to her ironing. He stands for a moment, taking in those smells he loves, the hot, damp smell of steam, somehow pressing sweetness into the pillowcases so that when he smells them at night, he thinks of Gwendolyn.

She switches on her radio. Her cigarette burns in a plastic ashtray somehow adding to the sweetness, not taking away. He waits for Gwendolyn to start singing as she always does, letting something rise from her gut, something that starts as a moan but spins finer and cleaner as it arcs into the room . . .

She stops abruptly and looks over at him. "What are you waiting around for? Go outside and play and leave me alone."

He knows she doesn't care if he stays or goes, but this time he decides to go, running down the stairs, with the sound of her voice ringing in his ears.

She'll be com-in' round the moun-tain
When she comes.
She'll be com-in' round the moun-tain
When she comes.
She'll be com-in' round the mountain,
She'll be com-in' round the mountain,
She'll be com-in' round the mountain,
When she comes.

He can see *her* as they sing, some lovely, wild-haired mountain lady, riding on the edge . . . he can see the cart careening on one wheel, her hands thrown up in the air, joyous, waving, whooping, and shouting "yee hah" as the horses charge around the bend . . . oh how he wants to go out to meet her, to greet her, waving his hat and jumping up and down, hopes she will notice him as she steps down from her carriage, full of vigor and fun, not one bit tired like his mother.

His mother and father exchange smiles. His father is driving, his hands steady on the wheel; the inside of the car is steamy, warm; the windows clouded and moist. His mother looks back and smiles at him as she sings, covers his hand with her hand as he bounces, not to tell him *stop,* but to tell him she is glad he's her boy. His mother's voice high and silvery like the fog, his father's deeper but not too deep, he sings all the words almost like he is *telling* the song. Sometimes his mother teases his father, *Mouthe the words.* That's what the bad teacher told his father when he was a little boy as little as him. All the children were singing, and she pointed to his father and said, *Mouthe the words.* That made his father very sad, very very sad, and he feels bad for his father and hopes his mother won't say that anymore.

No, now everyone is happy singing joyful, she is coming, she is coming, she is coming.

"Ira, sing something, sing 'Over There.' "

" 'O-ver ther-r-re, O-ver the-e-e-re. . . . ta da da Yanks are com-ing, drum, drum, tum-ming e-very-where . . .' I don't know the rest of the words."

"Would you like to sing it together? Should we start all over? 'John-ny get your gun, get your gun —' "

". . . get your gun . . ."

" 'Take it on the run, on the run —' "

His grandmother's voice, so loud, so insistent, poking at him the way he pokes the cat to keep it from falling asleep, so that he's got to join in. ". . . 'on the run, da, da, da . . . hear them calling . . .' I don't know the rest of it."

"I know. Let's show Aunt Kelly how you sing Beethoven's Fifth. She'd love to hear you sing."

"I would love that, Ira."

"Well, I'm out of that song."

"Why?"

"Because I sang it right in the bottom of the microphone."

Sing it deep, she said, so he did, letting each word sink slowly like a stone.

"I know how it goes," the aunt who is not his aunt says. "Da-da-da-*da-a-ah . . .*"

His beloved song ruined, the notes made light as marshmallows. *"No! Da-da-da-DA-A-A-H!"*

"Then what?" His grandmother hums the next phrase and suddenly he realizes the trick. They're just pretending they don't know the song. They know the song as good as him but they want to hear the way he sings his song so they can laugh at it the way the big boys do.

"Well, I'm out of that." He is startled to hear himself saying something his father says. He wonders if he should try doing what his father does next, grinning to one side and shrugging. *Fix you something different?*

"He's not usually so stubborn," his grandmother says.

"Perhaps he's tired." Aunt Kelly strokes his head. He does feel tired. He wonders when he will see his mother and father again, if he will ever see them again . . . He's tired of all the questions they ask him, of everything that they ask him to do. Why do they want him to sing? Why must he remember words? Why must he find the song over and over again once it has dropped away?

They have come to this city so that his mother can go to the special hospital where the baby will be delivered. His mother told him this. She did not say who was going to deliver the baby. He wanted to ask but he did not. His mother had many secrets that she would never tell him no matter how much he asked . . . He wondered if he could ever keep secrets as good as she. She would not tell him where the goldfish went after they died. She would not tell him but Gwendolyn did. Gwendolyn held him on her lap, her arm tight around him so he could feel her bones in his back, she dragged on her cigarette and blew the smoke the other way so his eyes would not tear. "Your daddy flushed them goldfish down the toilet so they could get back to the ocean." Then she described it to him so he could see how all the toilets in the city flushed into a big river and how the big river washed out to sea. "The goldfish missed their mommy?" he asked, struggling to catch her deep brown eyes. If he could see her eyes, he would know for certain if she was telling the truth . . . "That's right. They were missing the other fish, the family they left in the sea."

But about the baby even Gwendolyn was strange. "You can't know everything," she said finally, after he had been pestering her all afternoon. "All you can know is that you will have a baby the week after next. A little brother or a little sister. You can't know that yet, but you will soon enough."

Gwendolyn stayed home to get everything ready for the baby. He had seen the room before they left. In one corner stood a crib, *his* crib. He held on to the bars and gazed at the place that had once been his place and something inside ached for that clean soft place that safe soft place . . . Then Gwendolyn showed him the tiny bathtub and the plastic mat she would use to change the baby's diapers and he remember that too and his nose wrinkled, the slap, and the tearing sound of your wet bottom on the slick plastic as your legs shot up, helpless, the memory came rushing over him so strongly he almost burst into tears.

"You remember me changing you on this mat?" Gwendolyn was asking him. "You used to scream your fool head off, made me and your mama want to stuff cotton in your mouth."

Heels up in the air, his brown hole exposed like a bull's-eye . . . He couldn't stand to look at that mat any longer and he ran out of the room, promising himself he'd never go into that room ever again.

Tonight he will stay with Grandma Millie all by himself.

Like a big boy, his grandmother says. He will stay in the room that was his father's room when he was exactly Ira's age. His grandmother has promised to show him a picture of his father riding on a pony when he was Ira's age . . . He has stayed with Grandma Millie once before, when he was too young to remember. He doesn't like where she lives. It is very dark and there are many high doors that are always closed and are supposed to stay closed, his grandmother tells him. Her apartment smells sour, like the detergent his mother uses on the living room carpet. Whenever his mother uses that detergent, she and Gwendolyn open all the windows in the house and then they go outside.

Behind the curtains are windows that look out on bricks as dark as dried blood. He stands at the window staring at those bricks until his grandmother sees him. "Come away from there!" she says with so much alarm in her voice that he freezes, expecting a swat. "Come sit next to Grammy on the sofa." She pats the cushions invitingly so he obeys, sinking deep into soft cushion. But he's still thinking about the dark wall and the strange, sooty light, a cold light that makes him shiver.

His grandmother leans over him to switch on the lamp and it is as though she has waved a magic wand over the animals. They prance, two by two, across the coffee table. "I arranged them. Just like Noah."

Their motion is startling, strange, deer leap across the shaft of light, fish drift through strands of seaweed as bright as grass.

He is allowed to hold one animal at a time, each one smooth as water, yet firm and cool in his hand. He turns them over and over, watching the light play through them. His grandmother tells him that if he's good, he will be able to choose one to take home with him.

But will he be good? He asks himself. The question makes

him tremble. He thinks of the damp sheets that make his mother mad, that make Gwendolyn shake her head, that make his father stare at the floor . . . What will he do in the middle of the night when he feels his body getting so hot and full, when it feels like his skin's bursting like the skin of Gwendolyn's tomato when she lowers it into the boiling water. *Can't stand those skins. Make my teeth rattle.* So every tomato in their house is boiled, the skin pulled back so that Gwendolyn can eat them without the willies.

He has gotten into his feet pajamas, brushed his teeth and taken a tinkle, when the telephone rings. He and his grandmother look at each other, both frightened, before she leaps towards it to still it. The receiver cradled between her ear and shoulder. "Oh," she breathes. "A girl. A baby girl."

Sweetness trickles through her voice in a way that makes him think of an orange being squeezed into a cup.

"Phoebe? How beautiful. Like a Greek goddess. How is Eileen? Can I talk to her? . . . Well, then, give her my love." Her glance sweeps over to him, catching him in its net. "Ira's a good little boy. A little angel."

She holds the phone out to him. "Would you like to say hello to Daddy?"

He nods and takes the receiver from her. He has talked to his father before on the telephone when his father was on a trip. Always, his father's voice sounds so strange that he has to pretend that he is really talking to his father.

"Hello, son," his father says, his voice so loud that he could be in the room.

"Hello, Daddy."

His father tells him that he has big news for him and a big surprise. He will get his surprise tomorrow.

"Better than Phoebe?" Ira asks.

He hears his father catch his breath, then cough a little. "Why no. The surprise *is* your baby sister. What could be better than that?"

A ride in a space capsule. Or a boat.

Ira hands the telephone to his grandmother and goes back to the sofa. He hears her saying that she doesn't know how he knew except that he was listening. "He's a very bright little boy," she says, peeping around at him as if she has told his father a secret; then she asks more questions about the baby.

The doe wobbles in the palm of his hand, her head tilted slightly as though she is puzzled by something he's said. A girl, he whispers, a baby girl. *My sister.* For a moment the doe seems to understand, light blazes in her liquid eyes, but suddenly she is falling, twirling in air as if she's burst into flame, and then a crack, as she strikes the edge of the table and shatters. He sits there aghast. His grandmother, still on the phone, pauses, and opens and closes her mouth silently, then, "Don't move. Stay right there." She turns her back to him in that same secretive way as before to explain to his father what's happened and to ask advice.

He picks up one of the doe's legs, a perfect crystal toothpick as sharp as a needle, and touches it to his finger. *Keep the point away from your eye,* he can hear his mother saying. So he holds the leg at arm's length, watching the light dance through it. The second prick is as light as the first, but, to his satisfaction, there appears a spot of bright blood as bright as glass.

"I want my name," Ira demands, handing the flap of cheese back to his mother and stamping his foot. How dare she hand him an orange square of cheese and a piece of bread like that? Ever since the baby, she's been sloppy, like she's sleepwalking, or swimming through mud.

She sighs, wipes her forehead with the side of her hand. She's still wearing the faded dress she wore when her belly was huge. He looks away from her. The damp places on her front disgust him, like she's drooled there or the baby did, but the dampness is something worse, he knows because he saw them. Fat red nipples like the swollen ends of nightcrawlers. *Cut a worm in two and it grows back again, they said, but he and Tommy Cane whacked that worm hard as they could with the side of the shovel. They took turns and missed twice, but it was his blow that cut the worm in half. Wasn't clean, though, mushy, the bottom part didn't want to let go. They ran then, expecting the sides of the worm to rear up and bellow in pain. They ran all the way around the block and back to the square of sidewalk in front of Tommy's house, where the worm lay.*

Hunkering to get a close look, they saw the parts just lying there, no squirming at all. You killed it, You killed it, Tommy screamed like he was a murderer. He got down closer, then reached out with his finger and rolled one side away, leaving a squiggly line of guts and something shiny . . . dead all right, whoever told him about splitting a worm was lying . . .

He didn't know what they were at first. He was standing in the shadow of the doorway, across from where she was sitting, but he probably could have been standing right by her shoulder and she wouldn't have noticed. She was raising up her blouse, the baby cradled in her arms, and he heard the sound of something coming unsnapped, loud, like the snap when he undid his pants, then out poked the worm and the baby's head came up. He watched her guide the nipple to the baby's mouth, and the baby grabbed it, greedy. He ran.

"What do you *want* from me, Ira?" she says.

"My letters." He can't believe he has to explain. That's how his mother always serves him cheese, carving the letters of his name out one by one, each letter takes up a whole square.

"I don't have time for that today. I've got to feed the baby. Plain cheese today."

He stares at his mother. He can't believe she's doing this to him; once they breathed the same air, once they had the same thoughts, once he slept quietly in the balloon of her belly . . .

He slaps the cheese on the floor, then steps on it, hard, smearing the cheese with his toes.

She screams and is after him, but he's too quick for her, flying through the back door and across the yard, he throws himself under the lilac hedge, facedown, panting. He can hear her shouting his name, demanding that he come back.

He peeps out from behind his hands, afraid that if he sees daylight he will no longer be invisible. He can't see her, but he senses she's near. Can you stop your heart from beating? The big boys say you can't, that even if you ask yourself not to breathe you will, that even if you decide to hold your breath until you die, you can't. *No choice.* He tells himself not to breathe, he orders his heart to stop, freeze. He feels a chill race through him, and he thinks that he's done it, but no, his heart is still beating, louder than ever, as if to make him seem a fool.

"I am going to count to ten, and if you're not out of those bushes by the count of ten, you're going to stay out here without any supper."

Her voice has so much iron in it; when she speaks to the baby it is filled with feathers.

"One . . . two . . . three . . . four . . ."

He listens for a while to her counting, wondering if she will skip a number or forget one the way he does sometimes, but he has already made up his mind. He will stay *all night* under the lilac bush, *all night.* The thought stuns him in its grandness. In the dark with possums and moles and wolves.

Already an ant has befriended him. The ant crawls up his arm, the ant hesitates, feeling the air with its antennae as though it was blind.

"That's it, Ira. Good-bye."

He hears footsteps swishing through the crabgrass. He hears the back door slam. He could run around to the front door and see if she left it open. No, he's going to live under this bush all night, he's going to make the bush his home.

The house, once *his* house, looks so big to him now, it looks so big he can hardly recognize it. Moving slowly along one side, he looks up at the big windows, hoping to see his mother's face smiling at him or Gwendolyn's . . . He stops in front of a window and waves, in case they can see him, just so they know . . . know what? That he is out here. The windows have grown impossibly high and dark, like the frozen pond in winter, completely black.

He has never been in the backyard by himself before. Always before he had his mother or his father or Gwendolyn and Tommy Cane to play with. The backyard stretches wide as an ocean, so big it makes him dizzy.

He holds the chains of the swing the way his father taught him, fingers curled into his palms. *Pump,* his father always says. *Pump hard.* He heaves his body forward, back, forward, back, but there's no motion at all. The swing, instead of sailing up like a tossed skirt and back, twists sideways, his toe makes a pattern in the dirt.

A push. One push. He wants it so badly he can feel the tears well up in the corners of his eyes. *Pump.* He throws himself against that space in front of him, trying to part the air with his narrow chest. The swing moves, a little, enough to see the ground slip back, enough to get ahead of where he was. *One push.* His small, plump body too weak to do what he asks. *Pump.*

Her scream blasts across the yard, freezing him to his spot, freezing his fingers to the chain links burning in his palms.

"Get off that swing!"

He ducks his head this way then that, her fists stinging his ears, his back. She can't get to his bottom, stuck fast to the hard blue seat.

"Ira!"

Her nails bite into his knuckles, and he feels each finger pry open against his will, his palm exposed and shy, and he remembers the time the boys pulled his pants down, holding him from behind and his legs still running. *Hah, hah, hah. Big butt, big butt. Slapping as much as they could.*

When his father comes home that night, his mother rushes to him, lays her head on his chest like she is sick. "I think I'm losing my mind."

His father holds her closer then and says, in the same soft voice he uses to coax a boo-boo not to hurt, "Can't be that bad . . ."

Ira, pressing himself into the slats at the bottom of the banister, can't decide whether to make himself invisible or to run to his father to get picked up.

"Really, Michael," she is saying, her words coming out like a rope straining against itself. "I lost it, I really lost it today with Ira. I'm ashamed to tell you . . . "

His father pushes his mother away gently. "Let's talk later. I'm starving now. I've had a long day, too."

His father has caught his eye, and Ira knows he is next in his father's arms.

"Don't I count at all?" His mother clenching her hands to

her mouth and pressing her forehead to the banister, right above Ira. His father freezes, caught between the desire to take Ira in his arms and to help her.

"Of course you count, everybody counts. You count and I count and Ira counts and Phoebe counts. I just got home and I'd like a drink and I'd like to get out of my suit and I'd like to say hello to my son and my baby and have a chance to relax. I'm *tired.*"

His mother straightens, taking in his father's good sense, but it is as if she is fading too, from him, from his father. "Macaroni's in the oven . . ."

"Great," his father says, but he is gazing at Ira, stretching his arms for Ira. "How's my boy?"

He wants to run to him, wants to bury his head deep in the white starch smell of his shirt. He wants to tell his father about his afternoon under the lilac bush and out in the yard, but he can't tell if his father will hear it as a tale of woe, a tale of hurt and scorn, or a tale of bravery and courage. He wants his father to think of him as brave, but how can he do that without seeming to be a baby? He wants his father to be proud of how he treated the ants, letting them crawl on him like he was their jungle gym, he wants to tell his father about the swing, but his father might scold — *Never swing alone* — or his father might think he was a sissy boy too weak to pump. Most of all he wants to tell his father he didn't cry, but why would he if he was brave?

"My, you have a big hug tonight, Ira. What have you been up to?"

Ira looks at his mother, who looks right back at him. *Once they breathed the same air.*

"Ira had a big day today."

His father squints at him. "What did Ira do today? Did Ira go to the playground?"

Ira shakes his head. What will his mother say?

"Did Ira play with the big boys?"

Ira shakes his head.

"Did Ira get in trouble with Mommy?"

He holds himself completely still, waiting for his mother. Already he can feel something dissolving inside. That's it. He was in trouble, he wasn't brave, he was bad. He was bad and now his father will know and be angry with him.

"Ira had an adventure today," his mother says.

"What kind of adventure?" His father is looking at his mother. He and his father are both listening hard to what she is saying, and what she is saying they both know is not what she is saying.

Her hand moves from the banister to the top of his head. "Yes, Ira was a brave boy today."

He can feel her fingers pressing into the top of his head, she is telling him something through her fingertips. What's she telling him? She is scratching his head now very lightly. The scratching is telling him to keep a secret. To keep a secret from his father. He closes his mouth. His mother is telling him he's brave and he can keep a secret. He won't tell his father about the hitting, and his mother will not tell his father about the cheese. He knows all this through his mother's fingertips. He can understand her thoughts as though they were his own. His heart springs in his chest with a strange, aching joy, as though he were swinging alone, but not quite alone.

Mommy's coming to school today; Mommy's coming to meet your teacher, she told him. The news knocked him out. Thought of his mother in this blue-green room, sitting at his table, reading his walls, looking in his desk. Will she see the ink hole? Something he's been working on, started before him by some other boy, a big boy now, he's almost sure. A crater, black with ink, bored out in the corner of his desk. He takes the old fat pencil when the teacher's back is turned, works the pencil point round and round, slicking the sides of the hole, making them shine. Every day a little deeper, a little darker. Still many layers to go.

His teacher doesn't look around often, but when she does it's IRA, WILL YOU PLEASE PAY ATTENTION TO WHAT'S ON THE BOARD. They all look around at him, a dozen moon faces looking straight at him, so he shrugs, palms up: *What, me worry?* And that breaks them up. Not her.

"Not funny," she says, but she is lying because the boys laugh and the girls too, but who cares? She moves him up front, parks him between the two smartest girls in the class. "Look at the board and copy." Why *copy?* he wonders. Why not *do* something with these letters? The endless *A*'s annoy him, what can you do with just one letter, endlessly marching across the page like a string of paper dolls? He aches for *words,* real *words,* like the big boys get. You can't have the words until you have the letters. But the letters by themselves don't mean anything. He can read some words. He can read "and" and "cat" and "hat." He can read "the." No one knows this yet. His secret he discovered when his mother was lying down sick. My grain. My pain, she calls it sometimes, and he knows that is bad.

When he picked up his book, his favorite, the cat with the silly hat, and turned the pages, suddenly he was hearing her voice and the way she read the words and he could almost see the shadow of her finger on the page. Then all of a sudden he saw the word, it was like finding a shiny dime on a sidewalk and picking it up. "And" here and here and here, "the" "cat" here and here and here, "the" "hat." He was going to show her and his father that night, but she was too sick. He was going to show Gwendolyn, but she shushed him up. Everyone worrying about his mother.

He watches the two smartest girls, heads bent identically, close to their books. So serious, like the board is speaking to them, telling its secrets, like they have to catch every word with their pencils. He copies them for a while, head up, head down, wrinkles his forehead. The pencil, too fat, wriggles in his grasp. He tries two hands, one on the top to steer the end.

One of the smart girls sees him and points and giggles. Soon the other smart girl is giggling and others too. He sticks out his tongue. Who cares if she cries *boo hoo waa waa?* She does, and he is moved back to his old familiar spot, smell of rubber coats, rubber boots.

"Chair down, please." The teacher stops at his desk, crosses her arms and watches him so that suddenly his heart begins to flap. He wants to do his best. He looks up at the board, not at her, trying to hear its voice again the way the smart girls did. They are working on *R,* capital *R.* He draws the line straight as he can, which is not too straight, tipping kind of, like a chair pulled back. Teacher's watching him as though it's a test. He glances up at the board again, does not look at her, makes the fist and tries to swing the point through the curve, handle of a pitcher, or Gwendolyn's arm, hand on her hip when she's mad, the pencil slips, like the baby missing her mouth, the spoon flying clear over her shoulder. He laughed, but his father looked disturbed. *She's only a baby, his mother says. Can't expect her to have manners.* But he's not a baby anymore and is expected to have manners, to pick up the right fork and knife and hold everything the *right way.*

The teacher tugs gently at his pencil, then at his fingers curled into a fist. "Let me show you the way to hold the pencil,

Ira." Her voice is not unkind, but his ears are burning, hot as potatoes, his mother would say. They are like the small red lights on the back of their car, flashing his shame. She is still prying his fingers open one by one. *Relax.* Her own fingers, cooler than his mother's, slick with dust.

"Hold the pencil at a slant. Like this —" She demonstrates, holding the pencil in the air, and he nods even though he can't see anything, the shame like a red curtain across his eyes. Then she pokes the pencil through his thumb and forefinger, and, taking his hand in hers, squeezes as though his fingers were dough she expects to keep its shape.

It feels strange, like the pencil is floating, loose.

"Keep your wrist still. Just your hand should move."

His wrist and hand are frozen, his fingers feel like lumps of dried-out dough, useless. He cannot move the pencil then at all.

"That's better," she says, sounding tired. The other children, glancing around, eager for her attention or to witness someone's failure.

She is lying again, he knows. He has done nothing at all. His hand stays frozen in the position she molded for him. She moves down the row, nodding quickly as she goes. She doesn't stop at anyone else's desk. He is the only one.

He cannot move his hand. The letters march on without him. Still, whenever she looks in his direction, she smiles as if he has done something right. He feels nervous. What did he do right? She did everything for him.

A child gets up, mops the board with the eraser and sits down. His teacher rakes a fresh set of lines across the board, the chalk hissing in its frame. On the top, she draws a capital *S*, on the bottom, a small *s*. She gives directions as she draws. "The top curve of the capital *S* should just graze the top line, the middle passes through the middle line and the bottom curve touches the bottom line and comes up, like this." She gives the chalk a little extra twist as it comes off the curve.

He can tell she is proud of her letter. A perfect *S*. He would be proud of it, too.

As she bends over one of the smart girl's books, she flicks a glance back at him.

That's all right. He is ready for her. He is sitting exactly as she left him, holding the pencil correctly, still.

"Take a look," the teacher says as she pulls a composition book from the top of the pile and opens it to show Ira's mother. "You'll see the problem."

They are seated at a small round table at the back of the classroom. School has been out for over an hour, and the high-ceilinged room in the afternoon light has the loneliness and quiet of a library, Eileen thinks.

She strains to focus on what Mrs. Hammond is showing her. The book contains her son's attempts at copying the alphabet, each page devoted to a letter, uppercase and lowercase, the whole alphabet assembled within these pages, like a battalion of soldiers, marching down a red-and-blue highway.

"His hand-eye coordination is terribly weak. . . . His *A* for example . . ."

What Eileen sees is not an *A* but a pair of stilts inclined towards each other but not touching, the steps joined close to the base. Next to the stilts is a pair of young trees, bending across each other, their single limbs joined at a slant, and next to that is a man's top hat, and next to that, a chimney . . . the variations are dazzling . . .

"He eventually copied the capital *A*, but when we get to cursive —"

She pulls another book from the stack, flipping it open on top of the first.

Eileen looks closely. What impresses her is the darkness of the coil and its weedy fury, from that black cloud, you expect to see a posse emerge or a steam engine. She wonders if it strikes Ira's teacher as fierce.

"These are supposed to be *o*'s, Mrs. Hammond explains. "Those, *e*'s . . ." She keeps flipping pages, speeding Eileen through the evidence of her son's poor penmanship, his lack of coordination.

Eileen has noticed before, of course, Ira's wobbly letters, the way his signature seems to melt off the edge of his drawings. She never thought it was something important in a child his age.

"Is this *so* unusual?" she asks. "He's only six." Hastily she adds, "When I was his age, my teacher was still trying to get me to use my right hand. It made me a klutz at *everything* . . . "

The teacher tilts her head, wondering, no doubt, if Eileen is making a joke. "Ira's handwriting is illegible. He simply cannot do the work."

"Is it the way he holds his pencil?"

"Partly. He also doesn't sit still long enough to copy the letter correctly. There's the other problem I want to discuss."

The pain begins behind her right temple, loud as a school bell. The color is blue, a deeper blue than these books. Good, she thinks, the worst are red, hot, bright, red. "What do you mean?"

Mrs. Hammond smiles briefly. "The other day, for example, when I turned to help another child, Ira got up and started running around the room. I asked him to sit down and he refused. The principal had to intervene."

Eileen nods slowly. "Go on."

"That's happened quite a few times. He finds some way to

disrupt the class, whether by shouting out answers or refusing to do what the others are doing. If it's quiet reading time, he'll decide to draw and so on." Mrs. Hammond pauses. "Does he obey rules at home?"

Eileen draws a breath. This stage, she knows from experience, is like balancing a pot of liquid on your head. One false move and the headache will cascade over the rim into blinding pain. "Bedtime has always been a problem," she admits. "But my husband and I are very strict on manners. Table manners, and other kinds," she adds falteringly. "He's also responsible for helping to set the table and for making his bed . . ." She tries to think of Ira's other duties, but her mind is blank.

Mrs. Hammond has pale blue eyes that almost match the color of the composition books. Her face is lined with faint wrinkles, the kind caused by too much sun. She must go to the Cape in the summer, Eileen thinks, irrelevantly. She must go to the Cape and bake and bake in the hot sun and not think about children at all.

"Another example of his being somewhat out of control is the way he behaves on line. The children are supposed to line up before lunch. They take turns being the leader marching us to the cafeteria. But Ira *always* wants to be the leader. I ask him to wait his turn, but he runs to the front of the line and pushes whoever's there." Mrs. Hammond raises, then lowers a pair of folded reading glasses, placing them neatly against the edge of her desk blotter as though something inherent in them were helping her judge Ira's case. She utters a slight cough. "He's a bright boy. I like him . . ."

Eileen can hear in the teacher's voice that she has thought this over a good deal, that liking her son has been a struggle . . . *He must give her as hard a time as he does me,* she thinks. To her astonishment, a small part of her is glad.

"The truth is, if Ira doesn't improve, we will have to consider keeping him back."

"You would keep him back? For *handwriting?*" But even as she says this she has a defeated feeling, well, of course, this woman could do anything.

"Until his hand-eye coordination improves. That may have something to do with his behavior, his overall lack of maturity."

It is as though Mrs. Hammond has stuck out her foot to trip her. She can feel the pot tipping over. "What can we do to help?"

"I think you should set up a work schedule for Ira so that he practices every day. Do you have time?"

"I'll make the time."

"Are there other children at home?"

"A baby."

Mrs. Hammond nods sympathetically, but Eileen shrugs this off, assuring her they will speak to Ira tonight, that she is terribly sorry for the problems he's caused.

"We all want what's best for Ira," Mrs. Hammond says, yet her hand slips from Eileen's before the shake is done.

He would like to ask his mother what the teacher said, but doesn't dare. If you ask Mommy questions when she's sick, and sometimes when she's not, she yells at you hard and fast out of nowhere like the snap of a towel Gwendolyn makes to move him along, snap cracking at his bottom, she makes sure it never touches him, but his mother when she yells smacks hard and you cannot no matter what you do get away from her.

His mother stands in the kitchen doorway. She's wearing her

pale robe over her cotton dress and the beaded moccasins Daddy gave her for Hanukkah as though she wasn't sure if it was day or night, and her hair, usually so smooth and straight, is dark in places and mussed like angel's hair.

Gwendolyn said Mommy wouldn't be down, that Mommy had a headache since she got home from school, so Daddy heated the dinner that Gwendolyn made. Casserole and mashed potatoes and the beans that Daddy likes, shaped like tiny ears.

"Were we too loud?" his Daddy asks, wiping his mouth with his napkin, putting it down before he stands to pull out Mommy's chair.

She shrugs. "I could hear you. But it didn't matter. I won't stay long."

Fingers press the top of his head, kneading gently.

"I met Mrs. Hammond today."

He feels his stomach tighten, his heart moving in his chest like a crazy bat. *Not my fault the letters doing that stupid dance.*

"She told me she likes you very much. She says you work very, very hard." *So frightened,* she thinks. *Why?*

Ira pokes a bean with his fork, spears it, while his father raises his eyebrows, mouthes, "I forgot."

"Do you?"

Ira hesitates, then shrugs. "Guess so." *That all the teacher said?* He searches her face for a sign of what she thinks, what she knows, but his mother is not even looking at him anymore, her attention taken by her milk and bread. She chews slowly as if her teeth hurt, staring at the glass of milk, then drawing her finger down its slick side.

"She also said you give her trouble sometimes, that you talk out of turn sometimes, and don't pay attention. That you shove the other children."

Her gaze shifts back to him.

"Why do you do that, Ira?"

In his mind's eye, he sees the bodies of children, blocking him, bigger than he as he fights to get through.

"You cannot shove. We've told you that."

Bodies like trees, planting themselves in his way. On purpose.

"Ira, do you hear what your mother's saying?"

His father's hand on his, stopping the fork, the massacre of beans.

"She's telling you that you need to behave better in school. You need to pay attention to your teacher."

"That's *not* what I'm saying. May I please speak for myself?"

"But I thought —"

"But you always think, and talk. Where do you think he gets it from? Can't you please show your son how to *listen*!"

Pushed out. He and Daddy, pushed to the back of the class. Ira closes his eyes. The tip of the pencil, like a shiny nose, presses at the hole, presses through.

Ira is playing with his space capsule in his room, making it shoot into outer space like the Mercury capsule his mother showed him in the newspaper and he watched on TV, faster than you could ever imagine, his father told him. *Than the speed of light?* he asked, Well no. On TV the capsule looked as if it were moving slowly, floating in space where there is no *gravity,* his mother said, everything has to be tied down, plates, glasses, silverware, even the astronauts.

Ira zooms the capsule around the room, round and round until the walls blur and he's not sure what's up and what's down.

He and Tommy Cane play astronaut in the capsule that Tommy's father bought him. It's a *scale model,* Tommy's father said; when they crawl inside they are exactly like astronauts and they talk like astronauts, speaking one word at a time, growling each syllable like men, forcing their voices as deep as they go, trying to scrape something deep within, "roger," "roger and out," "base to control." Walkie-talkie talk.

The capsule has a control board and a window pasted over with a black paper filled with stars. He and Tommy mix up orange juice from powder, same as the astronauts, to take on the voyage and stuff beef jerky into their pockets. Ira's father has promised to buy them some freeze-dried food. One drop in your mouth tastes like steak and mashed potatoes with gravy. Tommy says he heard that they're making a pill that tastes like a whole dinner including a milk shake going down your throat. In the future, you won't have to chew at all.

He doesn't know his mom's been watching him until he looks up at her from the floor. She is leaning against the inside of the door, her arms folded, and he thinks, *I'm in trouble.* Slowly he stands, shoves his hands in his front pockets, gazes at the floor. Did he tease Phoebe today? Can't remember.

"Sorry to interrupt," his mother says, softly. She doesn't *sound* mad. "Mr. Meyer just called saying he'd like to take your picture for an advertisement. Remember the pictures I showed you?"

Vaguely Ira remembers his mother showing him a picture in a big magazine of a lady in a party dress standing in the kitchen, mopping like it was the most fun thing in the world.

"He remembered you from Jeffrey's birthday party and he thought you'd be just right for what he's working on. Isn't that nice?" And, because he is looking at her blankly, "Remember Mr. Meyer?"

He nods, but all his senses are on the alert: *This is what Tommy was telling about, Candid Camera.* He'd explained it to him a few weeks ago when they were orbiting Earth. At first he couldn't believe it, were grown-ups really that mean? Tommy nodded; he'd seen it, he said, on late after their bedtime. That was on purpose so that kids wouldn't find out.

Find out what?

The boy, their age, was sitting in a room with a man, older than their fathers, he looked like a grandfather and a very nice one, too. He asked the boy all kinds of questions, Art Linkletter stuff, like "What's your favorite thing to do after school?" Then more embarrassing questions, "Do you like girls?" digging more, creepy in fact, but of course the boy kept answering the man as he and Tommy recognized they would, too. Answer a grown-up when he asks you a question, their mothers have told them.

Then this is what happens: the room, the perfectly white room, begins to fill with water. First, just the floor is wet, and you see the boy sitting there starting to squirm a little like he's wondering if it's something he did. . . . His new party shoes are getting soaked and so are the man's, but the grandfather keeps talking, keeps asking questions in the same kindly voice. The boy is really squirming now, lifting his shoes one at a time, you can see him resisting the urge to shake them hard. When the man isn't looking, he whips out his pocket handkerchief and tries to mop them dry. What are you doing? the man asks. The boy looks scared. You know he's been told to keep his handkerchief in his pocket. Meanwhile the water keeps rising, ankle-high now, and the boy's suit, bought for TV, probably, is getting wet around the ankles, and now the grandfather does look concerned. "Anything wrong, son?"

"My pants," the boy whimpers. And the audience goes wild, pressing their hands over their mouths and stamping their feet. *"They're wet."*

The grandfather looks down and sees *his* pants are sopping, too. Pretends to be surprised. "You're right, son, I guess we should get out of the rain, and by the way . . . *Smile! You're on Candid Camera!*"

The camera draws back to show the audience screaming with laughter, even the boy's parents, who wade into the room, smiling and apologizing to their son, but wickedly happy, too. The mother, still silently laughing, hugs the stricken boy to her breast.

"Watch out," Tommy sang. "When you least expect it, you're elected, it's your lucky day . . . *Smile, You're on Candid Camera!*"

Since then he has been looking everywhere. Walking downtown with his mother he saw a man's shirt hanging on a metal pole, the kind that usually has a sign, but no sign that day, just the blue shirt. He kept his eyes straight ahead, holding his breath as they walked by, pretending nothing was different. *Can't fool me.*

And another time, a car parked so close behind them his mother couldn't get out of her parking space; she tried inching forward, then back, yanking the wheel in one direction, then the other. He could feel the air bunching around them and he knew it was about to happen. He wanted to warn her, but where was the camera? In the backseat? In the rearview mirror? In the light on the ceiling? His heart was beating fast, he was ready. When they yelled *"Smile!"* he would yell back, *You didn't fool me, I knew you were there.* But the lights didn't go off that time. Maybe because he was on to them. Instead, his mother rested her forehead on the steering wheel and said, "I'm exhausted."

The next time they met, Tommy was pretty sure he'd seen one, too. A woman crossing the street with a bag that all of a sudden busted open, spilling groceries onto the road. Cars screeched to a halt, and a man bent to help her, and he, Tommy, was holding his breath, he could almost hear the grandfather shouting, *Smile!*

The next episode did feature an exploding grocery bag. A different lady, but he and Tommy smiled at each other, knowing he had witnessed the test run.

Mr. Meyer is short and wide like his father, but his hair is wild and stands out from his head like he's been electrified. His mustache hides his lips, except when he smiles, and then Ira can see the shiny wetness of them as pink as Phoebe's toes. He greets Ira with a handshake as though he is a much older boy, a man, almost, and Ira thinks, *This is it. Candid Camera.*

"Thanks for coming, Ira. I'm going to take a lot of pictures of you and I just want you to pretend that you're not in a photographer's studio, you're outside at a picnic or a ball game. Ever been to a ball game?"

Ira shakes his head. *Key word is* pretend.

The man looks slightly disappointed. "You like hot dogs?"

He nods.

"Good. So I want you to stand here,"— backing him by the shoulders to some invisible spot that only the man can see — "and I'm going to hand you this hot dog, and I want you to take a bite and imagine it's the best hot dog you've ever had."

He's terrified all of a sudden. *What's going to be in the hot dog?* He sniffs it. Seems normal, the warm, salty smell, the wet splotches like it's been in the rain.

"Bite!" The flash pops in Ira's eyes and he's seeing purple circles inside of green circles . . .

"Don't look at me. Look at the stop sign above the door."

Phony sign. But he can't quite figure what the trick will be and that makes him nervous. He can feel a little shiver run through his fingers. *When do the cameras go off?*

The man is hunched under a black cloth attached to the

camera and Ira, following his instructions, is seated now on a stool in front of a white screen, the kind his father shows slides on. He is wearing a baseball cap, stuck on inside out and backwards. *Another trick?* And the hot dog now has a line of yellow mustard down the center. *Extra spicy mustard from the joke shop?*

When Ira experiments, dipping just the tip of his tongue into the mustard, the man yells, *"Great. Hold it."*

Again the flash, and again he braces himself for the *Smile* and the wicked grandfather bursting into the room, laughing as hard as he can at him and whatever stupid thing he's been caught doing.

The session seems to last for hours. Ira would like to pee bad but is afraid to ask permission. *Of course. The trick will be in the bathroom. The toilet won't flush or will overflow.* He remembers the humiliation in the restaurant bathroom when he saw his tight brown BM's floating over the rim of the bowl. He ran back to the table, afraid to tell his mother. Closing his hands over his ears, he expected to hear the sound of rushing water behind him and to see the little BM's go whirling past.

Finally, it's over. The man pats him on the back, removes the cap. "Guess you never want to see another hot dog again?" He's supposed to laugh with the man, he knows, but he's still on guard, still watching and waiting.

His mother has brought Phoebe with her, and as soon as they come in, Phoebe is poking at the equipment, sniffing at the plate of hot dogs, looking wide-eyed at the fancy lights.

"*Me* picture?" Phoebe asks, tugging her mother's skirt.

"This was Ira's session, sweetheart."

His mother shrugs at Mr. Meyer. "Don't put your daughter on the stage," she says, then, "Did Ira behave?"

"Very cooperative, but a little shy."

Phoebe lifts a hot dog to her mouth and is about to take a bite.

"Put that down," Eileen yells. Phoebe freezes, not quite sure what to do with the bite already in her mouth.

"I'm going to toss them anyway. But how about I get a shot of Phoebe eating a hot dog if you have the time?"

Ira's mother nods. "Don't go to any trouble . . ."

But the man is already crouching, offering Phoebe a hot dog, then shuttling her to Ira's stool.

Eileen puts an arm around Ira's shoulders, which he jerks off immediately. *She's going to get the surprise?* He looks up at his mother. *Does she know?* His entire body is stiff with anger. *Figures. Phoebe'll be the one.* But then he thinks, wickedly, *She'll be scared to death.*

The flash goes off, and at the same time Ira claps his hands together once. He looks around. *Where's the audience?*

"I'd like to take another," the man says. Phoebe giggles, and the flash goes off again and again and again. Ira's hands hang limp at his sides.

On the walk home, his sister bounces and smiles, holding their mother by the hand. He'd like to shut her up for once, make her really scared, like they were on *Candid Camera.*

The sound grows from deep within him. He can feel it boiling like lava, molten, spewing up, the roar a dinosaur would make, the kind with a mouth full of pointy teeth. He raises his hands like claws, swoops down on them from behind.

"Karrreeeeee!"

Phoebe shrieks, her eyes wide and black, clutching their mother's arm.

"What on earth are you doing, Ira? Stop that noise!"

But he doesn't stop. His body flaps loose around him like an oversize coat. He shrieks the prehistoric shriek louder and louder. *"KAREEEEEEEEEE!"* A few people coming in the other direction glance at him. He doesn't care. They can shine the lights on him full blast. He doesn't care.

The bus is big and yellow as a ripe banana and the seats are green and hard and they bounce. Ira heads for the back so he can see out behind and out to the sides. The girls in the class sit in the front, which is where the teachers sit, too. Only Mr. Jack, the gym teacher, sits in the middle, with his legs sticking into the aisle. He wears a silver whistle around his neck, the kind he blows to start Red Rover or to call time out, and right now he is facing the backs of the boys who are turned, like Ira, to look out the rear window.

"Down in back, sit down, Ira!" Mr. Jack yells. The whistle, clenched between his teeth, rattles and gives off a hoot like a kettle at the beginning of the boil.

So what if he blows his stack? Ira thinks. He would like to hear him really blast it, would like him to blow his stack, what his mother says she will do when she's mad. He thinks of a haystack exploding, shooting straw a mile into the sky.

Face to the window, Ira watches the school disappear. At the stoplight a large black car noses up to their bumper, so close Ira can see the driver, a lady about his mother's age, with a bag of groceries on the seat. When the light changes, the lady beeps and Ira wiggles his fingers in his ears, like antlers gone to jelly. The lady glares, but he just laughs. The bus is so much bigger than the puny cars; the bus is a giant and all the cars are midgets. The great joy of this makes him clap his hands and look at the others, who are clapping and laughing just as happy as he.

The bus dips suddenly, and Ira feels a jolt in his stomach as they head down a steep hill, which he recognizes even from this height and speed.

My house!" he shouts, and the boys crowd to where his finger touches the glass.

The whistle blasts. *"Ira!"*

But Ira is satisfied the boys got a good look at his house.

"Not bad," says Dick Tone.

"You own the whole thing?"

"Uh huh." He means his parents, of course, but doesn't bother to explain.

The boys nod, showing their respect, but Mr. Jack is coming towards them, palming the back of each seat as though he were swimming against a current. He grabs Ira's shoulder in just the same way, digging his nails into the bone. "For the last time, *sit down,* or you're going to find yourself next to me or one of the girls."

Shudders of disgust ripple through the boys, and a cry of "cooties" rises from the girls, their high-pitched girl voices sounding to Ira like the voices of alley cats.

"That settles it. You're sitting next to me."

Moving up the aisle, Ira catches first Roger Mansford's eye, then Mark Mahoney's, and they both roll him eyeballs, pure white, of their sympathy, but no one dares a snicker or any other sound until he has passed.

All the same, Ira feels gratified. A hero, if only for this moment.

The guide is about his mother's age, maybe younger, wearing shiny stockings and high heels and a soft white sweater and a shiny bracelet, and some of the boys say, *Not bad,* but not Ira, who thinks she is too old, almost his mother's age.

They follow her through room after room of paintings, pictures of grown-ups, grandpas and grandmas, kings and queens and generals on big horses, and soldiers killing each other. Ira straightens, walks chest out like the White House guys. He feels suddenly as he does at his parents' cocktail parties, nearly invisible beneath the canopy of conversation except when he asks in his grown-up voice, "May I take your ashtray?" "Would you like another drink?"

He brushes his hand over his head, bristles of his new crew cut spiky soft against his palm. *Swift.* His mother didn't want him to get one, but his dad said yes.

The guide told them the men in the pictures are wearing wigs. Tommy Cane told him Art Linkletter wears a toupee; Ed Sullivan could use one.

The lady stops, finger to her lips to shush and tell a secret. The line becomes a bunch around her. They are standing in front of high doors, higher than any doors Ira has ever seen. And the guide, when they are all quiet, says in the voice that grown-ups use to tell secrets, like they are remembering what it was like to play secret agent, "This is the Buddha Room. Does anyone know what a Buddha is?"

The question takes Ira by surprise. He remembers the store his mother took him to when he was little to buy a present for his aunt and uncle, a wedding present, a Chinese store, and he picked out a statue of a fat man sitting Indian style on a dark wooden platform. The man was smiling like a baby.

"That's a Buddha," his mother told him. "A god of good fortune. An excellent present." And the grown-ups went on and on, how remarkable it was, how strange, that little Ira chose the Buddha.

So now he waves his hand and the guide points to him and Mr. Jack whispers his name so she says, "Yes, *Ira?*"

"A Buddha's good luck," he says.

"Ye-s-s. Some are, yes. Anyone else?"

To Ira's relief, the rest of the class is silent.

"The Buddha was a man who spent his whole life trying to help people not to suffer. And a lot of people, Chinese people and Japanese people, and some Indian people, I believe, worship the Buddha and think he is God."

The word *God* makes Ira shiver, and he wonders if they are going into a temple.

"So in this room, you are going to see statues of the Buddha, all different to show the different sides of his personality. Now some of these statues may look scary, but remember, they're just statues."

The guide unlocks the doors and the children file in quietly. The room is almost dark except for a light that seeps in through one high window and creates a pool in the center of the floor, which most of the children step into, huddling against each other, as though it were an island in the midst of dark water. The room is ringed with Buddhas larger than men; Buddhas the size of elephants, Buddhas the size of dinosaurs.

Ira steps away from the children, glides softly across the speckled floor to stand before a gigantic Buddha, smiling exactly like the present he gave his aunt and uncle. *What's so funny?* Ira wants to ask. *What's the joke?* But he smiles, too, leaning across the velvet rope to touch the Buddha's knee.

Tap on the shoulder. The guide lady, frowning, shaking her head.

Next to the red Buddha is a monster with flailing arms and a wicked grin; he wears a crown of flames and dances with a skull balanced on his palm like a soup bowl. Ira steps closer, craning his neck to see if it's really blood or just paint.

"I'm scared," one girl begins to wail, then another, and immediately there is activity; the teachers crowd around her and the others, herding them out, while the guide apologizes, "I had no idea."

Ira lingers, letting the velvet rope slide through his fingers. If he hangs back, will they even notice he's gone? In front of him, a small Buddha reaches out to offer a string of beads.

"Ira Stein." Mr. Jack stands in the doorway, hands on his hips, the whistle steaming at a low hiss. "Let's go."

Don't dare blow, Ira thinks, *scared the Buddha's going to wake up.*

Ira runs back into the outer hall, where some of the girls are still sobbing quietly; behind him, the guide hastily locking up the doors.

Ira smacks his thigh. *Dumb girls.*

He asked his mom what the Buddha believed and she said she thought he believed something like everything you see is an illusion, that it's not the way we think it is, that we've only gotten used to seeing things a certain way, that we're fooling ourselves.

"The way the TV screen is really dots?" he asked.

Could think of it that way, she said. Or like a dream. To tell you the truth, it's beyond me.

They were Jewish, his father said. Jews believed in one God and that they were chosen by God to do what he told them to do.

What is that? Ira wanted to ask, but did not, because that's what the wicked son in the Haggadah did and was kicked out.

When he thought of God, he saw a huge man with a white beard, white eyebrows. It was hard to separate God and Santa Clause sometimes. Santa Claus brought Ira and Phoebe presents even though they were Jewish. He was very nice, his mother said, and Ira thought maybe he was God in disguise.

But who was Buddha then? A fake? If he said everybody was dreaming then how could he have been around?

"You don't have to worry about these things," his father said. "You're Jewish. You don't believe in Buddha, you believe in God."

"He can believe whatever he wants," his mother said.

Then his father wiped his mouth straight across like he did when he was mad. "He's Jewish."

"I'm Jewish and I've always believed what I liked."

"You're a Socialist like your mother."

"What's that?" Ira asked.

"Someone who doesn't believe in God. Like your mother."

"Don't tell me what I believe and don't believe. You don't have the foggiest what you believe, so why shouldn't Ira explore?"

"He can explore being Jewish," his father said.

His mother rolled her eyes. "So let's see you take him to a synagogue sometime. What a good idea."

Like it was a terrible idea, like she didn't mean a word.

"Your father hates going to temple, Ira. His father, your Grandpa Israel, who died, forced him to go and he hated it and used to wish he was off riding a train somewhere."

His father made a silly face then, his eyebrows going high up, his mouth like a goldfish. "True, true. I chafed terribly."

"So don't be a hypocrite."

"You're right, dear. You're always right."

And his mother was smiling then and picking things up quickly, plates, forks, knives, and looking like if you even touched her, she would snap your finger off.

Gwendolyn tucks the end of the pillow beneath her chin, pulls up the case like she was pulling pants on a kid.

"How do you know you're real? How do you know you're not a dream?"

"What are you talking about, child? How do I know I'm not a what?"

"Could be a fake. Ever think about that?"

"What's fake?"

"Everything. Everybody."

"So what difference would it make? Even if it's a dream, we got to *act* like we're alive. Don't have a choice." She plops the pillow on the bed, punches it from both ends.

"Well, what'd happen if God woke up?"

"What's eating you?"

"How can you tell you're not dreaming?"

"Pinch yourself."

He's been doing that. Every day just about. Pinching a flap of skin on his wrist, pinching so hard the skin turns white, pinching so hard his fingernails nearly meet and tears come to his eyes. Where his nails bit, two blood-filled crescents. Everything around him looks the same. But what if you're even dreaming that?

"How come you're real?"

"Huh?" Tommy Cane sits hunched in front of his chemistry set opened like a huge metal book on the desk in his room. On the right, a rack of slender test tubes filled with watery solutions; on the left, an array of small plastic jars containing lumps of chemicals. He and Ira are trying to figure out how to make an explosion.

"You could be dreaming."

"Look." Tommy pinches a flap of skin on the side of his wrist, pinches so hard the skin turns white. "See? I'm awake."

"What if you're dreaming you're pinching yourself? What if that's part of it?"

Tommy unscrews one of the jars, filters a little white dust into a tube, then adds some drops of water from an eyedropper. "Watch out."

They bend close, holding their breaths as a few bubbles break to the top of the filmy water.

"Dud," Tommy says.

"What if you're *dreaming* the whole time?"

"Who cares?"

He cares, he cares. Doesn't know why. *What if the world's a trick?*

At dinner, his father says, "I hear someone's had trouble in school today. Did something happen, Ira?"

He stares down at his plate, peas like tiny marbles; a mashed potato mountain; a strip of meat oozing blood.

"Ira?"

Smash the mountain, drag the tines of the fork to smooth it out. *Too hard,* he'd like to say. *Too fast.* The way the teacher expects them to copy this, copy that. Erases it all in a cloud of dust before he's finished, before he's hardly begun.

"Can you answer your father?" His mother looking at him across the table, then rolling a pea into his sister's mouth.

"Stupid," he says.

"What's stupid? Who are we calling 'stupid'?" His mother's voice contains a warning like an upswept hand.

Whole world. Whole world stupid kaka BM pee.

"Ira, who is stupid?"

Mother and father looking at him now. Forks down, knives down. Who is safest? Who is safest to accuse?

"Mrs. Kaka."

His father frowns. "Who?"

"Mrs. —"

"Stop being a baby and call your teacher by her name." His mother's voice, sharp.

"What's this about?" his father asks.

Ira feels his heart beating fast inside his chest as though

he's being chased across the yard. *Hands. Pushing. Eyes on the board.*

At the stove, his mother clangs a lid on a pan. "I've been telling you for months he needs help, and you keep saying —"

"No one said *you* couldn't help him."

"In my free time?"

His mother's voice rises, dangerous, and Ira glances at his father. He would like to warn him, watch out, but his father pats his lips with his napkin, picks up his fork as though he doesn't hear.

"You have some help, you know."

The frying pan crashes down on the burner. "Help? What help! You're never home to help."

"I've told you things are very tense right now. Crucial projects."

" 'Crucial' this, 'crucial' that. Everything's more crucial than your own family. Michael Stein, big hero, Savior of the Day, rah, rah."

His father grins for a moment, two front teeth overlapping like paws. "Calm down, Eileen. I'll help Ira."

"When?"

"Tonight."

"Too late."

"Don't say that." His father cuts a look at Ira's mother. "We'll go to the basement, the two of us. Practice our writing."

They sit on two stools at the shop counter, dim light from a single bulb, dangling from a cord.

Like a secret club, Ira thinks. But now they have to work.

His father places the pencil in Ira's hand, then folds his own fingers over Ira's, the way he taught Ira to ski, tucking Ira beneath his legs, their skis tracking parallel lines. Together they guide the pencil up and around the barrels of the capital *B.* Ira can feel the heat of his father's fingers, their strength.

At first it is like riding in a cart on a track, then it begins to glide on its own, neither Ira nor his father could claim to be controlling it. The pencil glides through a perfect *B,* the barrels like perfectly stacked snowballs.

"Now you try," his father says, withdrawing his hand.

Ira blinks. Already the pencil seems filled with its own, unwieldy power, seems to vibrate in his grasp, eager to carve its own idea of a path.

"What are you waiting for, Ira? What do you hear?"

He tightens his grip, fingers aching. *Make a* B, *make it straight. Stroke down. Backwards.* C. He can already see the screwed-up letter, the *B* knocked forward on its belly.

"Ira?"

In the silence, he can hear a crackle, a radio in the distance, or a cricket's song, or a space capsule orbiting the Earth. Maybe it's their radio he hears, *Earth to controls, Earth to controls, come in, Earth.* A faint scratching, kittens clawing the edge of a door, a teeny, weentsy voice, *Help me.*

"I'll be Big Buddha, you be Little Buddha," Ira commands his sister, who waits at the living room door for permission to come in. He points to a spot on the floor next to the base of the table.

"Whadda Buddha?" Phoebe asks.

"God," Ira says, and Phoebe is quiet as he crosses her legs, arranges her hands, palm up in her lap the way the statue looked.

When she is settled, he climbs onto the coffee table behind her, crosses his legs. The big red Buddha sat on a table just like this.

"I'm hungry," Phoebe whines, but there is no answer from above, only her brother's slightly hoarse breathing. She sighs, waiting for whatever is to come.

The fiery light of the late afternoon sun angles into a small patch on the wall above the baseboard. Quick as a blush, it spreads up to the ceiling, then across to the curtains and down to the rug. The entire room seems to rock in the red light, setting their skins aflame.

Ira squeezes his eyes shut, brilliant red of the flashlight held to his palm. Flesh glowing like hot coals. *In Russia there's a curtain nobody can get through, a curtain made of iron, nobody knows what it looks like on the other side. But me, Mr. Buddha. I can see what you see . . . blood in my eyelids and shadows of bones. Girls' legs beneath their skirts; Mama's boobs. Got X-ray vision. I'm Superman!* Flames burst on his forehead, his cheeks. Smoke wobbles from the top of his head like a starving snake.

In the kitchen, Gwendolyn or his mother clangs a pot lid, loud as a bell. An ambulance charges by. The sun moves.

Slowly his lids cool. Fire doused.

He squints. The air is filled with peppery dots, shivering specks of light and dark. He can hardly keep from crying out. *Atoms! Molecules!* He's seeing it, seeing how it all crumbles to tiny bits, jittery and scared.

They are sitting just as Michael imagined, in that cramped uncomfortable way people sit when they've been waiting.

"Sorry," he says, extending his hand to the woman who must be Ira's teacher and leaning quickly to brush a kiss over his wife's hot cheek.

"You must be Mr. Stein," the teacher says, letting his hand drop. "I'm Mrs. Hammond. Thank you for coming."

"Michael, please," he says, suddenly bashful. She reminds him of a teacher he had in high school, a similar horsey type. "I wouldn't miss this conference for the world . . ."

It's not a company picnic, Eileen thinks, avoiding her husband's eyes. *At least he made it.*

He joins them at the table, dropping his briefcase and coat as he lowers himself onto the small aqua seat. "Yes," he says confidently, letting his voice resonate as he does in his business meetings. *Your voice is key to your presentation,* his father would say. His father's voice a huge, intimidating instrument. "Perhaps Eileen has told you, Ira and I have been working together on the problems you last identified for my wife and I, uh, me, and I can say, cautiously, of course, but optimistically, nonetheless, that Ira *is* making some progress. Now, of course, he does have real *problems,* I'm not denying that, nor is everything completely solved, of course not, these things take time, but I do think . . ."

He pauses, suddenly aware that the two women are looking at him, their eyes glazed with a sort of pity or disbelief.

"I, uh, of course, should probably let you speak first . . ."

He glances at his wife, whose eyes have brightened to shiny brown and who has gone completely white around the edges of her mouth.

"That would be a good idea, Michael, since Mrs. Hammond had already started telling me about what is going on."

The teacher nods once, giving him a moment to recover.

"What is happening with Ira?" he says at last, his voice sinking, resigned.

The teacher inhales. "Well, I'm sorry to have to tell you that Ira's improvement, while certainly not *completely* unnoticeable, is not what we term *sufficient.* I would be happy to show you the exercise books again, but perhaps you can take my word that his handwriting is still quite poor, well, in point of fact, illegible.

"Even more disturbing, frankly, is his classroom behavior. Ira is frustrated, no doubt, with his lack of progress, and, as a result, he has found other means to make his presence known in the classroom. He is often the class clown and, at his worst, belligerent.

"I believe he is an intelligent little boy, but I'm afraid it's looking even more likely that Ira will be held back for the next school year."

He has been following the progress of her speech like a man riding in a tunnel who patiently awaits the return of daylight. Her conclusion stuns him. *"He has a coordination problem for Chrissakes. Is that a reason to hold a child back?"* Hearing no answer, he turns to his wife, who is sitting perfectly straight, her gloved hands caught in a fierce embrace.

"Let's listen to what Mrs. Hammond has to say." Her voice, though steady, hides myriad cracks.

"Thank you," the teacher says with a nod, as though Eileen has given her the correct answer. "The benefit, if everything is handled properly, is that Ira will graduate from the first grade next year as the most mature boy in the class, the best in many things, the leader he is capable of being."

A leader among men, he thinks. Who did that describe? Of course, his own father.

"You see leadership qualities in Ira?" His wife bends forward as though she didn't quite hear.

"During the year, he fell in with a group of unruly boys. But if he developed greater self-confidence and maturity . . . Which brings me to my other recommendation, that Ira consult a psychiatrist who specializes in treating children. His name is Dr. Goldman, Dr. Harris Goldman. He is a superb practitioner, and I can give you his number if you would like."

"*Psychoanalyze* him? At the age of six?" Michael ducks

his wife's glare, pawing the carpet with the toe of his shoe. *Can handle this.* "Well, naturally, in a situation of this *seriousness,* we would like to talk — not that we don't think you are qualified, of course, but I, *we,* think it would be a good idea to talk to the principal or somebody higher up about this decision."

He watches Mrs. Hammond's eyes narrow. "I don't know what difference that would make, Mr. Stein. Mr. Parelli, to whom you are referring, has not had the opportunity to observe Ira as I have.

"I've worked with children for over twenty-five years and can assure you, Ira is one of the most troubled I have ever seen.

"Frankly, trying to teach a class with your son in the room has been quite difficult. He has very poor manners, he is constantly making loud noises, he won't sit still for even a few minutes. Throughout the year, I've had to take time away from the other students not only to make him behave but to help him keep up.

"I know Ira is not a *bad* boy, and I don't want you to get the impression I don't like him, but we all have to help. He's a difficult child to reach."

"He's a difficult child for *you* to reach," Michael snaps, his rudeness invigorating him.

"I don't make recommendations like the one I'm making lightly, Mr. Stein. Whether you choose to follow them or not is, of course, entirely up to you."

"Perhaps there is another school that would be better for Ira, a special school . . ." Eileen gives Michael a hard look. She wishes he would just shut up and listen, instead of trying to impress someone all the time. All they have to know is the facts; they can make their decisions later.

"As you well know, the best-prepared students in this city

come from our school, the highest reading scores, the best college placements. Ira will never get this kind of attention in a public school." The teacher looks at Eileen. "Didn't you say you were enrolled here at one time? I don't have to tell you."

Eileen gazes at her lap. It's true, she loved the school once. "I was a very different kind of student . . ."

Michael shoves his chair back, sweeping up his coat and briefcase. "I don't see what more can be gained from this meeting, Mrs. Hammond. I appreciate your time and your effort, and I am, of course, embarrassed and sorry that my son has caused you so much trouble. Do you have anything you'd like to add, Eileen?"

She is still seated, her head inclined slightly as she studies the tangled pattern in the Formica. "I think that about says it . . . I'll see you at home." She looks up at him suddenly, and waves. She knows that he wants her to leave with him, to present a united front, but she plans to remain exactly where she is, thank you.

He hesitates for a moment, then turns. The chair, hooked by his coat, turns a somersault, its bowed legs curving in the air like horns. He does not look back.

The two women sit in silence, listening to the classroom clock tick the seconds as loudly as a metronome.

"I would like to get Dr. Goldman's telephone number," Eileen says at last.

"Of course. I have it right here."

Her gaze follows Mrs. Hammond as she hunches over her desk beneath the bright, limp flag. *As though that corner were a country in and of itself,* she thinks. She shifts around to take in the rest of the classroom, its low bookshelves and reading circle, its bulletin boards bursting with cheery messages and good advice: DRINK MILK! PUT ON A HAPPY FACE! THE MAGIC WORDS ARE "PLEASE" AND "THANK YOU."

Of this neat array of desks, which one is Ira's? she wonders. Instinctively, she scans the back row. She always sat in the front, the teachers adored her and wanted her and her friends near them like bodyguards, that whole front row a buffer from the middling and mediocre students, the bad boys.

"Where does Ira sit?" she asks when Mrs. Hammond returns.

She points, as Eileen suspected, to a desk in the middle of the back row. "We're going to have that desk replaced next year; it has a terrible filthy hole dug into it, something the children have worked on for years."

Eileen bumps her hip as she walks through the narrow aisle to Ira's desk. Sure enough, in the lower right-hand corner of the mottled blue Formica is a black hole, the diameter and depth of an upended quarter. She smoothes her index finger around the base of the hole, studies its smudged tip. Then she seats herself on Ira's chair. Inside the desk, a tangle of inked graffiti and stick figures stretches deep into the shadows. She is not able to make out much, a head, perhaps, mouth gaping like that of a crazed jack-o-lantern. What child wouldn't be more fascinated, buried deep in this row, by this record of the past, these hieroglyphics of other boys' doings and attitudes, than by the teacher's unfathomable instructions?

Mrs. Hammond hands her a sheet of lined paper with the psychiatrist's name and number in sweeping script.

The most troubled child she's ever seen. Eileen opens her mouth, and her voice comes out hissy, strange. "Did we do something — something wrong?"

Mrs. Hammond touches her fist to her mouth, clears her throat. "Obviously, you and your husband are trying very hard . . ."

Eileen blinks and says nothing. She is thinking of Ira's black hole, she is thinking of his frustration as he digs deeper and deeper, she is wondering if he ever wanted to disappear, the way she does. Now.

On the bottom bunk, his mother or Gwendolyn has laid out his good clothes, clothes so special that he feels waves of nerves just touching them. Gray wool pants, navy jacket and white shirt that is exactly like his father's, there are even slits in the cuffs with smooth sewn edges that his mother will fill with gold squares she keeps in the gray velvet box on her dresser. Cuff links Grandma Ellen gave him, *Grandpa Abbey's* cuff links.

His mother works the mysterious lever, like a drawbridge, then tugs and twists, making sure the cuff flaps out in just the right place, extending the plane of his wrist, so that his gold glints in and out of the snowy white cuff, a perfect jeweled yoke.

The tie is a disappointment, a trick tie, already tied, like the tie on a doll, it snaps dully under his collar. He would like to learn to tie a tie the way his father does, leaning so close to the mirror above the sink that his nose sometimes bumps the glass. His father is nearsighted, his eyes like shivery dark pebbles behind his thick lenses.

In the mirror left is right and right is left, his father told him. He cannot tell anyway, watching his father's fingers dance around the knot, and his father's neck lengthening and swaying like a turtle when he sniffs the air, wondering, *Is it safe to come out of my shell?*

His father says he will teach Ira when he is bigger and more coordinated. Then he blushes like he has said something wrong and his big hand comes down on Ira's head gently and stirs the hairs up a little and smooths them back down and he murmurs, almost in a whisper, like a secret, "You're a good boy."

They walk along the sidewalk that carries them past the stores, panels of bright, blank glass, curving at slightly broken angles like the cars of his electric train. His mother holds his hand tightly and does not stop to look at things the way Gwendolyn does, saying, "Don't hurt to window-shop." Once he echoed her "window-stop" and she laughed so hard he could see the very back of her pink tongue and then she explained *shop* not *stop*, but now she calls it "window-stopping" as does everyone else in the family, and Ira does not know whether to be proud or ashamed.

With Gwendolyn, he goes to the candy store, rows and rows of sugary pinks, yellows, greens, sagging back on each other, and smooth-skinned chocolates stacked like building blocks. He can choose one thing and he chooses licorice, not because it is his favorite but because it lasts, if you know how to make it last, pulling the whip slowly through your two front teeth, scraping lightly, letting the sweet red gum collect behind them like dirt under your fingernails. And always the temptation to bite, temptation as strong as an itch. He can make the whip last all around the Square and halfway home. But the last inch he chews.

No, they are not stopping at the candy store today, his mother says. So he walks, head down, afraid of the reflection of his suited self. Usually, he would be proud of the way he looked and sneaking glances at the watered curl at his temple and at the tie, even fake, positioned so beautifully, and the shiny black shoes, but not today. Today he is uncomfortable. The pants too warm for this warm spring day, the collar too tight, the tie lifting slightly as though buoyed by an invisible current. Even the beautiful cuff links seem tarnished and the cuffs twist annoyingly around his wrists.

His mother is taking him to see a man *who wants to talk to him,* and he has that sick feeling, like the flu, heating up all his senses, that he has been bad and that the man is a mean man, meaner than any man he has met so far. Meaner, even, than Mr. Parelli, the principal, who said to Ira only days ago, "Young man, your behavior in Mrs. Hammond's classroom is not tolerable."

But, brightening, he thinks, even Mr. Parelli was not as mean as he first appeared. He remembers the way the principal played with the ruler as he spoke to him, tilting it up on one edge and pressing the fingertips of both hands down on it as though it were himself he wanted to punish, not Ira. That made Ira feel worse than anything. The man was hurting himself on account of Ira. He saw the fingertips, a deep line sliced right into them.

Yet he had punished Ira. At least that's what he called it. But it wasn't what Ira expected. He didn't have to pull down his pants and bend for a swat. He had to clean Mrs. Hammond's erasers and think about the difference between "helping Mrs. Hammond and hurting her."

Had he hurt her? he thought with alarm. He had not meant to.

"Are you going to leave?" he suddenly asks his mother as she pushes open the heavy white door. The brick building and the heavy door look so much like the school that for a moment he is confused, as though a piece of the school had broken off and floated to this place.

Inside the same smell of floor wax, but to his relief no boiled smell of lunch, a cleaner smell, more serious, of typewriter ribbons, cleaning fluids, and carbons. The light is different, too, glowing in long tubes, yet strangely dull, the light trapped by something, suffocated by glass. More like the principal's office than the rest of school.

"*Are* you?" For she does not answer, pressing her finger to lips as though they are in the library, hush, hush, but this is not the library, doors of frosted glass speckled with shattered stars. A permanent mist has invaded the rooms and stuck onto the windows. His mother walks on ahead of him, pale in this cold light; his own hands float up eerie white.

"Look for two hundred and thirty-four. Two three four." His mother is counting the black numbers pressed onto the misty glass, so he pretends to do the same, then stops.

"*Are* you?"

Still gazing at the numbers, she murmurs, "For a little while. I have errands." She does not dare look at Ira, afraid she will lose her nerve.

He feels a shiver pass all through him. She must feel it too, because she pats his head.

"You will like the man. He sounded like a very nice man."

The man's office is not at all like the principal's office. It is like a living room filled with deep colors, blue, maroon, brown. There is a fireplace and a table heaped with papers and books; there is a window seat framed by gauzy curtains and a small table scored in black-and-white squares, and on this table stand carved figures like little dolls but not quite.

The man, who is taller than his father and darker, calls himself Dr. Goldman and asks Ira his name and if he would like to sit on the floor. But Ira is still looking at the strange table, the double rows of dolls, set up like soldiers, like they want to charge.

The man pulls up a narrow black chair, turns his head to see what Ira sees.

"Play chess?" the man asks him in a voice that seems to assume that Ira is a man.

Something about the way the man asks him, so direct and a little gruff, like he is embarrassed by how much he wants to play, makes Ira want to tell the man the truth.

"I'm only a boy," Ira says and waits for the man to recoil, to shake his head and pull back his chair.

"Yes. And I'm a man, like your father. Chess is a man's game, but I think you're old enough to learn. That is, if you would like to?"

Again the way the man looks at him, Ira knows he will say yes because this man wants to play this game, the way he wants to play a game sometimes when the only one around is his sister, his stupid little sister, but even she will do when he really wants to play, so he will say yes even though he is not sure exactly what "chess" is and he fears that soon the man will be disappointed with him just as he is with his sister.

"Good."

So they leave their chairs and go to the little table, the short-backed chairs.

"Now the object of the game is to capture the other man's king." The man taps a slender piece with a cross rising from his head. "At the same time you have to protect your king from *being* captured. You have a whole army to control, to both attack and defend. Understand?"

Ira nods; he is the general and these pieces are in his command just like when he was little and played with soldiers. But the cross worries him. *Does the man know he's Jewish?* He does not understand the cross, but he knows it a symbol of *Them* and the way to scare off vampires, and he has wondered if the vampire will be scared of *him* if he is holding a cross; because he is Jewish, the cross may not work for him. Perhaps he should tell the man he may not be able to play this game . . . but he doesn't because by now he wants to play the game whether he is allowed or not.

Choose a color, the man tells him, and he chooses black, the bad color, the color that is not *Them,* somehow the cross in black seems the opposite of Them, as he is opposite Them . . . But Gwendolyn is black and she is Them and not Them, too. She crosses herself with her finger like tying her chest with an invisible lace, and talks, rolling her dark eyes upward, to the Lord, and says *Amen* with a sigh, but sometimes it seems like she is only joking, pretending to need God's help, the way she pretends to need his mother's help when he knows she is perfectly fine on her own.

The man picks up the chess pieces one at a time and introduces them and tells what they can and cannot do. The tiny, bald-headed pawns remind him of babies, jumping all over the place, thinking they are brave and important, but, in fact, they are troublemakers, swallowed in an easy gulp, *no one really cares.* Next are the horses, in an instant his favorites, their taut, shining necks, dark lips, and bulging eyes tell him, *We are loyal.* The pieces that look like the towers of a castle, "rooks," the man calls them, are strange. How can a piece of a building move? The bishops with their nippled heads make him nervous. His mother showed him a picture of a man with a head like that. One of Them. So even though the bishops are his own pieces he will try to lose them as soon as he can. The queen can move *anywhere she wants,* a power so great that he wonders if *he* can move *her.* He feels sorry for the king, huddled, weak and fearful, at her side.

"One more very important rule," the man says. "When you are about to capture the king, you must say the word *check.* That gives the other player a chance to save his king. When there is *no way* for your opponent to save his king, you must say *checkmate.* Then you win the game."

Ira is amazed by this rule. No complete surprise. No Candid Camera. You get a fair warning. One. Then you fend for yourself.

Ira plays slowly, glancing from time to time at the man, who is watching him with his brow wrinkled like Ira's father's when he is on the telephone. He can't help wanting the man to approve of his moves, but he is cautious, too. Why should the man want him to do well?

"You have as long as you want," the man tells him, so Ira is extra careful, sliding his pieces forward and back on their slippery green pads while he makes up his mind. *Must be a trap,* he thinks, and sure enough, just as he is about to set his castle free, he sees — *why didn't he see it before?* — the man's white horse, grazing ever so innocently behind his white pawn, poised to spring on his castle should he let it go. Ira draws his castle back, his heart beating as though his own life were at risk. Instead, he inches forward a pawn; perhaps he can trick the man into gobbling it up with his horse and then he will capture him from the side.

When he looks up, the man is smiling at him.

"Good move, Ira. You play very well."

"Did you like Dr. Goldman?" his mother asks.

They are at the candy store, not at the counter but in the back, at one of the gray marble tables, smoother and cooler than anything in the world, he thinks, and sitting on the rickety chairs with their black wire backs like coat hangers twisted into back-to-back swans. These are chairs you would never tip;

sitting on these chairs gives Ira the same shivery, shaking feeling as sitting in a tree; when he wriggles his bottom he can almost feel the limbs shifting beneath him.

His mother reaches out with her long, thin spoon and catches a drip on the side of his dish. "Ah, chocolate." She sighs and he watches her eyes close slightly in a blur of delight that is somehow close to pain. "Like some of mine?"

He shakes his head at the green blobs she drops into his dish.

"Did you have a good time?"

"He teached me *chess.*" He tests out the word, wondering if she will know it.

"Chess. What a grown-up game."

He smiles more, stopping to spoon in more ice cream so he doesn't give away just how happy he is. "I learned *all* the pieces. Even the *queen.*"

His mother nods, smiling. "Powerful lady."

"It's like war. You capture people, but nobody gets dead."

His mother clacks her spoon lightly against her bottom teeth. "*That's* good," she says, her mouth clamping down on the bowl of the spoon and her eyes closing, so he knows she is thinking of the chocolate, not his game, and that she is wishing the spoon was all chocolate, could be drained of chocolate, like a slice of orange, between the teeth.

Then his mother straightens primly in her chair as though a teacher was coming into the room, and her eyes brighten to little pricks behind the lenses of her glasses. "Ira, I have to tell you something. And it's a little strange, but I want you to listen carefully.

"Listening?"

Ira dips his spoon into his dish, touches the glass bottom.

"I actually don't want you to mention Dr. Goldman or chess for a while. It's going to be our secret for a while. Okay?"

Whatever you say here is between us, the man said. *You don't have to tell anyone.*

"Even Daddy." Her voice so low it's like she's speaking to the table, not him.

Wings rise in Ira's stomach, stroking chills across his ribs. He nods slowly, remembering a long time ago, the day he was bad, the day his mother hit him. *Not angry now, though.* She puts her hand on his, white diamond, catching the light.

"Not forever. Eventually we'll tell him everything. And he'll be happy you're playing chess."

The sound of a vacuum roaring beneath him startles Ira awake. Stomach tightening, he clutches his blanket, puts his thumb in his mouth for a moment, removes it.

Wanna see shadow, he says aloud. Words popping into his mouth, words he has no use for, words that aren't his. *What's* shadow?

In the dream, Grandpa Abbey had the head of a lion, an eagle's claws, and when he snarled, Ira saw teeth pointy as a crocodile's, covered with blood. *His.*

Ira lets his breath out slowly, in little dribbles, so it doesn't hurt. *Don't tell,* his mother said. *Secret.*

What if she tells by mistake? What if she tells Grandpa?

From the stairs, Ira watches his mother bending over the vacuum hose and frowning. She drops the hose and falls to her hands and knees, pulling fiercely at the carpet the way Phoebe pulls at the grass wherever she sits.

"Why aren't you in some clothes?"

He freezes, startled. How'd she know he was there?

"You waked me up."

"The vacuum?" Her face softens for a moment. "Sorry. I'm in a tizzy. Got to get this mess under control before they get here."

He watches her eyes drift over the room, which is already cleaner than he has ever seen it. The carpet, usually buried under toys and discarded clothes, now glows soft and white like a field of snow, inviting him to play.

"Come down here. I want to give you something."

He thuds down the stairs slowly, making her wait for him. When he reaches her, she takes his hand and presses into it a soft wad of carpet fuzz.

"Toss this for me, will you? And ask Gwendolyn to get you some breakfast. Then I want you out of your pajamas and into a tub." Her free hand swats him gently on the bottom to set him in motion.

He opens his hand to look at the fuzz. His prize.

"When's Grandma coming?"

"And Grandpa," she corrects. "Do you remember Grandpa?"

Ira nods. Sometimes when he closes his eyes, he can see a hot white room, hot sun pouring over him, scalding his eyes, and Grandpa Abbey and Grandma Ellen sitting up straight in their big chairs, king and queen. *A king gave Grandpa Abbey a prize for being smart.*

"Grandpa's a genius," Ira says. Hard to say the word out loud. No matter how soft you say it, like crushing a tiny eggshell between your teeth.

His mother bites the tip of her finger. "I suppose so. People say that. Yes. Because he's my father I never *think* that way. But, yes, he's a genius."

Ira nods again. *Grandpa's a genius,* his father told him.

"What's a 'genius'?"

"Somebody who's very, very smart."

"Smarter than Daddy?" he asked, and his father opened his mouth as though he was choking something up, a kind of laugh.

"Smarter than your old daddy, certainly. Not that your daddy isn't smart."

But it made him sad his daddy wasn't as smart as his grandpa. Like Grandpa was sitting on top of a mountain, Daddy, at the bottom.

"No TV until you're dressed. Hear me? They're getting here this afternoon."

Still he stands there, digging his toe, trying to work the swirl of fear in his chest into words. He opens his mouth, but no sound. *Don't tell.*

His mother, on her hands and knees, peers under the couch. "Year's worth of crap under here. Doesn't anyone pick up?"

Chest heaving, he tries once more to pull sound out of the whirlwind, waiting for the moment she turns around, waiting to skip into the rope of her attention, but it's tears or silence that can't be shaped.

She wipes a strand of hair out of her eyes, pushes up her glasses. "Still here?"

Before he can answer, the roar of the vacuum fills the air.

"Now I've got a job for you," Gwendolyn says, shining her big dark face at Ira like a big dark moon. "An important job for a little man like you."

She spreads a newspaper on the kitchen floor and hands him a soft cloth that he recognizes as one of Phoebe's old diapers.

"Now don't go putting that to your nose. You can trust me. I don't hand you a dirty diaper. That one's clean as a napkin."

All the same, he takes a deep sniff that yields, to his satisfaction, a smell that is dimpled and clean as a baby's bottom after it's been powdered. The polish looks like pink milk, like it should smell of strawberries, but it doesn't. It smells like the sour breeze that rises from the diaper pail when you lift the lid.

"Be real careful now. That stuff is poison."

Poison. The word sends a shiver through his brain, and he peers again at the creamy liquid in the porcelain dish. Strawberry milk shake. Would Mrs. Hammond be fooled? Seeing himself bringing her the milk shake, putting it down on her desk. Yes. Except for the smell.

"Now you take that rag and you dip it in the polish and you smear it all over the side and the bottom and inside, too." She is doing it as she talks, and he begins to suspect a trick.

She notices and clucks. "Okay, you finish it. But don't spill none or get it in your mouth."

He clamps his mouth shut and rolls in his lips just to show her.

"When it dries, it gets kind of chalky like, see?" She points to a dry patch that looks to Ira like dried toothpaste.

"Then you rub it off. Just like new."

He takes the silver bowl onto his lap. Soon the poison coats his fingers and he wonders if it will burn them away. Right now it feels cool, like wet clay. He blows on the sides of the bowl to dry the polish faster; Gwendolyn joins him, blowing hard from the other direction so he can feel her breath on his cheeks and smell its smoky sweetness. *Got to give up my cigarettes,* she likes to say, but he hopes she won't. He likes the smell of smoke that is always around her. If he were blind, he would know exactly who she was. Even if she disguised her voice.

"Give it a rub now," Gwendolyn says, handing him a clean cloth. "Let's see what you can do."

He rubs, cautiously at first, then faster and harder, until the cloth in his hand turns an oily black and the bowl shines like the moon.

Grandpa does not want to hug, he wants to shake hands like a grown-up.

"What a big boy," his grandma says.

Not true. Smallest boy in the class, but he plays chess.

Grandma folds him up into a blue dress smelling sweet, then lets him go. Falling back, Ira's happy she's not the hard hugging kind, the kind that makes everything disappear and your face squash flat.

His grandpa is watching. His grandpa, who holds out his coat to his father and his hat and slaps his chest once and turns to the living room, though his mother has not said, "Let's sit down." But she does as soon as Grandpa turns. He sits in the white chair and to Ira's surprise says, "Ira, come here and talk to your grandfather. I want to get to know you."

Ira looks to his mother, who is smiling in a tight line and squinting, saying to him, he knows, but not out loud, *Go on.* He sits on the other white chair and cannot help but cut his eyes at his grandma and Phoebe, who is standing by his grandma's huge white shopping bags.

"Those our presents?" he asks.

His grandma answers, Yes, yes, these presents are for you. He longs to see what he got, but his grandfather's hand comes down on his shoulder and Grandpa tells Ira's father to bring another chair and now the room is only him and his grandpa and his father in the other big chair.

"What can I get you, Abbey?"

"Still make a decent Manhattan?"

"Not as good as yours, but I can try."

His grandpa smiling then, and his father smiling, too. Will Ellen want one? he asks. No, Ellen will want a martini, dry with a twist. His father smiling more and more. He and Grandpa Abbey and Eileen will drink Manhattans.

"Eileen drinks Manhattans?"

"Takes after her father."

Yes, yes.

Then his father goes out of the room, out to the kitchen, where presents are being opened and ice cracked and red cherries sucked and chewed, but he is here with Grandpa, the genius of the world. He shivers.

"Tell your grandfather what you're learning these days."

He is frozen; no words at all. He looks at his grandfather's pink forehead. His grandpa's head is bigger than any head he has ever seen, that's because of the brain, the big big brain that everyone talks about. He cannot tell his grandfather, the genius of the world, that he is learning a group of oranges plus another group of oranges. He isn't sure what it means himself.

"Nothing, I guess."

His grandfather's eyebrows go up and down. "Look at me. You haven't learned anything in your entire first year of school? You know how to read, don't you? How to write?" His grandfather's eyes shoot beams like ray guns from behind his thick lenses, zapping him into nothingness.

"I play chess with the man."

"Chess?"

"The man says I play good."

"Well."

The kitchen door swings open, squeals of his sister, and shut, and his father comes back with a tray. On it, a glass pitcher filled with liquid the color of tea and a row of glasses filled with ice, in each rests a cherry, glowing like a beach ball.

He watches his father pour a glass of the tea for his grandfather and smells the sharp sweet smell as it passes by and breathes deeply, *a drink.*

"Ira tells me he's playing chess."

"Really, I didn't know that. With whom?"

Forgot. A secret. "A man at school," Ira says.

His grandfather sips his drink, frowns.

"Strong enough?" his father asks.

His grandfather nods shortly, puckering his lips.

Ira's father takes a seat across from Ira and Grandpa Abbey.

"Playing chess. That's good," says Grandpa Abbey. "For a moment I was worried. Ira told me he wasn't learning anything in school."

Ira's father drops his head, his wrists braced inside his thighs, hands clasped around his glass. "Well, Ira's had his difficulties, certainly."

"But he tells me he's playing chess."

His father nods. "To tell you the truth, I didn't know that. Been so busy at work. Not home nearly as much as I'd like. You know how that is."

"What sorts of difficulties?"

Ira grips the arms of the chair, the fabric making a faint scratching sound as he pulls. *Don't tell.*

"Mainly mechanical, I guess." Then looking at Ira. "He's a bright boy, of course."

Ira can feel his grandfather looking at him, looking into his brain filled with spaghetti, grizzled meat.

"Why didn't you and Eileen mention this before?"

His father flushes. "Not anything terribly serious, you understand. His handwriting's poor."

"Oh." His grandfather's tone is dismissive. "Sloppy handwriting's a sign of genius these days. Look at all those doctors." To Ira's surprise, his grandfather is smiling at him.

"No, I'm pleased Ira's playing chess. Requires some of the same skills as mathematics — a capacity for abstract thought, the ability to juggle a number of variables." His grandfather turns to him. "Shall we play sometime?"

"Don't got one," Ira says.

"*Have* one," his father corrects.

"What? A chess set?" When his grandfather frowns, his eyebrows disappear behind the black rims of his glasses. He turns to Ira's father. "The boy's learning chess and you haven't gotten him a set?"

His father shakes his head. "Terrible, I know."

"Tomorrow Ellen will take him to buy a set. A good one."

Grandpa Abbey raises his arms for a moment just above the arms of his chair, then brings them down, gripping the ends firmly, squeezing them.

In the dream, Grandpa had the head of a lion, an eagle's claws, and when he snarled, Ira saw teeth pointy as a crocodile's, dripping blood. His.

Ira's father smiles again the goofy way, dipping his head and gazing at the floor. "Thank you, Abbey. Very generous."

Grandpa's king; Daddy's knight.

"Why thank me? It's for Ira, not you."

"We're going to buy you a chess set," his grandmother says, marching right up to the narrow glass door and pressing it open as though she expects a challenge.

He is excited; it is not a store he has been to before, though he has passed its window crammed dense as a cave with cigar boxes and razors and rows of elegant pipes fanned against blue velvet like specimens of exotic mushrooms.

In one corner of the window stands an Indian chief, somber prisoner of a log. At his feet, a chessboard set up with pieces of mottled green glass.

The store wafts towards them its scent of dust and cigar smoke blended with something sweeter. Ira feels embarrassed for his grandmother, who must grow armor not to notice how out of place she is in this shop, how loathed.

The clerk, a narrow man in fitted green vest, gold loop of gold chain dribbling from upper pocket to lower, a pair of rimless spectacles balanced on a thin nose, watches them. Ira wishes he could drop to his hands and knees, drop beneath the enemy's gaze. A long mustache cloaks the seam between lip and pipe stem. The clerk sucks twice, then removes his pipe to exhale.

Grandma Ellen's back stiffens and lengthens, as she readies herself, like a cat, for a fight. His grandmother is a famous fighter. Her battles with shopkeepers are legend. "Don't tangle with your grandma," his mother warns, but she always laughs.

"We're going to buy your chess set." Forcing the clerk to admit he's paying attention or risk losing a sale.

The clerk nods, staring at Ira for a second, then back at his grandmother. Ira, holding his breath, is grateful that the clerk won't tangle either or flutter admiration. A perfect match for Grandma Ellen. No nonsense, too.

"Come this way," he says, drawing them further into the store, though he stays on his side of the glass counter as if he moves on a track. Ira lags, examining the glass display, in which he hopes to find skulls of small animals, arrowheads, pots. He has only seen cases like these at the museum. But no, just boxes and boxes of cigars, lids propped open to reveal their neat loads of slug-shaped missiles in army surplus green.

The light is dimmer in the back of the store. The floor creaks, giving up dust motes with every step. Ira watches them sparkle in the shaft of milky light coming from the front door. Grandma Ellen reaches for his hand, pulls him around so he sees what she sees.

Behind them the tinkle of bells as a new customer enters, someone his grandma doesn't deign to look at, nor does the clerk, either taking her cue or giving her one, maybe they both want to look but don't out of stubbornness.

But Ira turns to see the new customer, an old man wearing a floppy hat whose stomach protrudes under a dull white coat. The man seems to understand that he will wait and turns to examine the rows of cigars as though he were a customer in a bakery examining cakes.

The clerk, meanwhile, has pulled a chessboard from a high shelf and is setting it up on the counter.

"Something that will last," his grandma says. "I believe in quality."

On the lowest shelf of the display, Ira notices a miniature set that folds into a small box. This is the set he would like to have. His grandmother's words unnerve him; he can feel chess pieces like stones weighing on his head. Dr.Goldman's set is a whole table.

"What do you think, Ira? Do you like it?"

The set is the same as the one in the window, green pieces carved from rock, not quite finished. He shakes his head. "Black and white," he says.

His grandmother smiles and puts her arm around his shoulders. The clerk looks blank as before.

"You said you wanted something that would last."

"I didn't say I wanted something so untraditional. Ira's right. This is a set that's going to be *used,* not a decorator's item."

Ira feels heat rising in his neck, but he is not sure if he is blushing for the clerk's sake or his own. His grandmother hates decorators, hates frivolity; his game is serious, serious business. Again he feels a weight like stone, this time the stone is in his stomach.

"I know what you want now," the clerk says. "Ivory."

His grandmother nods once, sharply. "Of course, ivory. I wouldn't consider anything else."

The set costs more money than Ira has ever seen. He blinks as the green bills flash by, reading "50" at least three times. *How come a piece of paper means so much?* he wonders. He has fingered the money in his father's wallet, some bills as soft as handkerchiefs, others stiff as construction paper. But it's not regular paper, Tommy told him, it's paper only the government can make. He and Tommy Cane have got to figure out how to make counterfeit money, Ira thinks. Then they'd be rich. It can't be *that* hard. Not if you could figure out the right machine.

His grandmother hands him the box wrapped in white tissue paper. It is heavy as a small suitcase.

"There," she says. "I know it was expensive, but it's worth it. Remember, if you can afford the best, you buy the best. That way you own something of quality, something that lasts."

Ira nods, and thanks his grandmother, who seems smaller and kinder now that she has gotten what she wanted.

"Thank your grandpa. He wanted you to have this."

The late afternoon sun spills fire across the living room floor, licks up the walls. Ira hopes his mother won't turn the lights on at all.

The chessboard is set up on the coffee table. The heavy white chairs drawn up so that, seated on them, Ira and his grandfather look down on the pieces, a bird's-eye view. Ira does not like this arrangement; he is used to sitting much closer to his pieces, pushing them forward as though they were his own feet and fingers. When he plays with Dr. Goldman, he has the sensation he is in their bodies or they are in his, he marches in their place.

His mother and father and grandmother have left them alone. One wave of Grandpa's hand; they are dismissed. Sighs of relief.

He looks at his grandfather, who is stooped way over, his white hair combed in solid waves as though the sea had frozen. His forehead, large and pink, makes two deep inlets into that frozen white sea. Ira has never been so close to his grandfather's brain. He wonders if he can hear the mechanism whir and click like the inside of a grandfather clock; his grandfather is synchronized like a clock, he moves so easily, makes decisions so quickly, Ira can almost hear the click-clock, two walnuts knocking, a pendulum swinging in even strokes. His grandfather pushes his pawn forward; as white, he makes the first move.

"Your turn." The voice grinds from somewhere deep. His grandfather does not look at him, not like Dr. Goldman, who winces, grins, almost a boy himself. You know he cares. It's only a game, he says, but teasing, to show that he knows, like Ira, that it's just a game and not a game, too.

Not Grandpa. Who makes his moves like a clock. Precisely.

Ira stares at the board. Dr. Goldman has taught him a few tricks. But he is uncertain now, certain only that his genius grandpa knows more. He moves, watching, not the board but his grandfather's face. He moves by his grandfather's expression, the weighted eyebrows, the twitch of one large nostril. Releasing the piece, it is as if his arm has disappeared, floated off like a cloud, dispersed in air.

His grandfather's eyebrow shoots up, just one, and down, up down, like a pump handle. Ira falters, grasps his pawn again, and moves back.

"You took your hand off, so it remains." His grandfather says sternly.

Ira feels the heat streak across his cheeks. Did he? He doesn't remember, but he pushes his pawn forward again and nods as though he meant the move all along. Inside he is trembling, and suddenly close to tears. He hates giving the old man what he wants.

His grandfather has tricks up his sleeve. Like a magician he makes Ira's pieces disappear. His knight comes forward, followed by a bishop and a rook. Ira watches his pieces drift forward and fall away as though under a spell. In no time, his grandfather's army dominates the field, an army of white, impenetrable.

Ira feels a pain in his stomach; he wants to save his men.

"Take your time. Take your time." His grandfather drums the table as he speaks, shifts in his chair, then looks towards the kitchen. "They're awfully quiet," he says. "Like a funeral."

Ira can tell his grandfather is pleased with himself, so hasn't he accomplished something? No. He's let his pieces down; the ones that are left are scared. He glances at his captured pile, touching the white bishop, his one triumph, but even when he took him, his grandfather seemed calm. Not like Dr. Goldman, who sighs as though he has lost a good man, one of his very own.

"You're not paying attention," his grandfather says as he takes Ira's pawn with a twitch of his fingers. "You see."

Ira blinks. He did not see that move coming, but he sees the next. There is no way to stop his grandfather's white arrow; poised to strike Ira's king, a blow to the heart.

"Check." His grandfather beams.

Dr. Goldman would add, "But look around you, you may find a way out."

Ira's grandfather won't give such a hint, or any hope at all. He sits back, laces his fingers over his belly. Turning his head again towards the kitchen, he calls, "Eileen? What's cooking?"

Ira fidgets, hoping they won't hear his grandfather, hoping they won't all come back to see his king in the throes of death, gasping beneath a knobby little pawn. His shame.

The door swings open. His father.

"How's everything? Need a snack?" His father's eyebrows lift, wrinkling his forehead, and he says in his exaggerated voice that makes Ira think of cartoons, "The *Victor*? . . ."

"Game's not over yet. Not quite," Abbey says.

Taking the hint, his father retreats.

Ira feels heat prickling along the rims of his ears and under his arms. He must find a way to save his king, he must, he must.

Afterward, he won't remember just how it happened. But suddenly the chessboard is flipping on end, diving sideways off the end of the table like a plane pitching into the sea, the pieces flying back.

Ira gasps.

His grandfather is staring at him; Ira watches the forehead turn a darker shade of pink than he has ever seen; he imagines the brain clicking at a fantastic speed. So Grandpa must know what Ira doesn't, but all he says, finally, is, "I guess we won't know who won."

He is to wait outside in the hall until they tell him to come in. Strange, the empty hall, empty of all the kids, a tunnel of shadow and light, floor shining, a molasses tongue stretched to infinity.

You're in trouble, Tommy Cane pronounced when he told him.

Guess so, maybe so, always trouble of some kind. The letters too fat too tall too tippy sideways, or his hands aren't to himself, or his voice's too loud or his ears don't listen. Always he's in trouble, though it doesn't feel like him the teacher's talking to, some other Ira, a boy in the mirror who tags along, clowning at him from behind his back, rabbit ears and holding his wrist, beating him on his head, *Why am I hitting myself?* "It's not *me,*" he pleads with the teacher, making her frown, making her say, "Then who is it?"

Cannot explain. Another boy. Jeff, he could call him, but doesn't. He shrugs.

When the door opens, his mother beckons him in, puts her hand on his shoulder, smiles a little, making a guppy kiss at him, her back to Mrs. Hammond, seated with her hands folded on top of her desk like when President Kennedy is on TV.

"Sorry to keep you waiting so long, Ira," Mrs. Hammond says.

He looks down at his feet in their Buster Browns, a shoelace untied, which he hopes his teacher won't notice. His mother guides him to a chair; she sits in one next to it, her knees nearly to her chin.

"Ira," his mother says. Her face looks sad, though she is smiling, eyes running teary behind her pointy glasses, and his heart starts to beat, thunk thunk thunk, like it wants to get out. "Mrs. Hammond and I have been talking about you and the trouble you've been having in class. Mrs. Hammond tells me she is very concerned about you. She says you try very hard to keep up, but that some things, like writing, and —"

He watches his mother's gaze veer to Mrs. Hammond for a second and back, like a kid wanting to check if she's done the problem right.

"Sitting are hard for you.

"Does this sound right? Are you having trouble?"

Not my fault the pencil won't work. Stupid fat old pencil. Tricky old snake. He shrugs.

"She feels you need a chance to grow more confident in your skills, to go at your own pace.

"Would you like that? The chance to go at your own pace?"

For the first time he notices the desk he's sitting at. Lucy's desk. Queen of the class. How's she keep the top so clean? Inside, pink pencil against the ledge, sharp as a needle. He rolls it into his palm, lets it drop.

"Mrs. Hammond thinks it might be a good idea if you repeated this year. Not to *punish* you, you haven't done anything wrong. So you feel comfortable." His mother reaches for his hand, which he jerks back. "You haven't done anything wrong."

"What do you think, Ira?" Mrs. Hammond asks. "Wouldn't you be happier if you could go at your own pace?"

Stay back. Andy Tomaso with his fat head, his Chinese eyes, drooly mouth. Blockhead, dummy, dope. The boys singing songs, pointing. Pinches and kicks. Secret jokes bending them double like they're going to throw up. Girls shoved, pretending kisses. Run, squeal, while the big dope turns happily like a big tomato.

Ira presses the tip of the pencil against his finger, harder and harder. *Mrs. Hammond's arm, her neck, her eyeball.*

"Can't make me," he mumbles and stands so fast his chair tumbles backward. Mrs. Hammond reaches for him and his mother, too, but he's too fast for them. Out the door, down the hall, running fast, fast as he can, dagger in his rib, heartbeat in his throat.

The door at the end of the hall clangs open as he bursts through. He pulls up a moment. Before him gleams the playground, a vast, oiled sea, two-dimensional, exposed. *Hide. Where?* He eyes the scrawny, sparse bushes along the brick wall of the gymnasium, deep scuffed paths between them where the kids dash in and out, hide and seek.

Any second, his mother and Mrs. Hammond will come through the doors.

He dashes across the yard for the opening in the chain-link fence, cars parked at the curb, black Buick, sleek Chevrolet. *Open the door, climb inside. Stow away for another place, another life.* In the window of the Chevy, he can see a shiny face, gapping jack-o-lantern teeth, his own.

The door swings heavy, smacking his belly like a wave, and he slips inside, takes his place curled up in the cavity behind the passenger's seat, cheek pressed against the grooved runner, clean as ice.

In the parking lot, his mother starts the car, making the engine roar a couple of times before releasing the hand brake. She drives fast when she's mad, as though she was Moses zooming through the Red Sea before it could drown her. Ira wishes they would drown, the sea at the windows, fish poking their noses at the panes, a diver with tanks on his back. Underwater he would find a cave, a treasure chest filled with gold.

She has not said a word since she found him, not a word except his name. When she hugged him, she was shaking, silent, her shoulders going up and down.

Mrs. Hammond turned away. "Thank God," she said. And stopping, turned again. "Should I call someone?"

His mother kept hugging him, shaking her head. Not a word. Mrs. Hammond went away.

He spots it before she does. A large rubber ball, rolling across the street. Girls line the curb. One reaches for her ball, her toe tilting into the street.

The stop bounces him forward and back, but he does not hit his head and his eyes open to an empty street.

Quickly his mother opens the car door and strides over to where the girls have huddled.

"Don't you ever, ever run in the street again. Understand? You could have been killed."

His mother's words jab into their heads, their chests, piercing them clean through. A girl bursts into tears, and Ira feels his neck heat up, his cheeks, his heart shivering in a surge of joy. *Stupid.*

His mother stares at the crying girl, then returns to the car, to her place behind the wheel.

"Frightened them," she says. She steps hard on the gas.

Ira sneaks a look back. The girls are still standing where his mother left them, looking after their car as if his mother has turned them to stone.

TWO

Paradise

IRA, 1967

He's been skating all afternoon. Not skate*boarding,* skating, what they call it here, so he calls it that, too, the association with ice sort of funny 'cause they don't have ice or snow here, not a single flake in a thousand years. When you skate downhill, though, they're right: it's exactly like ice.

He's always been a klutz, not really, but he always thought that, thinking his feet were like his heavy hands, but it's not like that, least not anymore. They've taught him *balance,* Jim really, he's the one who took the time, but the other guys are cool, Don and Matthew and Toby, who's a girl. But so tough they call her a boy, one of them, a special honor.

It's just balance, Jim says. For Jim it is "just," but for him, a magical floating dance, a hum, a song, an invisible force powerful as God. *Balance,* he breathes and can barely contain tears.

Jim's his best friend now, and Ira feels honored. Honored 'cause all the guys and Toby, too, like Jim the best. You can just feel it, though they're all friends. Jim isn't the leader type. Isn't bossy. Ever. He's kind, generous. Never laughs at anyone except himself. Ira wishes he could be more like Jim. Why does he always think of the cruel thing to say? The comment that strikes, draws blood, tip of Zorro's sword. Zip, zip, zip. Makes the others laugh.

Jim's the one who introduced himself one afternoon not long after Ira's family moved in. He was at the front door, hands in his pockets, embarrassed 'cause his mother had sent him. Ira was embarrassed too. He felt sorry for the guy, was glad his mother hadn't forced *him.* But hell, Jim said, he could tell right away Ira was *wick* when he showed him his chameleon in the glass fish tank in his room. They spent the afternoon feeding it bits of hamburger, watching the amazing tongue whip like a thread, the pink meat vanishing, the chameleon always still as a rock.

At school even, Jim stuck by him, introduced him to all his friends, repeating his praise: *Ira's wick; he's from the East.* No one cared where Ira was from, only cared what Jim said. Kids listened to Jim. You could tell.

Jim's gang was into skating, so soon Ira was into skating, too, practicing the whole afternoon in the empty garage. Jim teaching what he knows, wheelies, one eighties, three sixties. Lean back, flip your heel, spin. Ira was a natural, Jim said. Had his own style. Made Ira feel good, made him want to practice even more.

Ira isn't sure why he's Jim's best friend. He calls Jim at home and they talk about camping together, the two of them, in the High Sierras. They'd fend off rattlesnakes and grizzlies. Make campfires by rubbing stones. Not far away is a mountain called Grizzly Peak, where his sisters go to day camp. That's where we'll run to, Ira suggests and, to his amazement, Jim agrees.

The ride starts at the top of the hill, two miles of snaking curves, three, if you ride all the way to the flats. Steepest hill in the city. The others have done it before; this is Ira's first time. Everyone's scared but no one's admitting it.

They hop the bus together right after school. Toby's short on change, and Ira's happy he has some for her. He knows she's to be considered a boy, but he can't help thinking how beautiful she is. Her skin, tawny beneath a coat of dust, her jaw hard as a boy's. The tops of her calves round ever so slightly above pure muscle. Ira has no doubt that Toby's stronger than he is; she is even a little taller. The fact that he likes her, the way he isn't supposed to, is a secret not even Jim can know.

Toby squeezes the coins hard in her fist as though she thinks she might be able to crack them. She's always testing her strength and courage in little ways, he's noticed. She likes to bend soda cans in one hand and hold lighted matches till the blue flame shimmies down the matchstick, reaches her fingertips.

First time he saw her do this, he cried out, and she laughed. "Whatcha worried about? Don't feel a thing."

She held out to him her crooked fingers, which were rough to his touch, callused as the bottoms of his heels.

"I'm building up," she said.

From the top of Shasta, the city below is a collection of gleaming boxes. Far across the bay, afternoon fog advances like a giant mattress. Above them the sky's a pure blue that seems to leak into air. The others wear sunglasses, but Ira, who wears glasses, decides his clip-ons look too dorky. Now he squints downhill, glad that most of the way will be shaded by eucalyptus and redwood.

"Last one down's a rotten egg. The *g* sound floats back as Don slips past them, disappears around the first curve.

Ira's hands are wet, his stomach cramped. He waits as one after another his friends take off, reminding him of the way parachute jumpers leap from the plane, an invisible string between them, tumbling one after the other like looping beads. He and Jim are last.

"Okay, buddy?" Jim asks, rubbing his hands together, then smoothing them on his thighs.

Ira nods. "I'm cool." He's decided on the way up it doesn't matter if he dies. This moment's worth it.

He watches Jim dip into a crouch, arms outstretched like a surfer's. Then he, too, is gone.

The string goes taut, pulling, it seems, his very breath away. He steps on his board, placing his toe on the grip the way Jim taught him. All it takes is a slight shift of weight to set the wheels in motion.

For a second he isn't aware that he's screaming, it could be the steam kettle blast of a hawk above or a factory whistle rising from the bowl of Oakland. Then he realizes the scream's coming from his own lungs, whooping triumphant.

He crouches into the first curve as he's seen the others do and straightens and whoops again. The wind whips tears from his eyes. Car doors flash, a series of undulating mirrors, seductive, alive. *Keep your eye on the line.* The fall line, which he crosses again and again, shifting, shifting, rising and falling.

They're waiting for him at the bottom of the hill, beached on someone's wide asphalt driveway, a sheltering cove. Don runs full speed at the side of the garage, seeing how high he can climb without flipping over, while Toby sits on the curb, rocking her skateboard with one foot, ignoring the others as she smokes one of her mother's Kools. Matthew dancing one person to the next, thumping backs, whacking heads, saying *wick wick wick* like it's the only word he knows.

Spotting Ira, they utter a shout of greeting and gather for slaps high and low.

"Wipe out?" Jim asks, throwing his arm around Ira's shoulders like a father.

"Not too bad." He hit a crack in the pavement, opening a

small gash on his elbow, which he won't mention. Inside his head he's crowing, *balance, balance,* with a mad joy. "You?"

"Almost bought it. Fucking lady opening her door . . ."

Ira shakes his head, controlling a shiver.

"But he ducked it, man," Matthew says, arcing his body back, imitating Jim.

"Don the man here had a great ride. So did Toby," Jim says modestly.

Toby shakes her head and blows smoke. "Nah. Had to bail out a couple of times."

"No way," Don says.

Toby's eyes flash. "At Cedar."

"Red light. Doesn't count."

Toby flicks her butt into the gutter, and for a moment the boys are frozen watching it twirl.

"What next?" Toby asks. She rises, stepping onto her skateboard, nosing it out gracefully into the street, then bringing it around so she faces them.

"Jim's place," Ira says. To his relief, they all smile.

"Yeah. Jim's," Toby says.

And they go.

In the dark, the whole theater rustles, hoots, giggles. Ira glances down the row at Jim, Toby, Don, Matthew, plunging hands into the bucket of popcorn, blowing it into the air, beaning it, trying to catch it with their mouths.

Then lights down, almost a hush, then screams as the first chord breaks, train pulling into the station. Can't tell the screams of the audience from the screams of the fans in the picture.

Next to him, Jim's screaming too and he is too. Clapping,

stomping with the fans storming the big black car. *It's been a hard day's night . . .* Glimpse of Paul, digging it, glimpse of John, his favorite, also digging it. (When he and Jim play Beatles, Ira's always John, pasting a half smile on his lips as he looks way past the silly girls, the silly fainting girls.)

Paul's got a nasty grandpa. A dirty old man. Makes you snicker. Ringo's the only one who digs him. Grandpa Abbey's three thousand miles away now, but Ira never misses him, hopes he won't visit. Every week his grandfather calls, his parents acting like it's life or death that Ira get on the telephone. Every week, every Sunday, he calls asking the same questions, What are you learning in school? Do you know any science?

He thinks of his run down Shasta. *I know something about the speed of light.* But nothing worth telling Grandpa, so his tongue lies still in his mouth and his mother takes the phone away, saying, Ira's doing much better here, much happier.

It's true. Ira loves Berkeley, never wants to go back. Only place he's ever felt good, like he belonged, like he's special. Even school's not so bad. Principal knows his name, knows everyone's name, not just 'cause they're in trouble.

At recess, he hooks up with Jim and Matthew and Don and Toby, playing marbles. Talking Beatle talk. Talking Rolling Stones. Matthew being Mick Jagger, his hips going out and around like he's trying to shake a hula hoop.

Ira likes John better. With his crazy ways, his *cheek. Cheek*'s an English word. Means you don't care what other people think. John walks into the tailor shop, cuts the measuring tape for a laugh. He doesn't like taking things seriously, taking things the grown-up way. If you're too serious, you're an idiot. If you're too serious, you're square. John laughs at the worrywarts, the finger-waving grandfathers telling you what to do.

This is paradise, his mother says, pausing for a moment outside her study door, her hands clasping her cold mug to her chest. She stands completely still, as though she were listening to the birds or could actually smell the sharp scent of the eucalyptus or the deep sweetness of the rose garden or even the bitter tang of the orange once your thumbnail's torn the skin.

She closes her eyes and smiles. *Paradise,* she says again, though she's just standing there in the hallway, breathing deeply, breathing only the somewhat dusty air of the hallway, the smell of old carpet.

When she opens her eyes, it's as if she hasn't seen daylight in a long time. She blinks, like a cat waking up, still blind, and then, seeing him, asks, "How are you?"

He says nothing, slumping further into his chair. His heart is beating hard, but he doesn't want her to know he's been watching her.

"Isn't this a heavenly place?"

Heavenly. He thinks of clouds, a world somewhere up there that not even the astronauts can touch.

"What were you listening to?" his mother asks.

"What're you talking about?"

"I thought I heard music coming from the living room."

"Beatles."

She smiles and he wishes she wouldn't, wishes she didn't like his music. Dad likes it, too, and his little sisters. But not the way he and his friends do. His parents listen, sitting in their plump chairs, not moving at all, not even their fingers or their toes. They listen the way they listen to TV, heads tilted, frowning, like they got to learn something from it.

Once his mother asked him what the words were. "I always hear . . ." and he shook his head.

"Doesn't matter what they say."

"It doesn't?"

She looked really confused then, like she'd lost the whole point, the whole thread, the way you might look when the teacher asked you a question and you didn't have a clue what the answer was.

Now she looks down the hall. "Seen the girls?"

He shakes his head. "They're playing somewhere." Why should he keep track of Molly and Phoebe?

"Have you had anything to eat?"

He stares at her but doesn't answer. Where's she been? Lunch was a long time ago.

"I'd better go back then. Back to studying."

She's about to touch the top of his head, but he ducks. Still she manages to catch a few hairs with her fingers, fluttering them like a barber. "Long."

He shakes his head, shaking her fingers out of his hair. "I'm not cutting it. Ever."

She laughs. "You want braids? Like your sisters?"

Why's she bugging him? Why doesn't she leave him alone? But he can't leave her either. She seems kind of sad standing there, sighing about paradise like she can't even go outside.

"Why do you sit in here?" she says. "It's so lovely out. Look, the light on the patio."

He looks in spite of himself as she crosses in front of him to the French doors, walking right past him like a sleepwalker.

Heavy bands of light stripe the patio, turning the bricks into lanes of gold.

"To breathe that," she says, peering through the glass.

"Why don't you go outside, Mom?"

She glances back at him, startled, as though he has made the most incredible suggestion. "I might for a minute. Just a minute."

But her hand stays on the curved handle, and after another moment, she turns back.

Every vacation since they've lived here, they've gone to the parks. Dad rents a trailer 'cause Mom says she's got to have a bed. Her one condition.

Mom and Dad ride in the car, he and the girls in the trailer. It's illegal, so they hide when they get to the tollbooth. Under the covers, beneath the hinged table with its one good leg. Break out afterward, laughing so hard they can't stand up. And Mom turns in her seat, flashing them a smile through the rearview mirror, like she's a bandito, too.

The go to see redwoods so tall you can't find their tops. Find petrified wood so old it's turned to stone.

And they go to a desert called Death Valley, 'cause it gets so hot you could die just standing in the sun.

They go to the mountains, so big and old nothing matters to them.

In all these places, Ira feels so happy, so freed. Like the world's telling him, Be happy *now.* 'Cause you're just a tiny, tiny speck in the whole picture and you're not going to last so long.

He's a good skier, his father tells him. A natural. Exactly like Jim said.

His father loves skiing, too. But took him years to learn the balance. Even now he's just okay, not fluid like Ira, not a bird.

At the bottom of the slope, he waits for his dad, trying to pick him out. Got his eye on a speck that's moving slow, like a paper airplane making its wobbly descent on a draft of air. But no, can't be Dad. Too slow. Too creaky, careful. Like an old man.

Closer the figure comes, a man curving careful turns, afraid of the mountain, using his elbows to steer.

And now he can see, it *is* his dad, red-faced, nose running with clear fluid, eyebrows frosted white. He waves a pole, and Ira waves back, leaning on his pole, a hip cocked. He wants to laugh.

His parents are getting happy here, too. He can tell. Mom's throwing away her old glasses; Dad's washed the grease out of his hair. They've got friends. Jim's parents and Toby's, and Don's and Matthew's. Got all these friends, all *Democrats,* his mother says with relief, doing good stuff. Got a cause. Vote "Yes" on "G" for integrated schools. Mom spends all her time handing out bumper stickers, slipping leaflets under doors. She's not studying for her real estate license anymore.

And his parents dig this house, this house is a palace, perched like a cat in a tree, nearly invisible till you enter the tall box hedge, open the door. Then, Oh my God, everybody says. House curled around a patio and gardens rising in tiers. Roses, quince, plum. Eucalyptus, redwood, and orange. An old gardener tends the grounds for free.

He remembers the day they first came, his mother saying, "What am I going to do with all this house?" But he and the girls ran for the spiral stairs. "First dibs," he called. "I'm oldest."

Didn't matter. Every room had a balcony, a view of the bay.

At dusk the lights of the city come on, twinkling in the neverland below the hills; a sign on his door says: KEEP OUT

Everybody does.

Sometimes instead of heading up the hill, he and Jim slip down the curves of Buena Vista to Euclid and onto the wide concrete

paths of the university. Feels like they're slipping into another world, leaving the pretty paradise behind. Here jive things are happening, carnival-like and strange. Got an energy like Ira's never seen before. People shouting, people laughing, dancing like they don't care who sees them or what they think. Got a whole different language. Got *fuck* got *shit* got *ups and downs,* got other things: *weed, acid, trips.* Got a lingo about Revolution, about cops, call them pigs. Got no problem being happy, being mad.

And weird things happen. Like a girl comes up to Jim, real pretty with long straight hair, puts her arms around him, kisses his cheek, invites him and "his friend" to sit down on the grass with her and her friends, and no one seems to notice they're young, no one seems to care. Got a cigarette they're passing around, pinkie-long stick of soggy paper, evil-smelling tobacco. When it comes to him, he tries not to cough, but even when he does, no one cares.

Someone's got a guitar and a guy's blowing harmonica (down here's called "harp"), and he and Jim lay back, skateboard a pillow, and listen to the notes, cranky, weird, slitting the air like wisecracks, pinging sarcastic, then wide open waaah!

Exactly the music in his mind, exactly like it's talking for him.

He pulls the sheaf of leaflets from the back of his desk drawer. Without knowing why, really, he's hidden them behind the old cigar box of pens, as though there were something secret, forbidden about these papers. Now he unrolls them on the top of his desk to look at them. One has a stenciled fist and a slogan across the bottom: SUPPORT CHE! Ira stares at the word. What's *Che*?

He skims the others. Almost all of them want you to send money somewhere or to join them. Clubs? Ira wonders. They take kids?

The sheets in their hot, bright colors and heavy, black words seem angry. Just touching them, he feels the power of the anger, as if each leaflet's someone shouting at the top of his lungs the way he does sometimes as he skates down the hill.

He wishes he'd picked up more stuff. The leaflets give him a strange feeling, as if there is another world out there. One of the leaflets said, JOIN THE UNDERGROUND, like it's all happening beneath the floor. A world as crazy as through the looking glass, but somehow more real, clearer, more truthful than this one.

Reading these angry words makes him feel like someone is shouting at him to wake up! wake up! the way someone would if they found you asleep in your bed when your house was on fire.

There's another thing. Something about this other world scares his parents, they don't get it. Might think they do, but they don't. Not the way he does.

His mom's in a bad mood. You can tell. She's late picking them up from the Y and there's a traffic jam ahead. Mom squinting, leaning on the horn.

"Come on you, bastards. Move."

Little sisters clap hands over their ears. He sits back. Hey, hey, Mom, don't lose your cool.

"Oh, Jeez," she says, shielding her eyes with her palm. "What's going on?"

Ira sticks his head out the window, then most of his body.

"Get back in here," his mother says. "What do you see?"

"Some kinda parade."

Coming down the hill, coming down the street, people holding banners, signs, shouting something Ira can't quite make out.

Then police on motorcycles zip past the line of cars, so close Ira ducks his head in. "Whoa!"

"Sit down. Now." His mother's eyes are shining, her mouth set in the way it is when she's angry, as she noses the car out of the traffic, hangs a turn, heading down the opposite lane.

"Can't we check it out?" Ira looks at the rearview mirror. No sirens, no flashing lights coming this way. Only a whole row of cars, arcing out and around and speeding down the empty road behind them.

"So you were at a riot," their father says in his kidding voice.

"A parade," Phoebe corrects him.

"Did you see an elephant?"

"Not even a donkey," says Eileen in a grim voice.

Michael smiles and ruffles his daughter's hair. "I heard about it on the radio. Looks like the administration's really let things get out of hand."

How did it get out of hand? Ira wants to know.

His father smiles quickly. "They just weren't reasonable."

What's that mean? Ira wonders. His dad irritates him, he isn't sure why. It's as though his father, sitting there, chewing his steak and reaching for his water glass, thinks he could do better, act better, talk better.

But he wasn't there.

His father touches his napkin to his lips, lowers it. "You see, the students let their emotions get the better of them. If you're advocating free speech, you should allow others to speak. Respect's the key to civilized behavior."

But after saying this, his father looks to his mother, who's tossing the salad, not looking at his father on purpose, Ira thinks.

"What do *you* think, Mom?"

"Your father's probably right."

"Probably?" His father flutters his eyelids, making a joke of it.

The salad tools clack against the bowl as his mother scoops. "Well, the other way of looking at it is the administration's *not* allowing students to assemble, they're *not* listening to them, nor do they have any intention of doing so. Rather condescending if you ask me."

"Admit this, dear," his father says. "You've got to have *some* rules, *some* limits, otherwise the lunatics will be running the asylum."

"That's where we disagree."

"Oh my God, children. Your mother's become a radical."

His mother shrugs. Before his father can say anything more, she starts serving the salad in such a way that Ira knows the discussion is closed.

One morning they all wake up on the floor, books tumbled from the shelves. They laugh. Cool. Wick. The earth doing its own bump and grind, wiggling a hip.

School's closed so they can examine the structure, just in case. And Dad decides to call in a sick day, just for once.

They're going on a picnic, up to the park at the top of Shasta. Grizzly Peak.

Take sandwiches, take cold chicken. Iced tea and lemonade. Take cookies and the leftover hiking chocolate.

Pile into the Dodge. Like they're going on a trip. Got that

special feeling, 'cause they've all been sprung free, out of the blue.

They park at the very top of the mountain, where they've got a view of hills, of the city, the bay beyond. Dad points out the Golden Gate, flimsiest of clasps.

Mom wants to rest and read, but Dad says, "Let's walk, work up an appetite."

There's a trail through the woods, pounded hard by feet and hooves, but narrow enough so you can pretend you're the first one.

Girls dawdle slow. Mom even farther behind.

"You scout," his father says. "Let us know what's up ahead."

Eager, then, running through the evergreens, branches feathery and fragrant, screening the turquoise sky. Farther and farther he runs, like a deer, an Indian scout, a messenger picked for his fleetness of foot.

He stops to catch his breath, bent over where the enemy arrow caught him in the heart. Doubled over.

And that's when he sees the eyes staring at him, eyes tawny and luminous in the great pineapple head.

Owl on a branch. Staring.

His father makes the announcement at the dinner table. His project's over. He's being transferred. Back East to New Jersey. Big promotion, big boost in pay.

Never occurs to anybody to say no.

Mom in tears. Vote only a week away.

Little sisters in tears. They wanna stay.

Only Ira is still. 'Cause it's simple. He ain't going to go. No way, no how.

I know it's a blow, his father says.

Abyssinia. Ethiopia.

Ira, sit down.

He stands, shoving a chair out of his way.

Ira!

His father shouting, his mother saying, "Leave him alone."

She goes to touch him, gripping his shoulder, trying to speak.

He jerks her away.

Leave me alone.

And she does, falling back to the table, while he scoops up his skateboard in the hall, heads for the street.

This time of evening something heavy happens. Sky blotting up with ink, moon coming out, a shining C, sun sitting on the horizon, flaming dome about to be pierced.

He steps on his skateboard, tips its nose down the street.

Down and down he goes. Down and down. *How far ya going? So far you'll never catch me.*

Once he and Jim skated as far as the Fish Market by the ramp to the freeway, talked about how cool it would be to skate all the way to the bridge.

Kids stood by the side of the ramp, holding up signs where they want to go: S.F., Portland, L.A. *Could put a thumb out, but he's too scared.*

Skate to the Marina, to the edge of the bay. Stroking and gliding, wheeling around over broken glass, riding the pavement as far as it will go, like a wave played to its very last lick.

Let gravity take you, let gravity roll you right out to the bay, out to the strip by the freeway, where people harvest driftwood to make the fantastic: giant birds, heads like African masks, machines that do nothing but catch the wind.

Drift out to the driftwood people, patiently nailing their scraps by the edge of the bay.

* * *

He sticks his hand in his pocket, finds a smoke, but no matches. Sticks the cigarette in his mouth. King of the Hill. Riding down Shattuck, down University, like riding through a carnival at night, lights and sounds and people rushing all around.

But the Flats are quiet, deserted. Fog whirls in the street-lights like snow.

It's cold.

This is crazy, he knows. But a stubbornness is in him.

The sun's in the water. A crimson carpet lapping towards him, a lane of fire, dying away.

This is my home. Where I belong.

Gulls call overhead, white herons step barefoot on broken glass. A wind rises, cooling down his fire.

He tucks his hands in his pockets, bows his head.

No home now, no place for him.

Walking and walking, lights of the city heaped like a hive above him, a little beyond. Like the optical illusion of a glacier. Walls always seem so close, really so far. Stood on a glacier once, vast parking lot of ice and snow, so flat it made him want to walk to the end, made him want to cross that horrible blankness at a dead run.

How far you'd say that is? his father asked.

Mile or two.

His father laughed. *Ten. Fifteen.*

No way.

Yessiree. You'd die of thirst halfway there.

So they didn't cross. Walked a few yards here, a few yards there, got back in the bus with the other tourists, drove back down the mountain. Still he didn't believe.

Now it seems like he's been walking forever: feet sore, stomach yowling. But eventually the avenue begins to climb the face of the city, up past the campus and into the serpentine beyond.

He recognizes where he is now. Back to the sweet jungle of camellia and juniper, red needles everywhere.

Where've you been? his mother cries, rushing at him like she's going to knock him down.

Little sisters scramble like monkeys behind the slats of the banister. Dad coming out of the study, phone in his hand.

My God, he's back.

Got lost, he tells them. *Keep the explanations simple.* Wanted to see how far I could skate. Got dark and no money, no way to get hold.

Could've called *collect,* his mother shouts. You're not an idiot. We were frantic, frantic with worry.

Sorry. Got lost.

His father shaking his head. We called the police and they couldn't find you. We called Jim.

Parents look at each other. Little sisters sneaking down the stairs real slow like they want to catch Santa Claus.

It's okay, Mom tells them. Ira's all right.

Girls come fast then. Hug him round his knees, his stomach. He hugs them back.

Kinda hungry, he says.

His mother looking at him, cold as stone.

You'll never see her real face again.

All right, she says. We'll feed you.

THREE

Desperadoes

PHOEBE, 1968–1971

Ira wants to beat me.

Race you to the corner, he says.

Then he takes off before I'm even ready. It doesn't matter. I beat him anyway. I'm fast. Incredibly. So fast my feet don't touch the ground. I beat him and he says I cheated.

You're the one who cheated, I say.

Ira wraps his arms under my shoulders, cups his hands at the back of my neck.

Full nelson, he says, hunkering over me like a shell. One move and you're dead.

I hate you, I say.

Then I go limp. I know he can't hold his sister too long. It looks too weird. So I hang until his arms loosen. Then slip, whirl, punch his solar plexus.

Ira doubles over.

I run.

We sit in two rectangles of light on the wood floor. Ira's rolling a smoke, cupping the paper in one hand, sprinkling tobacco with the other. You've got to get it even, he tells me as he pats the row a little here, a little there, like he's tending a garden. I've never seen Ira so tender before.

Then he raises the little boat to his lips, licks across the edge. It looks like he's kissing the boat. He's still so tender.

"In Guatemala, peasants roll cigarettes in one hand 'cause they're not allowed to stop working," he says. I think he's making this up, I think he's practicing, hoping he can get that good.

I like to smoke, but it makes me nervous. One time Mom came upstairs, knocked on the door and, before we could do anything, she finds us smoking. She was furious, talking straight to Ira. "I'm disappointed in you," she says. "I thought you were smart enough to smoke behind the barn."

I don't get it. What barn?

She means the garage, idiot.

How come?

She means do it behind her back, but don't get caught.

It makes no sense. What's different about the garage?

Ira doesn't bother to explain.

"Take a look," Ira says. He drapes a magazine heavy in my lap, like an X-ray bib at the dentist. I look down and feel like I'm going to throw up. Pictures of girls in a locker room. Girls with pom-poms, cheerleader skirts, only naked on top. They don't know they're being watched, that their pictures are being taken.

"How'd they get these?" I ask.

"Hidden cameras," Ira says.

"Where?"

"In the ceiling, in the shower."

My stomach rolls. "I don't believe you," I say.

But I do.

I don't take my shirt off in gym anymore. I go to the bathroom instead. Change in there. Miss McKay wants to know what I'm doing, but I don't tell her.

Ira laughs. "They're got cameras in the bathroom, too," he says.

Our homeroom teacher tells us that the girls are staying in for recess.

That's no fair, I say.

Mrs. Pitt shoots me a mean look. "This assembly's just for girls," she says.

I look away.

They stuff us in one hot room, all the fifth-grade girls. Along with the teachers and the nurses. They're just going to show us a film, they say. But you can see how nervous they are, throwing each other looks and coughing like there's a big surprise. Then it's Jiminy Cricket teaching us the facts of life, how we're going to bleed each month and have babies. In the hot, dark room, it doesn't seem like anyone's breathing.

Why do they have to push us? Why can't we just stay girls?

In the front of the room, Mrs. Pitt's holding up napkins, holding up bras and harnesses to keep the napkins in place.

"You'll need these when you bleed," Mrs. Pitt says. She's trying to sound normal, but her eyes look glittery and her cheeks flame pink.

I raise my hand.

"Yes, Phoebe?"

"How come you can't sit on the toilet and let it drip out?"

Mrs. Pitt fixes her glittery eyes on me. "It's not like that. It's very slow."

The other kids laugh. Except Doris, my best friend. When

we're leaving the room, I whisper in her ear that I'm going to sit there until it all comes out.

After assembly comes gym class. I stomp around and won't play. Miss McKay wants to know what's wrong with me. She makes me go to her office.

"Why don't they leave us alone!" I scream once her door is closed.

"What do you mean, Phoebe?"

"How come they're teaching us this stuff we don't want to know." I kick the leg of her desk like it's a shin I want to break.

"Pull yourself together, young lady. There's nothing wrong with being a woman."

Yes, there is.

"Look at me. Look at me right now. *I'm* a woman."

Miss McKay wears purple gym suits with fuchsia tights. She's skinny like Peter Pan. And she walks like him, too. On tiptoe, like she could fly.

I used to like Miss McKay. Now I hate her. She's on their side.

I don't go up to Ira's room for a long time.

Then I do.

Ira hands me a smoke and a magazine opened to a full-page picture of a naked blonde with boobs so large and pale they look like they're going to burst.

Fake, Ira says. They're filled with silicone. A kind of plastic.

Why would they want to do that?

Makes them big, Ira says.

Heat pricks in my neck, my armpits. I don't want big boobs, I don't want boobs at all. At night, I lie in bed with my hands pressed hard against my nipples, so hard my hands ache in the morning, but it doesn't do any good. I wear T-shirts way too tight, try to make everything look smooth, but that doesn't work either. The nipples won't stay down. Even though they're soft, they've got a will of their own. I'd like to kill them.

"What's that?" I point to a sore-looking lump, the size of a quarter, on the girl's boob, the underneath part.

Ira pulls the magazine close to his face. "Pimple," he says.

It's not a pimple. It's *cancer,* I think.

"No," Ira says. "It's not cancer."

How does he know? "Do you think if I wrote Crystal a letter she'd get it?"

"Probably not," Ira says. "Anyhow, that's not her real name. They never use their real names or anything real about the person. That's not even what boobs really look like."

"It's not?"

"Real boobs are hairy. Like gorilla's."

"Not Mom's." I say.

Ira squints for a second before his eyes shift to me.

"You've seen them?"

"Uh huh." I can see Mom in my mind right now, jerking up in her tub, her arms flapping down close across her chest like she thinks I'm going to hit her. But I saw them. Two white islands, plump as knees, bobbing on the water before she punched them down.

"They're *not* hairy."

Ira smirks. "She shaves them. They all do."

I buy myself a bra. I buy napkins, too. I've got to be prepared. So I don't have to ask Mom.

Then I go to the bathroom and try on the bra. My fingers are trembling. I can't get it on. Somehow I hook it, look in the mirror. I want throw up. But I've got to keep going, I've got to put on my shirt.

There it is. The shelf. Like they've all got.

Then I rip off my shirt, rip off the bra. My hands are shaking, but my jaw is numb.

Stuffing the bra in the back of my drawer, back behind the jeans, I feel like I killed someone.

I run outside.

Ira's shouting he won't go. Without even seeing him, I know he's at the top of the stairs, shouting down at Dad.

It's not a matter of choice, Ira, Dad says. You're a member of this family, so you're going to Thanksgiving.

Dad's always trying to keep the family together, trying to get us to eat together, and to go on trips together. Ira's always telling him, Fuck you.

I pull the covers over my head, watching the blanket fairies spark and disappear. Thanksgiving's at Grandpa Abbey's. It always is. Ira's scared of him. We all are.

"I'm not a member of this family," Ira shouts.

"You're a member even if you choose not to be," Dad says back.

I put my hands over my ears. I feel bad hearing that Ira doesn't like our family. I wonder if he likes me.

The sky is very blue today and clear and the highway's almost empty at noon on Thanksgiving Day. This highway has lights every few miles timed so that if you're going the exact right speed, they line up green, green, green like the jackpot on a slot machine.

Thinking of those lights as gates, I hold my breath as Mom drives straight towards a red one.

"Shit! I forgot the cranberry sauce."

I wham into Ira's shoulder; Molly whams into mine. Our horn is blowing like a New Year's trumpet, our tires are squealing, as Mom, arms braced against the steering wheel, brings the car about in a full U-turn.

"Eileen!" Dad shouts.

Molly begins to cry.

Ira and I roll eyes at each other. We know Mom. She's crazy.

We squeeze together on the welcome mat outside the apartment door like we're squeezing into the frame of a picture. Only Ira stands back.

Grandpa Abbey answers the door. "Hi, hi. What happened?" He's wearing a dark suit as always, a dark tie. A red-and-white rosette tiny as a fish eye pokes from his lapel.

Grandpa doesn't hug. Ever. He leans shifting his weight from foot to foot, like somebody riding a train.

"Thanks God you're all right," Grandma says, coming up behind Grandpa. She's wearing her apron over her ivory suit. She doesn't hug, either.

"Traffic?" Uncle Robert gets up from his chair, but Aunt Beatrice stays seated, smiling at us through a mouth filled with nuts.

Everyone's looking at Mom, who's flushed so bright even her eyes are shiny.

"All I could think of was the cranberry sauce I left sitting on the kitchen table."

Ira raises his eyebrows, whisks invisible gunk out of the corner of his eye. "She nearly killed us," he mutters.

"What's that?" Grandpa asks.

"Mommy did a U-turn on the turnpike," Molly says.

"Oh well, I didn't want to disappoint my father." Mom's eyelids flutter like it's all compliments they're saying.

"Next time, don't risk your life," Grandpa says. But he's smiling. You can tell he's happy she did.

When Mom was a girl, she used to excuse herself from dinner after a few bites, go into her bedroom, and lock the door. That's why she was so skinny, she says.

Her bedroom's the guest room now, the darkest room in the apartment. It smells like mothballs and radiator steam. The windows look out on the brick walls of an alley.

We tiptoe in like there's someone sleeping on the bed beneath all those coats. I'd like to stay in here, too. I'd like to hide.

Instead, I take as long as I can to take my coat off. Ira's peering at the spines of books as though he were in a library; Molly's stroking the arm of Aunt Beatrice's mink.

Staring at myself in the mirror on the back of the closet door, I lose all hope that my party clothes have transformed me in any way. Two buttons shaped like logs are missing from my winter coat, my tights sag at the knees.

I'm wearing my green brocade, a shade I thought was the most elegant color I'd ever seen until Ira told me it looked like curtains.

I'm not very pretty. My cheeks are too thin, my eyes too small. I'm a green person. Green of a cocktail olive. Olive-skinned. Like an Indian from India.

I tilt my head, hoping to find a more flattering angle. I make myself smile. Every time we see Grandpa, he says, "Why does Phoebe look so serious?" I think it's a trick or a test. If I'm ever going to turn out to be a genius like him, I've got to be serious.

"Ira? Phoebe? Molly? Let's come out now." It's Mom in the hallway. It's the fake voice. "No hiding." A voice spun like sugar around a scorpion.

Molly gives Mom her hand. Ira mutters a swear, then shoves a book back on the shelf.

I face the mirror and flash myself a smile, a dazzler, like a Miss America type, with all of my front teeth showing. They learn to smile that way, even when they know they're going to lose.

Great-aunt Mildred's in the hall. She's even later than us.

"No cabs," Aunt Mildred says, handing Grandma a bunch of daisies.

Grandma hates daisies. She hates Great-aunt Mildred, too. Grandpa's younger sister. She's the only ugly person in the family. She's got buck teeth and a big mole on her nose. She likes to boast that her blond hair has never been dyed. Grandpa believes her; Grandma doesn't.

"My garnet twin." Aunt Mildred waves me towards her while the others go into the living room. "Let me lean on you."

We're twins because we were born on the same day.

"I have something special for you. But not yet. I'm still negotiating. A jeweler friend's helping me. We'll see."

I don't know what she's talking about, but I'm glad she's here, saving me a little longer from Grandpa. Her nails bite into my shoulder as she tugs off her dry galoshes and drops them on the Oriental rug.

"I was a schoolteacher for fifty years and was never late rain or shine. Ask Abbey. He knows." She lifts her chin for a second, listening to the sounds from the living room, listening for something. "How is my brother?"

"Fine, I guess." Once I asked Aunt Mildred what Grandpa was like when he was a little boy and she said, very matter-of-fact, "A tyrant, just the same."

Now she grabs my arm, squeezes my cheek. Her back makes a hump like a sleeping cat under her sweater. "Let's join the party," she says.

* * *

In the living room, the grown-ups are talking and drinking. Aunt Beatrice makes room on the sofa for me and Aunt Mildred. Ira and Grandpa are sitting next to each other. Grandpa, in his armchair; Ira, in the corner of the sofa. Mom's talking to Aunt Beatrice, but you can tell by the way she rubs the top of her leg and tosses her head she's really listening to Grandpa. Everyone's listening to Grandpa. Always.

"How's my brother?" Aunt Mildred asks. Her voice croaks and gurgles like a draining tub.

Grandpa frowns. "Fine, fine. I was talking to Ira."

Ira frowns, staring into his glass of Scotch. Five dark hairs adorn his upper lip, invisible from any distance, all the mustache he's been able to grow.

"How's my grandnephew? Drinking, I see?"

Ira nods, still looking down.

The tray of salmon sits on the coffee table in front of Grandpa. Plump silky slices sprawled over dark rectangles of pumpernickel. Salmon is the one good thing about Thanksgiving, the one treat. I wait for the moment Grandpa's head's turned, then dart my hand.

Mom gives me a little smile and gets up from her chair. "Grandma probably needs help in the kitchen." Ira gets up, too.

"Phoebe," Grandpa says. "Come sit." Pointing to Mom's empty chair.

I feel my heart beating fast in my chest, my legs shaky. He's going to ask me what I'm learning in school and I won't be able to think of a good enough answer. Every year when he asks, it feels like I've learned absolutely nothing, that I *am* absolutely nothing, that if I was a genius, like him, I wouldn't have to learn at all.

Grandpa clasps his hands across his belly. "How are you?"

"Okay."

"Such a darling," Aunt Mildred says. "My little girl."

Grandpa puts up a hand to shush her. "I want to ask my granddaughter a question."

I feel like I'm in an airplane about to crash. My heart's pounding so hard I can hear it echo. I wonder if Grandpa can, too.

"Do you know the story of Jacob and Esau?"

"Uh huh." I don't really. Something about a lambskin. One brother tricking the other, pretending he's a lamb.

"Which brother are you?"

I'm not either brother, I'm a girl, I want to shout, but his eyes are gleaming, his smile.

Once when I was little I asked my grandfather what a genius was and he told me, "Someone who asks questions."

I felt encouraged. It can't be *that* hard to be a genius.

But each time I wrote down a question, I crossed it out. My questions seemed stupid, not like genius questions at all.

"Esau," I say. *What does that mean about me?*

"Esau," he says. "That's what I would have guessed."

In the kitchen, Grandma's fussing with Mildred's yellow daisies, stabbing the stems into a narrow vase as though she hoped they would break. She says, "I loathe daisies." Then, catching my eye, she informs me, as though I were the one who brought them, that no proper guest brings flowers to a party.

"How come?" I ask.

"Can't you see?" Grandma cries, gathering the whole bouquet in one hand and shaking it. "Haven't I got a million other things to do?"

Grandma's tiny kitchen is bright under the fluorescent light. A washer and dryer stand side by side as a counter. In the corner next to the hutch, Molly sits on the kitchen stool and folds napkins.

We give each other a look behind Grandma's back. No one can please Grandma in her house. There's a right way to rinse dishes, a right way to dispose of garbage, a right way to crack eggs, to boil water for tea. The only way to get along with Grandma is to ask first.

But she has another side, too. She gives us chocolate apples, bunnies with our names in the ear, and clothes and money whenever she can. She has stock in each grandchild's name and every year asks if we would like her to reinvest.

"Here, find a place for this," Grandma says, handing me the vase of daisies. "Then come back. I've got another job for you."

The dining room table has already been set. Heavy white tablecloth, crystal glasses, silver. Little cardboard tents tell us where to sit. I circle the table, feeling like a spy. Who gets Aunt Mildred this year? Who gets Grandpa?

Molly's next to Grandma, then comes me. I switch the cards. No one will notice. Then there's Mom and Mildred and Grandpa at the head as usual.

Then I see Ira. Next to Grandpa. I want to switch him, but it won't work. Grandpa will say, I want Ira *here.* Every Thanksgiving Grandpa gives a speech about what each person in the family has accomplished. Ira's flunking math and science. What's Grandpa going to say?

I put the vase on the sideboard, under the portrait of Grandpa. He's sitting at his desk, holding a pen above a piece of blank paper. You can't tell by looking at him that he's a genius.

Molly and I follow Grandma back through the angled corridor past the living room, where everyone's still talking, past Grandpa's study with the framed tree hanging on the door, the tree Grandpa calls the "family tree," because the names on it, printed across the trunk like steps to a treehouse, and along the limbs and into the leaves, belong to scientists who got famous from using his research.

Grandma and Grandpa's bedroom overlooks a park and beyond that a river. Everyone talks about how lucky they are to have that view, but, glancing out the window, I see a river the color of stepped-on newspaper; across it, rusty, chewed-looking cliffs too steep to climb.

"This one for Phoebe, this one for Molly." Grandma hands us each a pillow-shaped bundle wrapped in tissue paper. "I found them in Russia on our last trip."

Grandma goes with Grandpa to all his conferences. While he gives papers, she shops. But a long time ago, she was an artist. The best in her life drawing class. She was even asked to teach. Then Grandpa asked her what she would actually do with her own studio. I couldn't answer him, she told me. I lacked confidence, she said.

The shawl's royal blue, wide enough to cover my whole body with material to spare. "Babushka," Grandma calls it. Her great-grandmother wore one.

In the mirror on the back of the closet door is a peasant girl with dark eyes and hair, olive skin and a ruby mouth. Natasha's just slipped away for this instant, away from her stall at the market, or from the kitchen where she's helping her mother make soup. Wrapped in her royal blue babushka, she's stolen to the farthest border of her world to peer into mine.

"Grandma, who's Esau?"

"Esau? You mean in the Bible? He was Jacob's older brother, of course."

"Why was he important again?"

"He was cursed by his father when he should have been blessed."

* * *

In the living room, Grandpa is shouting at Ira. "That the Earth moves around the Sun, that gravity is a force, that light is both wave and particle — the greatest scientific discoveries of mankind would not be valid without their mathematical proofs.

"Only an *idiot* would refuse to study math!"

Our mother is sitting with her eyes closed as though a plane is taking off, as though she would like to get up, but can't. And our father is standing at the mantel, his glass raised, his head cocked like he's in the middle of a funny story.

Ira sips his drink from a heavy glass, his eyes half-closed as though he's no longer in the room, as though he's listening to some music or voice through invisible headphones. He tips his glass way up, waiting for the last drop of Scotch to reach the tip of his tongue. It's as though he can't hear Grandpa.

Then Ira opens his eyes. "Why should I listen to you more than to any other old man?" he asks.

"Why? Because I'm your grandfather. A hell of a lot smarter than you!"

It happens so fast. Like a car accident. Grandpa standing up. His cane coming down. Ira's glass shattering on the floor.

In my old school in California, I was Queen of the Girls, the marbles champion, and the handball champion, too. I went to third grade for reading. Then we moved to New Jersey.

When we first came here, I wore my hair in two long braids, my dresses to the tops of my boys' sneakers, no flesh showing. And I had braces I was proud of, I liked to think of them as ornaments for my teeth. I was pretty cool, I thought, but the other girls decided I was a freak.

The only girl who looked stranger than me was Doris. She

wore hand-me-down dresses, and her hair frizzed like a dandelion globe around her head. Her nose was strange, too. It was small and soft. If you pushed it with your finger, it squashed all the way down. Eskimo nose, the other girls called it. No cartilage, Doris explained.

Doris's mother was divorced. No one else's was back then. That didn't happen until fifth grade, when everyone's parents got divorced except mine.

I think Doris's mother is cool. She wears black and smokes cigarettes and sends us on errands to buy her wine. On overnights, we start out with the wine run, then bribe her mother into letting us go for night walks on our own. Their house is on the edge of the college in town, and Doris knows the campus like her own backyard. Her older brother and sister showed her all the good places, the pool outside the quad where you can wade up to your ankles in water shot with light, the girls' bathroom in the basement of the dining hall.

We head first for the pine grove perched on a sloping lawn glazed with fluorescent light.

"Desperadoes," we cry, bursting from our cover under the branches. "Desperadoes!" We charge full speed down the hill towards the fence marked DANGER. Then freeze, breathing hard, our fingers twitching a quarter inch from the chain link.

Doris's brother told us we'd be electrocuted if we touched it.

"Desperadoes!" We wheel, charging back up the hill, back to our cover in the shadows of the pine.

Back at the house, Doris's mother is waiting for us, lounging on the velvet settee, a cigarette in one hand, a glass of wine in the other.

"Want some?" she asks when we come in.

I do, but Doris is blushing, shaking her head.

"Don't look so disapproving, dear. All the French kids do it."

Doris runs upstairs, and I follow, hoping her mother doesn't think I'm rude.

We don't talk about it, we climb into our sleeping bags instead. Turn out the light.

"Tell the Story," Doris says.

Okay. I slip the tip of my finger between my legs to find the place. We both know the Story by heart, but I tell it better. We're warrior girls, riding naked on white horses; the boys, wearing clothes, on black horses, are always trying to capture us. When they do, they parade us into a great hall, tie us to a stake in the middle of a giant lazy Susan, turn us around, pointing, poking, making comments.

When I tell the Story, I'm Leader of the Girls; the Leader of the Boys is Carlos, the boy I like. When I tell it, I can see it all happening like a movie. Carlos eyeing me, secretly liking me as much as I like him.

Beside me Doris is breathing hard and I am, too, heart bumping like I've been running a long time. My crotch tickles so bad I have to hold it with my hand, the tops of my thighs go numb.

At last the girls come to save us; we get away vowing revenge.

But when I tell the Story, I make sure we're captured many, many times. I know Doris agrees the revenge part's not as fun.

I'm sitting on the porch playing jacks. It's a strange thing for a girl my age, twelve, but I'm damned determined to beat the pants off Miss Geng, the new English teacher who wears miniskirts and frosted lips and didn't cast me in *The Night Before Christmas.* She cast Doris instead. Like she wants to split us apart, to build Doris's ego. I should be happy for Doris, but

I'm jealous, evil. Miss Geng said Doris leaps like a gazelle. I can see Doris falling.

I load up my fist, balance, shoot the ball and jacks into the air, sweep up jacks, catch the ball. I'm pretty coordinated. I'm good in fact. I can make it from onesies to tensies and back, through slapsies, knocksies, double knocksies and 'round the moon. I get stuck on Flying Dutchmen. You've got to toss throw catch catch. Sometimes I drop. Miss Geng is unbeatable. She could play straight through recess if the bell didn't ring. What's a teacher doing playing jacks all recess, anyway? I ask Doris. Why does she try to act like a girl? Why can't she act her age?

I'm practicing the Dutchmen when I see the police car pull up to the curb. I saw it before, going around and around the block, but I hardly noticed, a fly buzzing across the top of my screen. This time it's rolling down the street very slowly, like a whale hogging the whole street.

Ira calls the cops "pigs." He likes to lecture me about the Establishment and how it's got to be destroyed. In my mind's eye, I see a brick schoolhouse with white doors and windows, a steeple at the top. I see Ira and his friends with sticks of dynamite strapped to their backs, scrambling up its sides.

I still believe the cops are good, that they help you if you need them. Ira just laughs. He thinks I'm nuts.

Now I'm scared. They're parked where our walk meets the curb. The driver is talking into a microphone. He hangs it up, writes something in a notebook. Then he adjusts the mirror and his cap. His partner, in the passenger seat, just waits, fat face staring out the front window.

Then they each roll towards a door, just like on the shows, and I watch the passenger door open onto the curb and a leg stick out, and an arm and a head, like the partner has all the time in the world, like nothing is really bothering him, he can take his time, easing his big belly past the edge of the door.

The driver glances up and down the street. He's skinny and looks like he wants to stretch.

The cops are coming towards me now, up the walk with its tilted plates, its whiskers of grass growing between the squares. The fat one's in front; the skinny one hangs back a little, adjusting his belt.

It's a warm day for October and I see patches of sweat beneath the fat cop's arms.

I freeze. I mean to keep tossing the ball, to keep acting cool like I don't notice anything until they say something, but I freeze, the ball perched on my fingers like it's something I want to show them, and my heart is beating very fast, very hard.

The fat cop tips his cap. "Hello, there," he says. "Anybody home?"

He's got one shiny black shoe propped on the stair. His holster with its gun is right in line with my eye. I focus on the gun's grip, on its crisscross pattern that reminds me of the metal tread that keeps you from slipping between railroad cars, but in miniature. The gun doesn't look real, but it doesn't look fake either. It looks *useful.*

"Mommy home?" the skinny cop asks.

They think I'm a little girl. They think I'm stupid and in a way I am because I don't know if I'm supposed to lie or not.

"No one's home," I say. "But me." *"But I" my mother would correct. Or would she?*

"And what did you say your name was?"

"Phoebe. Phoebe Stein."

He smiles. "Phoebe, mind if we take a look inside then?"

I'm surprised. Were we robbed while I was sitting here? I should ask, but I don't. The police want to look inside the house. Do they need my permission?

"Okay," I tell them, then think of Ira. *Cops are assholes,* he told me. *Dickheads.*

Who's right? Me or Ira?

I let them in.

They stand in the hallway, looking up at the ceiling and then at the stairs, and the skinny one says in a nicey nice voice, "Now could you show us your brother's room?"

His room is so calm in the afternoon light. Bright bars of sunshine stripe the wooden floor. On his bed, a book whose title I can't make out lies facedown on the open sheet. In the one dim corner, a peace sign glows faintly on the drawn shade.

Once the police are in the room, they seem to know exactly where to go. The fat cop shines a flashlight into Ira's closet, then steps inside. "What have we here?" In his fists are two big garbage bags stuffed with capsules, tiny clear cocoons. Even full, the bags look light enough to fly away.

The skinny cop swears. "Look at this," he says. He holds up a Baggie of something that looks like green tea. I think it's pot.

"Hello! What's happening?" My mother's voice rises sharply from the front hall.

I go to the landing, lean over the railing as far as I can to aim my voice. "Up here, Mom. Hurry."

But she is already running, her footsteps like a racing heartbeat as she comes up the stairs.

After school, I go up to Ira's room. Climb up beside him on the bed.

"Can I watch?" I ask.

"If you don't make any noise."

I scoot down next to him, lean my shoulder against his to see the screen of the little TV settled on his chest like a lapdog. On it, a man is tap dancing like a wild puppet, pulling firecrackers out of his pockets, hurling them at the floor. Every time he taps his foot, there's an explosion. Crack, crack, snap tap crack. He lights the fuses off his cigarettes like he's playing pan pipes. Digging it, as he whirls his arms, twirling across the stage through a storm of fire.

Maniac, I think, but Ira is grinning, his eyes glued to the crazy man.

When the number's over, Ira shuts off the TV. "Fred Astaire," he says. "Very cool."

I'm jealous. Ira used to think I was a good dancer. He even asked me to teach him once. I didn't know how to dance myself, but I pretended I did.

The Twist was playing on the radio. Chubby Checker all friendly and loud. I was trying to remember what I'd seen on TV, the way you keep your elbows at your side while your whole body twists down.

"It's like skiing, almost," I told him. That was something Ira could do.

I was showing him as I said this, twisting my hips and shoulders, shaking my butt, then going up on one toe. I was starting to get it, to let my hips slip, my waist turn. I was twisting all the way to the floor, my knees touching, and up, while Ira just stood there like his body was tied in rope.

Then the song was over and a slow dance came on. Ira moved close to me. His thighs clamped over mine and his arms came up around my back. He was wearing a flannel shirt, soft on my cheek. Under his breast pocket, his heart was thumping. I could imagine a little boy trying to punch his way out. Wow, I thought. Ira's as scared as me.

Juvenile delinquent, the judge called Ira. That doesn't describe him at all. Can't they tell he's brilliant? So witty, our mother says. She doesn't say it about anybody else.

Ira's being sent to a special school. Not even Grandpa knows. But it's better than jail, Mom says.

They're taking Ira away from us. For a year.

It's all my fault.

IRA, 1971

There was no one he had to say good-bye to. Strange thought. George, his roommate, dead, the girls gone. Who else mattered? No one really. Which was cool. It was an evil place. A circle of hell.

And they wouldn't miss him, wouldn't even notice he was gone until the weekend tally of runaways. Old Duncan, the head head in his WASP costume of baggy tweed and penny loafers chatting up the parents as he peers at them bleary-eyed from behind the wire rims, coughing and sniffling into his linen handkerchief, nostrils red as an orangutan's ass. He could see Old Duncan now: Ira? Ira Stein? No one's seen Ira Stein? Perhaps he's *meditating* somewhere? Perhaps he had to meet our latest shipment of dope at the bus station? Does he need a lift?

And another week would go by until he made some half-hearted call. The children come and go, talking of angel dust and snow. Someone told him Duncan's dope was the very best, the very purest shit around, that he kept it in the cellar like old fine wine.

It's bigger than he remembered. The kind of house people called a mansion and he didn't even bother explaining his parents weren't really millionaires, that the ceiling fell down in the living room every year, that the only room they could afford to heat was the kitchen, that his mother lived almost permanently in that shabby room with the stove on high and the oven door open, that she and his sisters sat around the scarred kitchen table, holding mugs of hot tea for warmth.

Your parents live in a fucking mansion, his friends would say as he led them up the gravel driveway and around the back porch. Windows blazed with light; his father loved light, loved leaving lights on in every room. He could see his mother following his father through the house, turning off whatever he turned on. His father had a thing about electricity. Light made him feel rich.

They would gather behind the shrubs at the end of the yard to smoke pot, swallow hits. His mother complained until he asked would she prefer they get busted on the street? (She didn't know about the acid.)

But shit was she scary when he did get busted, screaming like some kind of Greek lady, like some fucking Clytemnestra or something, like he'd murdered her daughter or something, *I thought you went behind the bushes.* Not that time, that time Pamela freaked, right on the street, and he, like an ass, gave his name, his real name. Why the fuck did he do that? Because he was scared. Not of the pigs, but that Pamela would die, fry right there on the sidewalk in front of the five-and-ten. He gave them his name in exchange for an ambulance.

A week later they busted him, not badly, empty capsules and less than a dime of weed. Enough to get plea-bargained to Nirvana Acres, we're happy to rehabilitate your hippie for ten thousand a year.

Not when your father's here, she used to warn him. Which he didn't have to worry about much since his father was never home. He'd lost another job and had taken a new one, moving scrap metal around South America. Not exactly the Peace Corps. His father was in the Amazon somewhere pawning off trinkets to the chiefs like some fucking Columbus. It was embarrassing to watch him pack those silver dollars and T-shirts of astronauts.

You don't understand, his father told him. They love this stuff. It's very important to them.

His father was very sanctimonious about that shit, couldn't see it any other way. A fucking missionary.

No cars in the driveway. Good sign. Though he could always stow in the shed no one ever went into.

It was a dull afternoon. Early March. Not great hitching weather.

Phoebe jumped, pushing back the chair so fast it tipped over, hitting the floor with a bang, and then she was hugging him so hard he could feel her nails in his shoulders, and he thought of the game Little Sister used to play. The Black Stallion Against Man! she screamed, raining blows on his chest, and he trying to catch her fists, trying to tame Little Sister, the fury, but he could not, he was laughing too hard, bent double, gasping, holding his sides.

Now she was sobbing and he held her close almost like she was a girl, not his sister. Someday she might be pretty, but now she was weird looking. The glasses. The way she parted her hair. But she didn't know and that made her kind of attractive, kind of cool. He admired her for that. She didn't care, it didn't matter to her. Then he thought he remembered getting a letter from her saying a lot of boys had been bothering her and he wasn't fooled, he was glad. Little Sister deserved to be loved.

She wanted to know what he was doing there and when he told her, she got teary again and he started to get nervous. He had a bunch of things he wanted her to do for him and he didn't have much time and he didn't want to run into Mom and Dad.

"What're you going to do?" she asked.

"Say good-bye to some people and split."

"Where are you going?"

"California."

She looked like she wanted to know a lot more, but instead she asked about his friend George. And he told her, George was okay that he might come down, too. That they might hitch together. And her face cleared and she said how great, and went on about how she'd been practicing *gimbri* ever since George showed her how to work the bow and then he felt like shit and finally he had to say actually George isn't coming, actually George is dead.

She did not take it well, not well at all, and he wanted to kick himself for his big mouth. But Little Sister had to know. She had to know stuff, didn't she?

She was the Wise Child, his little sister, not a kid anymore, so he told her about the OD and how the vein popped, and he should have stopped there, but he couldn't, it was the first time he'd told anybody and words kept rolling out, dropping and spilling like stones, clattering down and down and by the end he was sobbing too, cross-legged on the linoleum, and Little Sister was holding him, or trying to, leaning across his legs and grabbing his shoulders.

"You've got to tell them," she said. She meant their parents. "You've got to tell them exactly what you told me. Exactly the same way."

She kept saying that word *exactly* and she kept saying they would understand.

They won't, he told her.

But she kept saying it over and over and he got the feeling if he didn't agree with her she'd keep saying it until it got too late.

Just leave it alone.

Please, she said. Please, please, please.

He thought Little Sister was crazy or just naïve. He thought that but also it blew his mind the way Little Sister could say things like that. She was serious. She was totally fucking serious. He promised he would think about it.

It was a place Crazy Harold had told him about in a basement of one of the dormitories. Crazy Harold had drawn a map on a piece of napkin. He had a photographic memory, he said, and, of course, everyone thought it was more Crazy Harold bullshit, but he drew with a steady hand through the twists, turns, angles of the catacombs. The map showed a twiggy branch with *x*'s for landmarks such as the vending machines, the furnace room, the laundry. Harold knew the place because he'd hidden out there himself. You might meet some banditos down there, but don't worry, everyone's cool, he said.

It was Crazy Harold who told him to stay hidden until late afternoon, or even better until night. They look for runaways and shit down there, he said. But there are rooms no one else knows about. These rooms he'd marked with triangles.

Ira took the map out of his pocket. He knew the complex on the far edge of the golf course. Pamela liked to folk dance in the quad with her friends. In summer, they hung Christmas lights and dragged a phonograph outside and danced in a dirt circle in the courtyard.

She was always bugging him to come folk dancing. She didn't know that he watched sometimes. Smoking a joint and sitting on the stone wall, just beyond the light. He liked watching Pamela and her friends dance when he was stoned. They danced in a tight circle like peasants, their tits swinging beneath the tucks of their blouses and the weird music spidering up the sides of the buildings. He liked watching the men go crazy, leaping, hooting, slapping their thighs and twirling white handkerchiefs. He might have joined them if he wasn't such a klutzy dancer.

So far Harold's map was right. He had passed the vending machines and the laundry, the furnace room on the right. So far he hadn't seen any students, no one at all. They were probably eating dinner around now. He had forgotten to stow food and his stomach was aching. He might eat the joint in his pack, too risky to smoke.

The door had a heavy creak, which was good, he thought. He'd have some warning. He didn't bother to look for a light. He could make out a stack of boxes on one wall, a row of old desks like the kind they had in elementary school. No light except from the passageway and he didn't want to leave the door open. He would not be able to stay down here for long. He'd have to find something to eat.

He took off his jacket, rolling it into a pillow, then rummaged in his knapsack until he found the tiparillo box. He would sleep a little and go out later. In the meantime, the pot would take the hunger away.

He stretched out, letting the pot take its time. Meanwhile he was thinking it was funny that all he had to his name was this ratty little pack, his harmonica, the clothes he was wearing.

Back home, he had a closet full of stuff the old man had given him. Weird stuff. A stack of old *Evergreens,* which were pretty boring except for the occasional picture of a naked girl. His grandfather was into that shit. He could tell. He could tell by the weird way he had plunked the stack down and said kind of offhand, "You'll find some interesting reading." Creepy. Because the reading was not interesting at all and he knew that. And then right in the middle of the stack, like he'd just forgotten it was there, a real porn magazine, none of this high-toned intellectual bullshit.

And the old man's pipes. He wouldn't have minded cigars, a box of panatelas, but instead he makes an ass of himself trying to light up in front of Jimmy Colcord. The kids cracking up watching him suck away and no action. Just the sickening flavor of old tobacco and spit filling his mouth till he nearly pukes. Don't you know you can't smoke a used pipe? No draw. So he got tricked into saying some stupid shit like he knew it, he just wanted to see if Jimmy knew it. And, of course, Jimmy saw right through him.

He took those pipes and shoved them to the back of the closet. The rack was too nice to throw out. Maybe he'd get some new pipes someday.

The bronze fish, he had to admit, was pretty cool. It was Japanese. Some emperor or somebody had given it to the old guy. The ruby eyes were real. Maybe he should get Phoebe to bring it to him. He might get a lot for it if he decided to pawn it.

It was also weird the way the old guy had handed over these things. Always shuffling back to his study and making a big deal as though he was handing over the family jewels, the keys to the family treasure. A stack of porn magazines, a set of old pipes, and a fish. What a legacy. And the guy was supposed to be rich.

He'd been looking through some of the magazines, nothing better to do, and he'd noticed some of the pages were kind of wavy like they'd been dropped in a bathtub or something. Did the old guy whip his pecker out at night? Probably. While his grandmother was sleeping. He'd seen the masks. They both had them. Black silk. Like raccoon masks. She probably had one on in the dark so she couldn't see what he was doing over there under the covers . . .

The old man thought he was such a big deal. Played it to the hilt. That's what pissed him off. The way the old guy wallowed in his power, happier than a pig in shit. Grandma cooking any little delicacy his heart desired. Everyone worshiping him, down on their knees.

Old man didn't seem all that smart. His father seemed just as smart or smarter. At least his father knew a few things about camping. And he could quote Shaw as though he were his best friend. Dad's problem was he was too modest. Mom, too. You could see she was scared of the old guy. Every time she was around him she got all quiet and started stuffing food in her mouth. She was always chewing something. It was pathetic.

The old guy was a queen bee, all right. The family, a bunch of drones feeding the old guy's ego. A bunch of suckers.

Well, he refused to be a drone. No way, no how. He wasn't going to get down on his knees to suck the old guy's dick. Not like the rest of them. Not like his mother and his father. Not like his grandmother. He hoped the kid would wise up. Not likely. Not without some help. But he was leaving. Time to split before he turned into a drone.

He wanted to make it clear that he was not chicken about the F's. The F's had nothing to do with it. He could see the shrink at school saying in his wake that Ira was ashamed of his failure, that he couldn't face the old guy and his expectations, all that shit. That wasn't it at all. It had to do with survival. If he didn't leave, he would die. That simple. That was the revelation.

The revelation was thanks to the old guy. The old guy was the teacher. God, that was a weird thought. Everything fit, after all.

It happened Thanksgiving when they were all sitting around the living room. At first, it looked like everyone was just sitting around a living room waiting for Thanksgiving dinner. But it wasn't. It was everyone sitting around the old guy waiting for Thanksgiving dinner. It was like the old guy held you in a kind of orbit. Shit, he couldn't remember any of that physics stuff, but it was like magnetism or gravity or something. No one in this room could cut loose from their orbit around the old guy. The old guy was the sun.

You could make a diorama of the family in their orbits. Grandma, Mercury, was the closest to the sun. Then crazy Aunt Mildred, Venus. Then Mom, the Earth, and Dad, her satellite, the moon. Uncle Robert hung a little further out with Aunt Beatrice, but not really. They lived two blocks away from the old guy when they could live anywhere in the world. So what did that make them? Mars and Jupiter, or something. Even his little sisters were in orbit, playing with the old guy's medals every time they went to visit. He wanted to yank the medals off. They're going to weigh you down, man. Watch out.

But as of that day, he was a planet cut loose, a mad star, self-exploding. He had taken himself out of the orbit. Broken free. It cost him his life. That life. That life was over.

He'd been scared shitless of what the old guy would say when he heard about the F's, scared so bad in fact he puked in the maid's toilet the first thing he arrived. Then the next thing, he's having a revelation.

The old guy was pissed, of course, shouting he was so ignorant, shouting science was the foundation of intellectual thought, shouting science was the foundation of human civilization, shouting without science we would all be ignorant asses, worshiping stone gods. The old guy was superpissed, pounding the chair with his fist, getting up without his cane.

He had to admit, for a moment, he felt weird, like he might cry or do something totally strange, but then he saw the picture clear as though he were standing outside the room, looking in a window, or at that diorama, and he said so calmly — he'd never felt as calm in his life, or so clear — "Why should I listen to you more than to any other old man?"

He didn't say it to be rude. He said it because it occurred to him. A gift from God.

The old guy took it hard. Stared at him a moment. Looked as if he might hit him. Whacked the glass instead. Then sat down. For once in his life, no words. The aunts and uncle were stunned. His dad, clapping his hand on his knee over and over again like he was keeping time to a song in his head. His mother looking like she couldn't tell if she was scared or pissed. Total silence. Then Grandma, oblivious to revelations, anger, planetary motion, stood in the doorway, tinging a little bell.

"Dinner is ready," she said.

He's been thinking about George. *Where the fuck was he?* Heaven? Hell? Someplace in between? He didn't believe in God. What kind of sadistic asshole was he? He was a killer, is what he was.

He was glad he'd given George the twelve-string, even

though George had a problem with it. This is *valuable,* he used to say. So what? You can *play* it, man. I can't. In exchange, he got George's six-string, some Spanish number, all scarred and scraped. George had owned it since he was ten or something. He liked George's guitar better than the Martin, so it wasn't a true gift. His grandparents had given it to him. Someone, his mother or father, had told them he wanted a twelve-string, and one afternoon it arrived by truck, a huge box, stamped FRAGILE, and inside the guitar locked in its black coffin. George was the first to play it, his fingers gliding, plucking, thrumming, making it sound as though it were five guitars. He'd never heard so many notes weaving and unweaving in air.

If only he could talk to Crazy Harold's friend, the priest. He wondered if he could find him. Would it be worth going out? The priest was the one who said atheists are the true believers. One thing clung to the other. It made sense, it made sense to him.

Little Sister was not an atheist. She told him she prayed to God every night. She said she saw him everywhere, in blades of grass, in trees, in flowers, even in horses. He told her she was a pantheist, and had to explain what it meant, but she said no, it was all God. One God in all those places.

He wished he could see God like that. He remembered when he was a little kid sitting in a chair at dusk and watching the room disintegrate into dots of pepper and thinking he was God, he was seeing *everything,* atoms and light. *In the beginning was the light,* and then it was dark and everything disappeared and he did, too.

Where the fuck was George? Would the priest know?

The funeral was maybe even happening today, right now, or yesterday. In Connecticut someplace. His teeth were chattering. Did George do bad shit? Or too much? (Some asshole asked him before he split: Hey, what's going to happen to the guitar?

And he'd answered: He's going to be buried with it, Jack. Wanna dig it up and play it? The place'll be marked.)

They thought he was crazy in that place. *Just a question, Stein. Stay cool.* Well, he'd cooled out and checked out. Left those bourgeois self-medicated fuckers in Wonderland where they belonged.

He sucked in a deep breath. *Screaming would be a mistake.* He came so close, so close. But they couldn't dull *him,* lull him. Hah.

Some girl said: God only gives you as much as you can handle. And he answered her: God's a fucking pimp. *Aint' got no — duh, duh, duh — satisfication.* The notes thrummed in his teeth. None at *all,* baby. None.

He woke with a start; something had run across his face. He shivered and sat up. He had been dreaming he was fucking Pamela on the lawn of the high school and the whole school filed out to watch, like a school assembly or graduation or something, a retinue of teachers and students in long black robes. He was drilling her so hard, she was screaming, but no one said a thing. Silent rows of black falling in around him, black as crows.

He swore. He could feel the stickiness on his thighs. He'd come in his pants like a little kid. Unzipping, he tried to blot the semen with the ends of his shirt. Should he call her? Would she want to see him? She might still be in that loony bin they sent her to, she might not be home at all.

The first time they fucked was in his room. She must have figured it out, but she didn't say anything. It wasn't her first time. She was on the Pill, she said.

Afterward, he thanked her, and she laughed. *Your aura's blue,* she said. *Before it was white.*

But it was his windowpane she freaked on, and he hasn't talked to her since, not since that time in the hospital when she looked like shit, tubes stuck up her nose, needles in her wrists. Her eyes still bright and dilated, just like an animal's. She blinked once at him and turned her head the other way as though just looking at him caused her pain.

Sitting in this room in the dark by himself, he was remembering shit. He was remembering a time when his mother and father took him to visit his grandfather. He was remembering how the old man just looked at him, didn't hug him or anything, just looked at him and palmed the back of his shoulder with a little push. He remembered his grandfather saying, "Perhaps Ira would like to look at the Prize," and he didn't know what that prize was or what it was for, but his parents started nodding. Oh, yes! they said. *What a treat.*

He could feel his mother's warm breath in his ear, a little damp, like the breath the sea gave off if you stood where the wave pushed foam up onto the sand. *It's a prize for being a genius.*

His grandfather was smiling, humming, as he puttered into the back. They could still hear him humming even after he left the room.

He came back carrying a velvet box, which he placed on the coffee table. His grandfather asked him to open the box, but he couldn't, the spring was too tight, so his grandfather opened it for him, the way his father opened clams, slipping a knife blade between the halves and prying up.

Inside, a large gold disk pillowed on a folded ribbon, and his grandfather said: *This is the Prize, would you like to wear it?* And his father said, *Let me see, I've never seen the Prize be-*

fore. His father's voice was trembling, but his mother was sitting deep in her chair, her fingers laced over one knee, and his grandfather said: *Want to feel what it's like to wear the Prize?* And he wanted to say no but they were all looking at him, even his grandmother, who said, *That's a bit silly, isn't it?*

His father lifted the medal out of the box, raising it and lowering it on the flat of his hand as though he were weighing it, and he said: *How much is it worth? Just the gold alone, I mean.*

About a hundred fifty, his grandfather said, and he wondered if his grandfather meant thousands or millions.

Then his father handed the Prize to his grandfather and his mother told him to stand up and his grandfather spread his hands slightly apart and lowered the ribbon with its medal over his head, which he bowed slightly, and then he straightened, attench hut, the way he and his friend Tommy Cane had practiced, and the grown-ups gasped, their eyes on the medal twisting slowly between his knees.

"Hey, what's doing, what's happening?" In the dark, he could hardly see their faces, their faces bobbed in and out of the leaves like monkeys' faces, whole families chattering in the night.

"They spring you?"

"I split."

"Cool."

There were slaps high and low down the wall.

"Not much action, man."

"No strikes?"

"Nah. Nothing."

It was the usual crowd, none of his real friends, just dudes.

"I got a joint but I can't smoke out here. You take it."

The whole line of sitters turned gleeful. Cool dude. Cool.

The first guy, he thought his name was Joe, flicked on his lighter, took a deep inhale and passed it on.

"Anyone know where I can score some cash?"

The monkeys quieted, became thoughtful. Gee, man, that's difficult. Got to think on that. And, of course, there were numerous offers of names of people who had scored recently, people whose parents were wealthy.

"How much, man?" one kid asked.

He was going to say two C's but thought maybe that was too much. "Whatever you can handle, man. One C might do it."

"That's cool. Where you hanging?"

"In the grad basement by the golf course."

The kid was kind of plump and pimply, his hair combed in a slick field across his scalp, somewhat narc-like.

"Well, hey, if I can score anything, I'll stick it under the Coke machine." (No pun intended, he added.)

"Thanks, man." The kid's joke made him nervous, too corny. Probably was a narc.

"Thanks for the weed."

It's all right with him that there's no groove for him here, no place to fit in. That's okay. Just another sign.

"Anyone know what's going down with Pamela?"

"Bingham?" It was the narc, trying to sound casual, but Ira could hear the excitement in his voice, like a little kid who likes to be in on the adult conversation.

"Yeah."

"I heard she freaked. I mean completely. Breakdown city. Out of it."

He swallowed a couple of times. His heart was suddenly pounding. "Is she home?"

The boy cackled. "*Home?* Are you kidding? She's fri-i-ed."

He knew the guy was a fucking narc. "Where is she?"

He shrugged. "Still in the nuthouse, I guess. Shit and she was a *fox*. Wasn't she, Dylan?"

"Who?"

"Pamela Bingham."

Whistles broke out along the wall, but the Dylan kid said, "Jerk off someplace else, asshole."

"Fuck yourself," the kid replied.

More monkey glee.

"You know where exactly?"

"County Mental, or maybe her folks sent her to a private tank. Aren't the Binghams loaded?"

Ira shrugged. He wanted to split fast. "All right. Take it easy."

The kid named Dylan raised him a high five and the others followed. He slapped them all, except the narc. That kid should fuck himself, he thought.

Loping past the enormous houses with all their home fires burning, it seemed right to him that they'd started out in this place living on the third floor of a boardinghouse, a German shepherd barking at the foot of the stairs, whether to keep them in or out it wasn't clear.

Every night for months, the family trooped downtown, what there was of a downtown, an old tired strip of dusty storefronts displaying clothes that weren't even remotely in style. Passing by, he'd stare at those disembodied torsos of lime plaid and charcoal, those banana yellow sweaters with blue stripes. Golf sweaters his mother called them and even she made fun of the stuffy clothes, tsking at the dowdiness of a navy skirt or a gold-buttoned blazer.

They ate every night at the counter at the back of McPhail's

Pharmacy. Safe at last, barricaded from the street by the revolving displays of hair clips and hairbrushes and postcards of the town so artfully taken that he didn't recognize the place. In these cards, it seemed the autumn leaves were glowing with separate fires, the sky a startling blue. The photographers' favorite shot the chapel with its white steeple, the cross glinting in the sun like a hood ornament. His family did not go to that church. They went from time to time to the synagogue, a disappointing building of red brick, surrounded by poured concrete.

Seated at the counter, they slouched into their hamburgers and milk shakes, their grilled cheese and tomato, their French fries drenched in catsup. At the counter, you did not have to talk. No attempt at family dinner conversation. His father didn't even ask if they'd had a nice day at school. No, they sat and ate as comfortably as five strangers at a counter, not a family at all.

They'd moved in the summer, in blazing heat and humidity so heavy it felt like you were carrying the sky on your head. Fall brought locusts, millions of them, dragging themselves up from the bowels of the earth, coming alive to fuck and die, leaving their tea-colored husks behind.

This is a WASP town, his mother used to say as if to explain their isolation, their hopelessness. He turned on his stool and expected to see insects floating around, those heavy bodies, looking dense as iron, suspended by invisible threads. She meant that people in this town were blond and thin and spent a lot of time suppressing coughs. What she meant was she wished they were back in Berkeley. Back in paradise. Instead of this place of dead-still air and greedy bugs.

The room was hot and close, so hot he felt wrapped in layers of feathers, musty, hot feathers. He beat the air with his fists, thinking he was beating away thc old green bag, the mummy bag, his father got in the army. He blinked, there was no bag. His head rested on a balled-up pile of clothes. His own odor curdled in his nostrils; he was drenched in sweat.

He could hear voices beyond the door. Phoebe and someone else. Fuck. A trap?

He lay back, wiping his forehead with his sleeve. The smell made him laugh. Of course he could trust her. He remembered the morning his father had called Phoebe and him into the bedroom. "I want you to tell me in all honesty, Phoebe, does your brother smell like he needs a bath?"

He'd lifted his arm around his sister's shoulders as she fitted her nose snugly into his armpit. "Smells like Ira," she said.

"It's me, Phoebe. Are you in there?"

The knob turned slowly and he stepped into the shoulder of light. She gasped, clapping her hand to her mouth.

"Who's with you?" he said.

"Doris. She won't tell."

He nodded and stepped back.

"You scared me," she said. She sounded pissed.

"Did anyone see you?"

She shook her head.

He was kneeling over the knapsack she'd handed him, checking the contents. He didn't look up.

"You've got to tell Mom and Dad," she said.

Fuck that, he told her, catching her wince.

"Please," she said. "You've got to tell them. They'll believe you."

"They'll say no."

"Of course, you idiot. They *have* to. But if you accept the no and tell them your plan, like about going back to school in California and everything, they might say yes. I'm almost sure they will."

He looked at her face, so solemn, as though what she was asking was life or death or something. She had a way of looking at you, so intense, as though she really did know.

"When are they getting home?"

"Dad gets home around eight. We eat before that."

He nodded, remembering all the times they'd had to wait for his father, wondering exactly what had changed.

Then she stepped up to him, her arms went around his shoulders and her head found the hollow beneath his chin. She was making a kind of gurgling sound. Shit, he wished she wouldn't do that. He tried prying her away from him, but she wouldn't budge.

His sister's hair smelled of dried grass and something else, something even sweeter, the remnants of a little girl smell. He could feel the wetness now in the trough of his throat, trickling down his chest, sopping the flannel. He could feel her sobs resonating in his own throat.

Pamela had cried this hard once. They were getting stoned in his room, and he told her he expected to die young. He had meant it as some jive to impress her, some stupid shit that had popped out of his mouth 'cause he liked her so much. But it was as though he'd told her he just swallowed poison. Her face went blank and she started weeping. He never knew a girl could collapse so fast. He kept telling her it was bull and apologizing and all, but she went on sobbing. As if she knew something and had decided not to tell him. As if he were already dead.

"Will you tell them?" his sister asked. Her voice was hoarse.

"They shouldn't have sent me to that place," he said.

"They had to."

He looked at his sister. "You'd better be right," he said.

A delegation came to see him. Petey, a kid he used to jam with, and Katinka, his girlfriend, a round-eyed girl wearing an army jacket. They brought a friend, Tom, skinny kid in a paisley shirt and baggy jeans.

They'd heard from the dudes on the Wall that he needed dough, but all they had was a jar of peanut butter and a loaf of bread, a few apples.

Still, they were brothers. They embraced. Then the round-eyed girl started talking about this puppy she knew her neighbors were beating on. She could hear them in the yard. The guy, this real asshole, came outside every night bombed off his ass and started whipping the thing.

"It's like brutal," she said. She put her hands over her ears.

"Let's rescue him," Ira said.

The others looked at him.

"Where are we going to keep it?" Katinka asked. "My parents would freak."

"What do you mean, kidnap him?" Petey asked.

"What time does the guy get home?"

"Six, seven."

"All right, so we have plenty of time."

The puppy flattened to the ground, a golden doormat, its eyes wild in supplication.

Don't worry, Little One, we'll take care of you. Ira and Tom grabbed the puppy's front paws while the others pushed him from the back. The dog refused to budge.

"Give me your coat," Ira said. "We'll carry him."

They trudged along the sidewalk, each holding a corner of the sling, synchronized as pallbearers.

"Where're we going?" Tom asked.

"My house," Ira said.

The others shrugged. Everyone always said Ira Stein was a true freak.

Phoebe was waiting for him in the front hall and saw them turn up the walk, carrying what looked like a dead fawn.

"What's that?" she asked when she opened the door.

Ira was grinning, the others scattering fast, waving, as they leaped across the lawn, tore down the street.

"A puppy."

"Mom and Dad'll kill you."

"Where are they?"

"Upstairs."

"We'll put him in the kitchen and feed him cat food or something. I'll tell them later."

"Do they know anything?"

She shook her head.

His father's standing where it seems his father's always standing, in front of the dresser, peering into the open cuff links drawer like a jeweler contemplating his jewels, and his mother's lying on her side of the bed, wrapped plumply in her quilted robe, a book and a half-filled crossword puzzle at her side.

At this moment he feels like a burglar, frightening them as they have never been frightened before, yet he's the one who's shaking, shivering so badly his teeth buzz in his head, and all he can do to keep from collapsing is to repeat his mantra, beneath anything they can hear, *because they love you.*

"What?" His mother's on her feet fast, throwing her arms around him, while his father, still moored to his spot, asks, "Is anything wrong?"

He takes a deep breath and suddenly he sees what they see: he sees a son who smells like shit, standing in front of them in clothes that are torn and dirty, and he sees a kid, lost, a runaway, and he sees they're afraid, that they have no stomach for being jailers.

He remembers once asking his father what happened to *his father,* why he never talked about him.

My father died of cancer, he said. I was ten.

Did you remember him? he'd asked.

Of course.

Did you like him?

His father had looked uncomfortable. Stroked his mouth, then his chin.

He was a stern man. Very strict. He wanted me to be a rabbi; I wanted to be an engineer.

Were you sad when he died? Tell the truth, Dad.

All right, his father had said. No, Ira. I wasn't sad. Not in the normal way.

"You told me one time you ran away." Ira is speaking to his father now while his mother sits silently on the edge of the bed.

His father looks surprised. "I didn't actually."

"You wanted to." *Had freight schedules for the whole country, planned to jump trains nonstop from New York to San Francisco.*

"What does this have to do with the honor of your presence?"

"I'm hitching to California. I'm not coming back." He watches his father speaking, but doesn't listen. His father's saying no because he has to, because he loves him, because he doesn't want him to have to run away, because he doesn't want his won to hate him as he hated his own father.

In the end, his parents say yes. He can go. He can go with their permission.

Before they go downstairs to tell the girls Ira is home (he never tells that Phoebe already knows), Ira turns to his father, "Thank you for saying no."

And his father looks at him. There are tears in his eyes and he does not know what to say.

ABBEY, 1971

Abbey strides, whistling, swinging the cane he does not need. The few students who pass him smile, but he does not acknowledge them, like a woman who knows she is beautiful, he basks in their tokens but does not return them. Famous Abbey twinkle and all that. He basks, knowing that he is quite irresistible in his way, at his age, which he hardly considers unless he must impress on some young man, some pip-squeak or other, just who he is talking to.

She lives in an inconspicuous part of town, which he likes. A neighborhood not too far from Eileen's but completely different in character. In Eileen's neighborhood the large houses, matronly comfortable, spread their girth over ample plots. What isn't porch is iris.

Here the houses lean in, willing to exchange a nod. Comfortable, lower class, though not a bit like the slum Abbey grew up in. Senator's parents on the corner and her own house, a large slate blue Victorian, set back, with a backyard, filled, unlike the others on the block, with grass, not garage. She does not drive. Impossible, he told her. I don't. She smiled. Someone else can always do the driving.

He starts humming, the words sometimes asserting themselves, his alma mater, always his song of victory. But what did he conquer lately. Back then it was the flu and Ellen, of course, espied on the school tennis courts, flashing a shapely calf.

A-courting he will go. That's what makes him skip lively as he can at seventy-five and rap the brick sidewalk with his stick.

Does he feel guilty? he asks himself. He is in the habit of querying himself, is known for this quaint habit, and emerges with phrases like "I've debated with myself," "After having given some thought to the matter . . ." He has decided that it is the difference between *should* and *does.* Should he feel guilt? No. Not because every Frenchman has a similar arrangement. Something else. Does he? He does. Occasionally. *How is it, sir, that a man who has devoted his career to campaigning against the government's secrecy, who blames that secrecy for destroying the scientific community could, in fact, be living a secret and duplicitous life?* Pause while the heart drums up a response. "You've studied light, haven't you? You know that light behaves as both wave and particle, don't you? Well, I am like light. I cannot be explained simply."

The surprise to Abbey is that he loves Diana. This love, a phenomenon, a law, overriding "should" and "does."

He opens the gate, whistling even more loudly, then stands at the door and pushes the bell. All this to show that he is not secretive in the least. See, here he stands for all the world. And the houses lean in. Yet nobody sees. In this neighborhood, shades are drawn and curtains pulled, not like the daughter's neighborhood, where honey light glows the evening long, shades pulling back their tongues at dusk so that you may admire the chandelier, the cascade of fine books, the crowd of heads tied in the party knot.

Here people value their privacy, value each other's. *Some secrets to be revealed, some concealed.* So Abbey likes to believe.

She is a subtle woman, yet one who does not beat around the bush. She is wearing the kimono he bought for her, silver and pink fronds on black silk. He has never bought his wife a robe like this in all the years they have been married. In the robe, Diana's as pale and pink as one of the fronds. Her hands go to the sides of his head, drawing it down. No reserve, ever. She knows she owns. Like a child. Her narcissism charms; equals, he senses, his own.

He tries to remove his hat, but she's there first, flinging it off and away. She leads by the hand, up, up, the cool black stairs.

He might feign protest, but why bother. Why? Not with her. Her hips are slender as a boy's beneath her robe. He is a small man, but she is smaller than he, bones bending and bound like fine reeds.

She does not sleep with anyone but him, she's told him, and he believes her. Yet tonguing the slippery silk of her mouth, he finds himself wondering who else, besides the husband, has swabbed its milky surfaces.

He breaks from her. "A drink?"

She shakes her head; the porcelain eyes are on him.

"Strip," she says. And he obeys, shedding his suit, his underclothes with the ease of a much younger man.

Her hair in his hand is three shades of yellow silk, the lightest, pure white like his own.

I'm going white, she says as she draws his hands to the hems of her robe, makes him take hold, parting the curtains.

"Ah." *His goddess in white marble.* He pulls her to him, feeling her breasts flatten against his chest, her smooth belly, her hipbones like tiny elbows thrust against him. He is giant now, stirred and roaring, embracing her.

He must plunge in.

Her eyes widen, the luminous blue of a refracting lens. "Darling."

She is the most extraordinary woman. She is completely golden.

Later, lying in bed, he snaps the lighter for her cigarette, then lights his own. He loves smoking in bed with her, watching the light sift through the room. Her room has beautiful light in the afternoon. You could be anywhere, the angle of the window and the bright blue sky, gentle noise that could be the sea, you could be in Italy in a seaside town . . .

She shakes his arm gently. "Hello?"

"I want you again."

"You'll be late."

"No matter." But he falls back on the pillow, deterred. "You think Edmund enjoys looking on?" Ordinarily, the photograph on the bureau does not bother him. Finds it proper rather. She threatens to prop him up there too, but he says no. On the bureau next to Edmund, he'd be taken as the father. No amount of genius protects him from that.

She gets up, tips the photograph facedown on its leather frame. "Do I see you again this trip?"

"If I can."

"Can't wait by the telephone."

"Don't."

They both know she will.

"Your next conference?"

"Month or so."

"That long?" Her eyes fill with tears of the kind that do not break.

Remarkable, he thinks. Ellen has never wept for him. Never. She considers their marriage a contest of ice against ice, which, he has to admit, has kept it interesting.

"I'll write," he says.

"Every day." She does every day put something in the mail. Professor Stark, Stone, Stymy. She is always Professor S. Professoress. Their joke.

He worries sometimes that Ellen will hear the envelopes hissing "mistress." *The French way, of which Ellen might approve. Because she does approve what's civilized.* Yes. And Ellen values privacy. Believes in it as he does. In this way they are alike.

Biographers seek him out, propelled by that most human of desires — if you're not one of the great ones, attach yourself to the great. He interviews with them all, without the slightest intention of granting them access. Real access. But he's curious to peer into their mirrors. Their distortions interest him.

No one can understand unless they've been born in your skin, he tells them. You could never capture the texture of the light, the place. You could never understand fully the moment in history, in its context, why assembling a radio in that neighborhood in the fall of 1912 was exactly what it was, so important.

The biographers humor him, offer gifts of their insights, of new facts that have come to light. The true history of the atomic age is itself just coming to light. And he doesn't mind letting these eager young men do the detective work, finding a secret file here, a secret file there.

They don't know his secrets.

Then this morning, the young man from Chicago, particularly confident, though he's done nothing with his physics degree, he confides to Abbey (almost a brag), thrusts a well-folded page across Abbey's desk. "This will make your eyes pop."

Abbey glares at the young man. Takes in the wide bland face, thin lips, an infant's white-blond hair. The terrible thing about being a fraud is that you know it in others, some special power to detect the signs clearly as if an *F* glowed faintly in the center of the forehead, an evil eye.

The sheet is small, rectangular, typed on an old machine. Something familiar about the cramped elite, making a modest march across the page.

It is without hesitation that I recommend Professor Abbey . . .

Abbey's heart explodes into beats, his palms into moist pads. A voice minces in his head, vaudevillian tenor. *How d'you know when you're a genius? When Einstein tells you so.* He slides the paper back across the desk. Careful to keep the poker face. Why give this nobody the satisfaction?

"Forgery," he says, ignoring the crumpled expression on the young man's face. *But it's real.*

As soon as the study door closes, Abbey rests his forehead on his folded arms, allows himself three heaving breaths. All these years he'd thought it a fluke of some kind, a prize given out of desperation, a lack of choices. All these years he'd considered himself a fraud. He's not.

Must call Ellen. Somehow it's a prize they've both won. The approval hers as well as his.

Phone purrs in the old-fashioned way (Ellen refuses to buy a new model). Three times, four.

"Hello?"

"Ellen, it's me. I've something to tell you —"

"I know already." Each word chipped, hammer to ice.

Know what?

Then all hell breaks loose. *"Goddamn it, you tricked me! Tricked me! . . ."*

Thighs quiver as he stands, hand shakes as he holds the receiver away from his ear. Caught. Even as a boy he'd dreaded that moment of helplessness, that moment of shame when some grubby finger poked your rib, your back, as a voice crowed, rapacious, gloating: You're It.

"Coming home," he says.

She is sitting in the armchair by the window. Dressed, he thinks, for the part. The silk shantung, the chignon, her very toughest look. And the it-ness is wearing off. He has a position, after all. His own charge of recklessness to answer hers. Waiting until he was abroad to have her breasts removed. In secret. Both. Just in case. So she didn't have to be bothered.

He takes his usual place in the armchair across from hers. Another mistake on her part. How did she think she was going to gain power?

"Who the hell is she?"

Only one tack, complete disclosure. "Stanley's widow. Stanley, who worked in the lab."

"How long?"

"Years."

It's like a blow to her jaw, tipping her head abruptly back.

"Does anyone know?"

He shakes his head. "I've not confided in anyone. Nor has she." He is, in fact, lying. He has told Alain, his oldest friend, though it was Alain who confided first that he had a mistress.

"Why?"

"Why what? Why haven't I told anyone?"

"Don't play stupid."

"Ask a psychiatrist." Even if he tells her, she won't understand.

"Blond, I suppose."

"Yes."

"The sort of woman who has to take someone else's man."

Strange, only an hour ago, he wanted to share his new honor with her. Now he wants to kill.

"I've been thinking about it all morning, Abbey. I'm not going to stand aside, pretend I don't notice. You have to make a choice, Abbey.

"Only let me tell you something, I'm going to be expensive. Very. The women in my family live to a very old age."

"I don't respond well to ultimatums." No one has ever dared, not even his father on the day he informed him he would not be bar mitzvahed.

Still she sits, chin high, eyes pinned to him, eagle-fierce.

"You should have been an actress." *But there's color in her cheeks.* He lifts his elbows to the arms of his chair, his fingers coming together in a tent. "How much money would it take to satisfy you?"

He has never seen her move so fast, except as a young woman, chasing a tennis ball, her expression deathly fierce before she smashed her racquet down.

In a second she's above him, her fists beating his head, his face. Pounding with all her might, though he tries to fend her off.

"Ellen! Stop!" An arm crooked to protect his forehead, a hand grabbing to catch her wrist. Still she manages to land blows sharp as stones.

"Tricked me! Tricked me!" she screams.

Trick trick trick, her knuckles battering his skull, until at last he is forced to rise, to rage.

"Stop it!" he commands.

She can't. Or won't.

He lunges, butting her stomach with his head, shoving her in one motion back into her chair. Now he's above her, gripping her wrists, looking into eyes lit with hate, with hurt, like a child's.

"Ellen."

"Get away!"

"Ellen." He forces his pitch down.

She turns her head away, chin thrust, neck strained like an animal's, searching for freedom, a last breath.

Then her wrists slacken, and he feels the flesh soft between his fingers.

He lets go.

"Mugger," he tells his secretary to explain the bruise to his eye, his cheek. "Coming out of the subway at 116th."

Oh! she exclaims.

Word gets around fast. Colleagues popping in all day. Congratulating him as though he were a hero.

"Didn't do much. Went down and that was it."

Clucks, nods. He's a hero all the same, for having survived.

This morning Ellen stayed in bed. No breakfast, no egg and toast, no coffee, no paper.

No apologies either. Her form beside him a shriveled, mute lump.

Seated at the diner counter, he shakes out his paper, pretends to read. Headache perched in his brow, a spiked cloud.

Why can't she negotiate? Compromise? Why can't she see that each woman can have her place? Her sovereignty?

If I hadn't found out. If you'd kept it a secret, as you should have.

As he's staring at the steel coffee urns across the counter, an image comes to Abbey, the command center deep beneath the earth he'd been taken to, prefatory to some consultation or other. A vast waterworks of pipes and scaffolding, of elevators raising and dropping their weights. On a wall, the shadows of planes cut arcs across the hemispheres of a brightly lit map two stories high.

Seated on a balcony, at the far corner of the map, at a desk empty save for two telephones encased in glass, one white, one red, a general in full uniform, braid gleaming beneath the beam of light.

The guide, smiling, caught Abbey's eye, pointed to the telephones. "The White House; the Bomb."

— *She lives in a separate state, bears no relation to yours.*

— *She owns the night.*

— *Nonsense. Not every night, not every day.*

An image floats there now. Not of the telephones. Of the general, stolid as a statue, sitting at his bare desk. How could any human endure such boredom? How could anyone stifle entirely the desire to pick up that phone, destroy the world forever?

There is only one thing Abbey is terrified of and that is writing. It is not that he cannot write or that he has no time. "People write for immortality," he scoffs, and his listeners nod, thinking, as he does, that Abbey's immortality lies in his scientific work. "I don't care to be immortal."

Now a foundation has asked Abbey to write his memoirs. "Write anything you like," says the head of the foundation, a certain Dr. Blythe, former student of Abbey's, a second-tier physicist who has found suitable employment, in Abbey's eyes, as a fund-raiser. "The check is blank." But it's not money that Abbey cares about. He started with nothing, made something, investing wisely, a genius, too, at the inexact science of stocks and bonds. (His hypothesis: it's a floating crap game.)

For a short time, Abbey contemplates writing a history of his family, an autobiography after Ben Franklin's. (Abbey, as a boy, modeled himself after Franklin and wonders if some bright boy might not model his life after his own.) But the more he thinks about it, he realizes, not the family — the rise from humble beginnings cannot be properly understood by audiences today. They judge too much by their own experience, and they see you, lush and comfortable, flourishing, heaped with honors, with wealth, and assume that you are exaggerating the depth of your poverty, the humbleness of your origins.

Well, Abbey thinks, he would not be exaggerating, but, in truth, his biological family has never been as important as his scientific one, never will be. The history of the world is *not* the history of the family, much as some writers would like it to be. It's the history of ideas, the history of science. Although he has played only a small part in this history, he admits he is proud of that part. If he writes anything at all, it will be of that.

But now Abbey has another writing task, more pressing than a memoir or a history. Abbey must write to Diana. A letter is the form in which to break this news, he thinks. He could not face her and he knows that hearing her voice on the telephone, distanced, marred by static, would make her vulnerable, make him vulnerable to her. He is, in a small way, grateful to Ellen, for knowing what she wants, for eliminating all feasible options.

Unfaithfulness is not his sin, he thinks. His sin is laziness. Not just in love but in other things. His work felt like pushing a stone up a very steep gradient. Not Sisyphus-like. No persistence. The thought of the boulder coming back at him made him moan, feign sleep.

He was lazy not about ideas, just about following through.

Working out dctails, buying equipment, rigging it. Waiting. He'd always collaborated for this reason, happy to share the credit, give it away if only someone else would do the tedious work of every day.

At home, Ellen pushed the boulder, willingly, with extraordinary ease. Mistress of domestic details, making sure he was free to think.

Could Diana do this? It wasn't her style, her way at all. "We'd hire someone, darling." Who would? She or he? Who would keep domestic life ordinary and calm?

It isn't Ellen's so-called price that's holding him back; it's something else, not so easily defined. A system, an order. She keeps their life in order. *Their life.* The plural dissolved into singular. He has to take this into consideration: they have a life, a family. To destroy this marriage is to destroy the family as well: to throw the planetary system awry.

The blank paper is a white field into which he must fall. He turns to stacks of letters — fanning them with the tip of a finger, wishing that one of them contained an opening sentence he might use.

My Dearest,

A tragedy has befallen us . . .

He crumples the page rapidly and tosses. Too melodramatic. He should be direct, the letter should be brief, but tender.

Dearest Diana,

We are discovered and must break it off. This pains me more than I can say — (or would that be write?)

Abbey crumples the paper again, turns to the telephone, lifts the receiver, then lets it drop. No, it must be in writing — irrevocable and true.

Diana,

Ellen has found us out and I must break it off. I trust you to understand this as you do everything in my heart.

A.

Abbey picks up his ebony letter opener, a slim black sword, Diana's only present to him, and snaps it in two. Then he seals the envelope.

FOUR

Devotion

IRA, 1972

At first the freak show was exactly what he wanted. Smoke and toke and howl Revolution till the cows came home. He was among the big boys, the bad boys, the Big Daddies of it all. He dug it. He could listen for hours, cross-legged, knees propped against strangers' thighs, just grooving on that mad dog kind of rage. Or standing or marching, arms linked, roaring like the stung gorilla, the tortured beast. HELL NO, WE WON'T GO.

But after a time, it got tired. It was people howling to hear themselves howling while the deals went down backstage and outta sight. The world was a hustle like the X said. They were all hypocrites. Every motherfucking one of them. They all dug the hype, shot it up, sucked microphone deep as it would go. For effect. To preserve the illusion.

He learned something. People liked to shout. No one gave a fuck. The more FBI, the better. The more narcs, the better. The more pigs, the better. Without those fuckers there'd be no audience, no ray-zin d'être. Prostitutes for evening news. I don't get no satisfaction, if I don't get your big reaction. *But they tried and they tried and they tried and they tried for the Big Erection, the nighttime connection. One and the same.*

In an accent not at all American, the man asks, "Howya doin', folks?" The accent is strange, held back in the throat and lopsided. German or Russian or something? He's a strange-looking dude. Big head shaved smooth as an egg and round all over like an egg man. Propping the fiddle on one plump thigh, he says, "We here's the Mandala Sun Mountain Band. Bringing you live music and a little dharma, too."

They are supposed to laugh at the hokey accent, but the man follows with a neat bob, hands folded as in prayer. He's praying politely, nodding to *them* as though *they're* the gods. Then a wink. Or maybe not. He bares his teeth, eyes burning like fires in a cliff as he saws the bow across the strings. He's sawing away and stomping so hard the platform shakes. The band bends in around him, the women wear white kerchiefs; the men, maroon berets, vaguely military. A tall woman thumps the bass with her long fingers, and a dude in aviator shades gets down on the banjo. Four fiddlers saw in unison behind their leader.

Ira turns the harmonica in his pocket, the metal cool in his palm. What the hell? He's back row anyhow and the band's rowdy enough. The wood at his lips tastes smoky; he licks the notches quickly, each as familiar as the gaps between his own teeth, and then he is wailing along with Buddha band, jamming with the man, the stomping Humpty-Dumpty, the fire-breathing egghead. His eyes are closed but he can feel the man smiling at him, or maybe it's a god. It feels good. He plays on.

Afterward someone slips him a card. Not the leader, who is busy mopping his head, chugging water from a canteen. Ira sneaks a glance. He looks fatter up close but just as fierce. The whole head round and square at the same time, like a bulldog's.

The man who hands him the card is the second bass player, a tall man with scooped shoulders. He seems a little nervous, but is kind.

"Take this. You may want to jam with us sometime." He looks over at the leader, who wipes his eyes with his sleeve then gestures at Ira with a flip of the hand. Been paying attention all this time, Ira thinks. Eyes in the back of his head.

Ira is trembling. Why? Just a bald dude with a mean arm.

"So," says the man in the same guttural accent. "You're the peanut gallery. Trying to distract us with that caterwauling?"

Ira mutters something, blushing. But the man's tone is not unkind.

"Let me see that." Again he flips his hand.

Ira doesn't usually let anyone hold his harmonica, but now he hands it over, curious what the man can do.

"I'm a string player, myself." He twists the harmonica in the air as though he has never seen one before. "How do you blow one of these tin whistles?"

Ira takes the harmonica back and starts to demonstrate, cupping one hand over the other. But the man does not want his instruction. Waving him off, he takes back the harmonica. Ira watches him suck it so hard he expects the harmonica to disappear. Evening snack.

A chord blasts the air like a steam whistle. Ira shakes his head, but the man ignores him, blasting a few more ferocious, earsplitting, notes.

Then he hands the instrument back to Ira. "You play the thing. I'm just a banshee."

"What do you want to hear?" Ira asks.

"Anything. You pick the tune."

The other band members are packing instruments and unplugging equipment. Ira's glad they're not listening. He takes a breath and launches into a blues riff, raunchy waa-waa notes slithering then strutting out, flashing here a pelvis, there a thigh before he sucks them back in, spins them out again, this time wailing, *screaming* for attention, for someone to listen the right way. He feels, he does not know why, as if he's auditioning for something, not a gig, something else. He feels as if he must show this strange man exactly the condition of his soul.

After a time, the man, perfectly still, holds up his hand. From deep in his blousy shirt he extracts another business card, bent at the corners and slightly damp from his sweat. "Stop by," he says.

He doesn't know whether to call first then thinks the hell with that, the man said drop by and jam sometime and so he will. Now looking up at the modest Victorian, he pulls the card from his back pocket to check the address one more time. Nothing about this house indicates that inside resides a troupe of handkerchief-headed, bluegrass-playing Buddhists.

There's a light on in the hallway, but he can make out little else through the lace curtains. To the right of the front door hangs a sign above a wicker basket: Please leave cigarettes, firearms, and drugs before entering.

He glances inside the basket, half-expecting to see a revolutionary's temporarily stashed Uzi. The basket's empty.

Ira fumbles in his jeans pockets, finds a butt. Seems ridiculous to drop a butt in there, so he pushes it further into the seam and wipes his hand on his thigh. *Bloody hands.* He smiles to himself, but he's surprisingly nervous.

He can hear the bell sound in the house, not a bell actually, but a harsh raspberry of a buzzer, a sound he remembers suddenly as the buzzer he pushed to be admitted to his shrink's waiting room when he was a kid. Dr. Goldman. Whatever happened to him?

A sound of swishing steps and whoever it is pauses before opening the door. Ira wonders if he should buzz again. Then the door opens a couple of inches of taut chain. A woman wearing a white kerchief tied back beneath her hair stands in the inch of light.

"How may we help you?"

She has a serious face, made more so by a pair of wire-rimmed glasses perched on a delicate nose.

The syntax is polite; the tone, not particularly.

Ira holds up the card. "I, um, heard you play a couple of weeks ago and, um, your leader —"

"Rinpoche."

Ira nods. "Yeah. Well, he invited me over whenever. To jam. But if this isn't a good time . . ."

The woman nods, but Ira can hear the chain sliding off.

"Come in," she says. Her voice only slightly warmer. "Practice isn't till eight thirty. We're eating dinner."

Leaning into the doorframe, Ira smells curry spices in the air. At the far end of the hall, people are talking in loud kitchen voices above the clanging of metal pots. Still, he hesitates, not knowing whether the woman's statement is an invitation to dinner.

"I'll wait out here."

The woman frowns. "Suit yourself. You're welcome to eat with us." Then, as though she has assumed his answer is yes, she points at his feet. "Shoes outside."

Under the woman's gaze, he unties the laces of his hiking boots, fumbling slightly, his coordination has never been good. He wishes she would just let the door close.

"Do much hiking?" she says.

"Much as I can."

She nods as though he has answered a test question correctly. "We do a lot of hiking," she says. (As though he should know who *we* are, he thinks.) "Rinpoche says mountain is mantra."

He wants to ask about this word she keeps using, *Rinpoche,* but decides not to. Must be the bald guy. The leader. In Ira's mind he is Chief Egg.

The woman glances back once as she leads Ira down the narrow hall lined with closed doors. He can't tell if she's checking on him or looking past him as though expecting someone to be following *him.*

"Rinpoche's finishing *puja,*" she says in a half whisper as though to explain. And it is then he realizes she's been glancing back to the staircase, anticipating Rinpoche's step. "When he's done, we'll eat."

Ira nods idiotically, finding himself eager to please. He doesn't understand a word she's saying, but it makes him strangely happy that she expects him to.

"So what is this? A kind of commune?"

"We live together," she answers rather stiffly.

"You hang out and play music?"

The woman stops and blinks at him for a second, trying to decide whether he is joking. "We're Buddhists. You didn't know that?"

Ira shrugs, glad that the dim light hides his blush. "Figured something was going on," he says, pantomiming scissors near the top of his head.

The woman nods and Ira thinks, *I've blown it.*

"It's complicated," she sighs. "Rinpoche will explain."

The dining room is spread with an Indian print cloth that covers almost the entire floor. Ira stands awkwardly in a corner and watches the disciples set out the food. There are heaping platters of puffed breads and saffron-colored rice; small dishes of coconut, raisins, peanuts; and a huge covered tureen, dragging a spicy current.

A few of the men acknowledge Ira, nodding gravely in his direction, as though he shares a secret. All of the disciples are wearing white shirts printed with an insignia, a strange rattle topped with bishops' hats at either end, and green fatigues that tie at the ankles like genie pants. The men wear maroon berets on their shaved heads, making them look to Ira like French paratroopers. Still Ira is struck by the nakedness of their shaved scalps, the strange newness of those shadowed heads.

The women smile as they pass by, setting plates, silverware, napkins. Ira offers to help them, but they brush his arm away politely.

A bell is heard in the distance, a deep ringing clang, and suddenly they are lining up against the wall, the men sweeping off their berets as though royalty were approaching, and Ira hears a rushing whisper: Rinpoche.

The man's as round as he remembered but more imposing. Still flushed from his activity (What was it? "Pooh-ja"?), his skin has the heated look of a man who has been engaged in a strenuous sport. Tonight he is wearing a crimson cape, hooked with a bronze chain, crimson pants, tied like the fatigues at the ankle. The light illumines the drops of sweat that line the top of his forehead. Rinpoche pauses in the doorway, flicks his thumb along this line, and offers it to a woman on his right. She shakes her head, smiling, and the others groan.

"Jeez guys. You know how to make a guy feel welcome."

Laughter ripples through the group, and everyone is immediately loose-limbed, hustling at some small but seemingly important task.

"Why don't y'all sit down?" Rinpoche says in the put-on accent Ira remembers from the performance. "I's hungry."

Again laughter. A young woman pulls round cushions from the sideboard which are passed around. The first goes to Rinpoche, who settles himself with legs tucked in a bulging lotus position.

Ira is handed a pillow and clutches it to his stomach, not knowing where to sit. The woman who led him down the hall gestures him to sit right where he is.

"Hey! Who's this? The obstreperous harmonica player?"

Ira nods. His palms are sweating and he can feel everyone's gaze turn to him.

"You've come back to blow your horn, have you?"

Ira nods. He isn't certain how to address the man.

"Until then you'll be silent and mysterious." Big wink. "The girls like that, eh?"

Ira can feel heat rising inside him like a cloud. But Rinpoche leans forward, extending a hand. "Seriously, now. Welcome. We're very pleased you're our guest. What's your name?"

"Ira. Ira Stein."

Rinpoche repeats his name in such a way that Ira feels as though it is not a name he has ever recognized, as though his name by some alchemy has been changed into an obscure rock, a rock from the moon.

"Where do you hail from, Ira?"

"Berkeley."

"A student?"

"Just hanging."

"And playing mean harp."

Ira freezes his gaze on the frayed heel of his sock.

"So what ya waiting for?"

The question surprises him. It's exactly the question he's been asking himself, standing on the corner of Euclid and Hearst with the bundle of *Barbs* under his arm. He thinks of saying, *Some days for suckers, some days for saints.* No, every day for saints, teachers, deliverers. From what?

"You're a Wandering Jew, a-searching for a path. And you've gone astray . . ." Rinpoche shakes his head. "There's a spiritual energy in Jews. Why do you think you scratch a guru and you find a Bernstein?" The group laughs, and it strikes Ira that Rinpoche is saying this for their benefit, not his.

"How do you like hanging?"

"Sucks."

Rinpoche raises his brows. "So you're considering a monastery instead."

And though he doesn't quite get it, Rinpoche's remark sends the rest of the group into gales of laughter.

After that Rinpoche turns his attention to his food and does not speak to him for the rest of the meal.

"Where have *you* been?"

She is sitting at the kitchen table, her back to him, and all he can see is her cascade of red curls and a ribbon of smoke rising as though she were sitting in front of a small campfire.

Rinpoche said, "We're a fire-walking group. Can you dig that?"

"Out," he says, softly. He's not trying to start anything really, but he's not sure how to explain. He pinches her shoulders gently, until she shakes him off. He draws a chair. The rims of her eyes are red against her pale skin.

"You weren't at school. I called . . ." She takes another long drag of her cigarette, blowing the smoke away from him. "Why do you keep doing this?"

He shrugs. Before crashing with Rita, he'd been sleeping in

the back of Jim's old Buick, a monster of a car with overstuffed seats, cartoon dials, and a hood that rose in waves of black shiny metal. Every night he'd pulled his coat tight around him, seeing in his mind's eye a tiny kid, locked in the car while his mother went shopping. Every night, as soon as he wedged himself into the crack along the back of the seat and breathed in the oily smell of plush and leather combined, he'd felt himself shrinking, shrinking, fighting the urge to suck his thumb and weep.

She was older than he. Ten years. And she was from Cambridge, where he'd once lived. She told him she'd been standing in the middle of Harvard Square when all of a sudden she thought, What am I doing in this place? It seemed everything that was happening was happening in the West. She'd been pregnant, she told him, and it had been drop out and have the baby or have an abortion and stay. She'd had the abortion and split. Her parents still hadn't forgiven her.

"Who are you fucking?" she asks. This time she lets the smoke stream through her nostrils. "No bullshit."

He reaches for her free hand, covers it with his own. Her knuckles, all bone, poke his fingers. She is bony all over, knees, elbows, clavicle. He loves this about her, that when he touches her, he feels her skeleton, her form, the mysterious cage of who she is.

"You won't believe it," he says.

"Believe what?"

"I met this man, this crazy man, this teacher —" *We walk on hot coals, he said, not 'cause we think we're Jesus, just to make sure we're awake, to keep on our toes.*

"What kind of teacher?"

"A holy man."

There is something in the way she is looking at him that reminds him of his mother. Of how frightened she always was, of how she held herself steady even when she was scared shitless, as though she were telling herself, Keep cool, cool, cool.

"Well, who *is* he? This teacher?" She cannot help biting off this word. Once *she* was his teacher, in many ways.

"Rinpoche."

"What's that?"

"I don't know. They just call him that."

"Who are 'they'?"

"His disciples. They live in this house in San Francisco, and they play music and climb mountains and other shit." He doesn't want to tell her about the fire walking, not yet. *We don't let this get around, Rinpoche said. There are people who aren't ready, not that any unenlightened schmuck couldn't do it, but it would freak their minds.* Not his. "They believe you can become enlightened in this lifetime."

Rita whirls her index finger in the air. "Whoop-de-do. Then what? You walk on water?"

"You help all sentient beings become enlightened." He sees his words passing through her like flames, and he knows that she is thinking, *He's leaving me,* and, to his surprise, he knows she's right this time. He's leaving even though he still loves her. "Come here, Little One." Usually this makes her smile at least.

"You're the shrimp," she says as she moves to his lap.

"Crustacean, sheathed worm."

"Imbecile." She kisses the top of his head.

They make love swiftly, on the kitchen floor, as in the old days, when he would take her wherever she stood.

"Will we ever get together?" she asks.

"In the biblical sense?" He strokes her back, tracing the outcroppings of bone with his knuckle. "It's not Siberia. You can visit any time."

"Same," she says.

That night he dreams he is chasing Rinpoche up the mountain, his plump calves working fast as he tries to catch up, awkward as a small child at his father's heels. When he reaches the top, Rinpoche is motioning him to come, come. But he cannot see what the man is pointing to, and when he reaches the spot where Rinpoche stood, he cannot tell where the man has gone.

Maybe it is the father thing. But what a father. Not like any father he'd imagined. Ever. No Ginsberg, no gray-haired poet. No Whitman. No Watts even. No Jerry. No Jesus, for that matter. Makes him laugh to think of it. He's a Buddha, man. Stepped off the page. The stomping Buddha. The man can stomp, and twang and saw his fiddle like nobody's business; he popped three strings the night they jammed in the basement, and the sweat flew, drops springing off him like off a shaking leaf, and it might have been smoke coming out of his nostrils the way the man was playing.

He would switch it off, switch on a sweet, almost silly smile, a welcome to our house kind of smile, a grin that was somehow all wrong, somehow too sly.

After the jam, Rinpoche invited him upstairs to the temple room for a private audience. They sat on cushions in front of a fireplace, embers still glowing in the circular hearth. Rinpoche poked at them with a long stick. He was smiling, delighted with something. The fire? Or what Ira was telling him?

At first, when Rinpoche asked him to talk about himself, he struggled. It was like an audience with his grandfather, except that Rinpoche seemed to take it all as a joke, the interview itself, his own performance.

Ira mumbled something.

"Speak up, man. I'm not going to chuck you in this fire if you make a mistake. Tell me something stupid, tell me something silly. I want to hear it all." The man was grinning. He handed the stick to Ira. "Here, stir it up."

Ira obeyed, shooting sparks into the air, watching them fly up the chimney. They were being watched all around by Buddhas, hanging on the walls. Little flames danced among the embers. He could make out images here and there, a ring of round, grinning heads. It seemed as if the whole room was listening to what he had to say.

He started telling the man about when he was a kid, about the dots, about X-ray vision. He told him about this question he'd always had: How do you know we're not dreaming? He was getting into it. Almost like he was stoned. He said it's like looking at clouds. When you're a kid, you think, of course, you can stand on a cloud. They're solid. Then your parents tell you no, it just looks that way. It's condensation or something. But couldn't reality be the same way? The world only *looks* real, but it might be a dream, an illusion. If we'd been told that everything we see is as insubstantial as a cloud, then we'd see things differently, wouldn't we? The way they really are.

Rinpoche was grinning. "Well, well," he said. "You've probably been fortunately born a few dozen times or so. How old were you when you worked this all out?"

Ira shrugged. "Seven, eight. Something like that."

"A little dharma bum." He laughed, creasing his jowls. Then he grew serious. "Ira Stein, you are getting by instinct or by birth the essence of the Buddha's teachings. What this group is doing is trying to realize exactly what you're talking about. We're on the bodhisattva path. We vow to put off our enlightenment until *all* sentient beings are enlightened. It's a heavy pledge, the bodhisattva vow. We're not futzying around. We're working our balls off to reach enlightenment in *this* lifetime.

"So here's what you're gonna do. You're going to talk to Rita. You're going to tell her you've found your new path. You're going to collect your belongings in a little rucksack or a U-Haul truck or what have you, and you're going to get your butt over here to San Francisco.

"We're going to teach you a little tantra magic. You're ripe."

At the ashram, he was learning to walk on fire. No big shit, Rinpoche said. "We's not here to prove we're Je-e-sus." You walk through salt, then step lively. Any schmuck can do it.

But you have to keep focused. Be there or be square. No drifting, or you begin to hear the snap, crackle and pop. That's a toe, Joe.

The pit on the beach was no larger than a grave, but deep, six feet at least. The men worked in shifts while the women carried logs down a path carved into the cliff. Then came the lighter wood, doused in kerosene.

Next they fitted wet logs close enough to form a bridge across the top of the pit. Someone's job would be to keep an eye on those, turning each log before it caught fire. If a log began to smoke, it was pulled out and thrown into a barrel of water. Gyalwang was the master log handler. He pulled those suckers in and out as though he were ringing changes in a bell tower. All rhythm and motion.

Flames licked up his ankles, the air filled with that fearful smell of burning hair. Rinpoche was shouting something that was drowned by the crash of the surf beyond. It didn't matter what he lost. He was moving, moving, no thought of anything but that.

By the time they'd finished their passes, the tide was up. The waves poured into the pit, sending up a roaring hiss as they extinguished the flames, the coals, and retreated, tugging the logs out to sea.

PHOEBE, 1972

We stand at the bus stop, stomping our feet, blowing our hands, freezing our butts. The bus is already ten minutes late, and Doris's bummed. She wishes she had a boyfriend.

Isn't all *that* great, I tell her. She doesn't believe me. She's got a crush on Tom Marsh, cutest guy in our school. Wants to sleep with him real bad. She doesn't care about love.

That's a mistake, I think, but what do I know? So I promised I'd take her along to get the Pill.

Across the street is a statue of a man reading a paper on a bench. "Remember the time I thought he was real?"

Doris turns to me, laughing. "'Look at that poor man, sitting in the snow,' you said. You thought he was homeless."

When Doris laughs you can see her big white teeth. It's amazing how long I've known Doris, how long I've known her teeth. When did she get such big teeth? Such beautiful eyes?

Doris shakes a cigarette out of a crumpled pack. "Want one?"

"I quit."

She coughs deep into her fist, then lights her cigarette. "I should, too."

I'm sorry now I didn't bum a cigarette. Just to be smoking with her.

"At least you're actually sleeping with somebody." She flicks her ash, watches the wind carry it away.

"I don't know about that," I want to say. Mark's my first lover; I think I'm his, but I've never asked. We don't talk about love or making it. We hardly talk at all.

The bus is almost empty and unbearably hot. We sit near the front, close to the driver, so we can keep checking for our stop.

"Hey no smoking back there," the driver calls over his shoulder.

Doris gives him the finger behind his back. Surprises me. She used to be so shy. Still, she drops the cigarette on the floor, squashes it under the toe of her boot.

"He's got to tell you that. It's his job," I say.

Doris breathes a shadow on the window, then draws with her fingertip. "So why can't I get Tom Marsh?"

"You'll get him."

I watch Doris corral initials in a heart then rub the window with her sleeve, soaking it. "Right," she says.

My visit doesn't take too long. I give the lady my name, she reaches into the drawer, pulls out packets of pills that could be pocket combs in their plastic jackets.

"How many?"

"Six," I say. It seems greedy to ask for more.

She slides them across the desk, and I put them in my knapsack fast. Afraid she'll want them back if I take too long.

I wait for Doris in the lobby, watching the people come in. Mostly grown-ups, women. Some with kids, some not. Some men, too. I sit with my magazine. Try to look invisible. It embarrasses me to be here, like I know everyone's private business and they know mine.

Doris comes out, looking pale.

"What took you so long?"

"Come on," she says.

The bus's already at the stop. A minute later, we'd have missed it.

Doris sits down, all quiet.

"What's the matter?" I ask.

She rests her head against the window and acts like she doesn't hear me.

"Come on."

Doris turns to me, her eyes shining.

"Fucking lady didn't believe I'm fifteen."

I roll my eyes. "What'd you say?"

"Even if you don't believe me, I can still get pregnant."

"Brilliant."

"It's true."

Mark picks me up in his car and drops me off at school even though he doesn't go anymore. I don't know what he does all day. Probably smokes reefer. Rides his skateboard. He wants to build a tepee. Someday live on his father's land.

He used to know Ira, and I keep wondering if Ira liked him. I think so. He's very gentle, doesn't like to hurt anyone.

Sometimes I ask Mark about Ira. What'd Ira do that was so cool? I want to know everything I possibly can about Ira, about the stuff he did when he went out. The stuff he'd never tell me.

But Mark just shakes his head and says in his soft voice, "Cool dude."

We fake the big good-bye almost every night. Then Mark sneaks back into the house, back up the stairs into my room.

My parents sleep across the hall, but they hear nothing, see nothing.

He starts by kissing me, his eyes closed. Then he's unbuttoning, unzipping, and I take off my nightgown. When Mark makes love to me, I'm always the watcher, a lone cloud floating free. Over and over I watch a herd of bulls stampede over a prairie, dashing headlong toward a cliff. Afterward, I rush to the bathroom, stay there a long, long time, telling myself it's not his fault he's a man.

In the morning we wake to the sound of Dad taking a shower in the bathroom next door. Mark gets his clothes on, sneaks down the stairs while I lie listening to Dad's one-note drone.

Seven days a week my father gets up at six thirty A.M., thumps through the four-star level of the Royal Canadian Air Force exercises. It's taken him ten years to reach his goal: thirty push-ups, fifty jumping jacks, seventy sit-ups, ten minutes' skipping rope. While he's jumping, the whole floor shakes. He says he's not vain, but sometimes I wonder. He looks so proud of himself standing there in his shorts and T-shirt, huffing and sweating. He doesn't see the red skin, the snot dripping from his nose like tears.

This goes on for months. Then Dad disappears. Business in Africa. His letters arrive on blue paper, one for Mom, one for me and Molly, typed so we can read them.

When he comes home, we crowd like curious natives around his open trunk in the hall, watch him pull out lengths of blue cloth batiked with stars and smelling like cat piss.

"You can wash it," he says.

Beneath the cloth are layers of gifts. Dad hands me a carved wooden boat, the rowers held in place with pegs. He hands Molly an ostrich egg, ivory-colored, impossible to crack. For each of us he has a picture made of butterfly wings, women carrying pots on their heads, children following.

"Horrible," Mom says. (After all, he's been gone for over three months. And his words, trapped in thin, blue aerograms, have felt as insubstantial as those shimmering wings.)

Finally, he comes to the jewelry, and we grow hopeful. From the pockets of the suitcase, he pulls ropes of malachite beads, nickel bracelets that lock and unlock with tiny keys, worms of silver shaped into rings. Heavy clunky stuff, not really in style.

But for Mom: filigree pendants, silk blouses from Paris, a bikini.

Each time he hands Mom a gift, he looks at her with a funny expression, like a boy giving his mother something he's made himself. He watches her silently unwrap. It's all a test. When she smiles, he starts talking as fast as he can, telling us bits of stories, mentioning African names and places, distant hotels and deserts, pausing only to say, "I wished you were all there, of course . . ." or "I thought of how much you would've enjoyed riding those camels . . ."

At the bottom of the suitcase, a long narrow bundle nestled against the back seam, a present for Ira, which Dad sets aside.

Throat tight with jealousy, I wonder what Dad got him. It's different from our stuff, and *wrapped.*

"Heard anything from Ira?" Dad asks.

Mom frowning, holds the bikini's skimpy bra against her chest. "Seems fine."

"What's this?" Molly asks, picking up the bundle, weighing it in her open palms.

Does she have to give everything away?

"We'll call him tonight. Let him know I'm back," Dad says.

"WHAT IS THIS?"

Dad looks at Molly, hearing her for the first time, but even Mom's listening.

"That's a spear. A chief gave that to me when I told him I had a son."

Ira never calls Dad back. And he never comes home. Even though Dad keeps inviting him.

This time, his birthday, a woman answers the phone. Her name's Rita, Ira says. They're thinking of getting married.

The door to Ira's room shivers, then bursts open. Smell of old smoke, burnt matches.

I rip back the bedspread. Underneath, a bare mattress with piss stains the shape of continents. I hoist myself onto the high trundle, flop on my back.

In the dim light, words glow in fluorescent paint on the window shade, faintly green, FUCK YOU, PEACE, BEATLES FOREVER. All I've got left of Ira.

"Phoebe," Mom calls.

She's standing in the doorway of the bathroom. Just a slip on. She gives me a little wave.

"What d'you want?"

"Come here."

She doesn't sound mad.

"Could you show me how to put on eye makeup?"

I'm surprised. Mom and Molly are always teasing me about my "lizard eyes." They make it sound like I'm really disgusting.

We stand in front of the vanity, and I open the top drawer. All my old, half-used pencils and shadows. A frosted lipstick and a glossy rouge. Stuff I bought at Woolworth's years ago with my allowance.

"You can't use this. It's too cheap."

"I only want a little bit." Mom takes off her glasses, blinks at herself in the mirror. She can hardly see without her glasses. Her eyes are terrible.

"I'll show you how to put it on. But you have to promise to buy new stuff."

She nods. "You're so good at these things."

I am? I dip my finger into the gray shadow and begin to smear along the crease of her lid. "Your eyes are set-in," I say. "This will pull them apart, make them seem larger." I hear myself sounding like a beauty magazine. Can't she tell it's all fake?

She leans into the mirror, and I try not to notice the hollow between her breasts, their plump edges. We don't ever get undressed in front of each other. We're an incredibly modest family.

Dabbing a new color at the corner, I say, "Always shade. And smooth in the direction of the skin."

She smiles. "I'm so glad you're doing this. I noticed all the other women in the office wear makeup."

They're younger, I think. I don't say it.

By the time I finish making up my mother, she really does look younger. Perhaps because, when she sees herself, she begins to smile.

"Oh! Look at me!" She flips her hair behind her ears and sucks in her cheeks. "I can't do this every day."

"Why not?"

She shrugs. "What brand do you recommend?"

"Something more subtle."

"I've never bought makeup before," she says.

"Even as a girl?"

"I was too beautiful for makeup."

"Well, it's kind of fun. Like playing with a watercolor set."

"We'll see." She closes the drawer and bends to the mirror. "How does it come off?"

"Why don't you leave it?"

"I can't go around with this stuff on. Your father will think I've gone bananas."

"So what?" But I can't stop her. She smears the white cream over her face, wipes it off with a tissue.

When the color's all gone, she says, "I'm me again."

Mark puts me on his skateboard, pulls me along like a string toy.

"Practice balance," he says.

He's incredible. He can go down anything, up anything. Jumps curbs, barrels. Like his feet are glued to the board.

I'm not like that. I'm scared of speed. When I start rolling, it feels like I'm going to crash. No matter how slow, how safe.

"Bend your knees. Use your arms."

"What's it like to balance like that?" I ask him.

"Like flying," he says. "Like you're soaring through air."

"You don't get scared?" I'm remembering a time stuck at the top of a ski slope, looking down at the snow, white as porcelain, stretching into the valley, thinking I was going to die.

But Ira had said, "The mountain's holding you. The mountain's your friend."

Then I was over the lip of that run, screeching like a bird, hearing Ira in my head, and I wasn't afraid. The only time.

"Oh, look!" my mother says. "Letter for you. From Grandpa."

From Grandpa? We only live an hour away.

Small white envelope, a rectangle. My name scrawled in black fountain ink.

"Why isn't there one for me?" Molly asks. "It's not her birthday."

I take the letter into the front room, the one that gets the morning light. Ripping open the envelope, I'm nervous. What is this about? My grandparents don't send letters, just the occasional postcard when they're traveling, written in Grandma Ellen's neat hand.

There is no letter. Only a photograph. A girl wrapped in a silk babushka, staring silently with sad black eyes. Me.

On the back, my grandfather has written something, the handwriting shaky as though written in a dream: Who is this?

Who is this?

"What did he send you?" my mother and sister want to know.

"My picture," I say, showing them just the front.

"Odd," my mother says. "But you'll write to him."

Will I? What would I say? It's me, the Thanksgiving before Ira left. The last Thanksgiving is how I think of it.

Stupid to write all that. Of course Grandpa knows it's me. Of course he does. So what does he *really* want to know?

I'm sitting at Mom's desk downstairs in her study, talking on the phone to Doris while my hand surfs through the junk like it's got a mind of its own. Doris is riffing about Tom, her depression, the usual. I'm not listening too closely, watching instead my hand bobbing in and out of the clutter, watching my hand come up with paper clips, Scotch tape, a Chinese menu, watching my hand come up with a stiff, cream-colored envelope, address handwritten: Eileen Stein. *Invitation?* I watch my fingers remove the card, the same stiff, cream-colored cardboard of a wedding announcement, and watch myself reading, not paying attention to Doris or to the voice in my head saying, *It's not your mail.*

Black ink, slightly blurred.

You were wonderful, Eileen. Looking forward to Saturday. Todd.

Todd? Who's Todd?

I blink, stuff card in envelope, bury card. Heart exploding my chest.

"Got to go," I say.

"What? I haven't gotten to the good part."

"Sorry."

"What's going on?"

All our friendship, I've told Doris everything. I can't tell her this.

Call you later, I say. I slam down the phone.

I know where I'm going. Just know. Like a mission I've been sent on.

Weird niches all over this house, weird hiding places, secret places. The trapdoor in the living room floor, the closets under the eaves, a loose brick in the hearth in my parent's room where Molly and I used to pass notes.

Other places. Rooms filled with junk and closets in those rooms stuffed with jigsaw puzzles and rackets, mittens and stuffed animals, board games, workbooks, checkbooks. Stuff Dad brought home from the army — knapsacks and mummy bags that smell like metal, masks of stiff black felt, huge boxing gloves filled with down.

Even in the almost dark, you can tell her room's a mess. Sheets are on the floor, dirty clothes piled everywhere.

"Mom?" I whisper, my face already set in false surprise. We're not allowed in this room. Even when we were little, seeking comfort in the night, she kissed us, turned us back to our beds.

No answer.

I crouch, wiggling the brick in the floor of the hearth like a loose tooth until it comes up, then slip in the envelope, drop the brick back where it belongs.

Maybe I'm imagining things, maybe I'm the evil, disgusting person she thinks I am.

Moving to the bureau, I slide out the top drawer, stare down at the compartments corralling their hordes of underpants, stockings, bras. What am I looking for? Cream-colored notes, more evidence. Am I dreaming?

I take out a rose-colored bra, satin. Mom's breasts are smaller than mine, rounder. I stuff it back, reach for underpants, nylon, white, crotch stained with shades of tea, balled up stockings. I sniff the sooty toes, the sagging heels, examine the stretched calves that held my mother's legs all day.

If I wasn't scared she'd find me, I'd examine every item on the floor, in her bureau, on her nightstand. I'd rummage in her medicine chest and in the quilted bag that holds her toiletries. Ban roll-on. Chanel No. 5. Gold clip-ons like the sliced domes of gumdrops. Boxes of unworn ivory. A gold filigree pendant delicate as a Christmas ball. Junk that amounts to nothing, details that can't explain. Who is she, this woman, my mother?

Doris unlocks her flute case at the same time I unlock mine. It's been a long time since we played duets. Since Mark came along, and Tom.

Now Mark's gone for a few days. He hitched to Atlantic City to surf. I don't miss him.

"That's where it happened," Doris says, tilting her head at the mattress on the floor, now perfectly made up in three shades of purple Indian print.

She looks incredibly tired. Lavender pouches under her eyes, her pale skin tinged with gray. Even her room looks tired in the weak afternoon light. The treasures on the bureau, her eagle feather, her Dad's bow tie, the purple knob she found one night at the bottom of the pool in the quad, gone dull.

"What was he like?"

"He didn't know I was a virgin."

I watch as Doris snugs the mouthpiece under her lip, blows a long A.

Desperadoes, we used to cry. Desperadoes, running full speed down the moonlit bank to the fence marked DANGER. *We thought if we touched the fence, we'd die.*

Doris stops blowing for a second. "He's kind of a jerk, if you really want to know."

Hairs prick on the back of my neck. *What'd he do?* I concentrate on matching my A with hers. Some things she can't tell me.

Mom pretends she doesn't notice. Voice full of good cheer. Eyes flashing. It's been weeks like this. *Don't think you can get to me,* she's saying. She knows I know.

We're in the kitchen. Me, eating toast (Dad's away again; we don't eat dinner anymore); she, making tea.

Suddenly I feel hands on top of my head, pressing, smoothing.

"How are you?" my mother asks. "How's school? I never see you."

I shake off her hands, narrow my eyes. Pour on the guilt.

"I guess there's something I'm not understanding," she says.

"Guess so."

Mom turns abruptly from me, dunking her tea bag, then dropping it in the sink.

"Can't you dispose of that properly?" Perfect imitation of her.

She stops, looks at me. Then picks up the wet tea bag, throws it with all her might at my head. Splat. It lands past the end of the table. Nowhere near.

Without a word, she leaves the room.

I look at my toast, but can't eat. Heart beating too fast, too hard. I might be sick.

Then I hear it. A shriek from the hallway, and I run. The mug's hitting the staircase wall, a flume of hot tea spewing into the air.

"Stop it. Stop punishing me," she screams.

Pee fills my crotch, warm, almost comforting. Even though I can see the mug on the floor, it still feels like it's going to hit my head.

"Sorry," I say, "sorry sorry."

She's not looking. She's sitting on the stairs, her face in her hands, her shoulders bouncing.

"Sorry," I say, but I can't move, and I don't even know if she can hear me.

IRA, 1973

He woke crying, the pain forcing him on his back. Stakes through the eyes, acid, searing. He screamed and Chimay came running.

Milarepa? What is it?

Holding his hand.

Migraine?

Words from a distant planet, words falling like tin pieces on his ears, shiny cutting sharp. Without content or dimension.

Rinpoche summoned.

A glass of water held to his lips; pills from Nepal pressed onto his tongue. Mantra mimicry screeched parrotlike, unceasing, in his head. A million jagged mirrors drummed their razor edges into his skull.

Keep it dark, he heard someone say. Wait it out.

He waited in that black room of pain, waited for impermanence to work its magic, for a gale to blow the pain to smithereens.

The high lama was coming today. Coming all the way from Dharamsala to teach. Rinpoche's main man.

He was feeling a little better. A week since the first bomb went off in the brain, though the successive headaches came roaring on, a squadron of dark missiles falling; he, cringing beneath. Holding out his mantra as armor; they struck, pow pow pow.

Always pain, but not quite as bad as that first mother of all bombs.

"You're to do nothing but rest," Chimay told him. "Rinpoche's orders."

"Give me some brass, some flags or something."

Chimay with that no fucking way smile, always surprising in her stern face. "Nothing, Milarepa. Rest."

"Come on."

"Boss's orders. Lie down."

No use arguing.

He could feel the whole house moving beneath him, an ark filled with tramping animals. Everyone getting ready.

He wanted to help. He couldn't.

Someone somewhere was practicing the fiddle. Long sour notes that sliced through his skull like a wire through cheese. On and on the fiddle whined, whipping its silver wire so close to his head he thought his ears might fall off.

Above him the cracks in the ceiling were undulating, hairy arms of seaweed dragged by some strange current. I'm tripping, he thought. The revelation giving him the courage to prop himself on an elbow.

Pain smashed him between the temples, knocked him right down.

"Okay," he said aloud to no one.

He had only time to grab the nearest receptacle, a brass bowl usually brimming with carnations, now chalky white with polish, when the nausea hit. Afterward, he was breathing hard, tears in his eyes at the shock of his gut's betrayal. He hung his head, mouth gaping over the bowl.

In the bathroom, he flushed the bowl's contents down the toilet, found a washcloth, rinsed his mouth. His fingers trembled on the stem of his toothbrush and his face seemed to float in the mirror, wobbly like a face staring at him from underwater.

The flu.

He could call someone, but he didn't want to. If he spoke, clouds of yellow gas would emerge, puffs of poison. *Better keep your trap shut.* He'd make it back, crawling down the runner the way as a child he'd paced the rug outside his mother's study door. Fingers flexing in the rich pile. *Open up, open up. Or else.*

Jim once told him, picture rainbows when the trip's going bad. Rainbows. Where'd he get that?

Had a dream. A dream he'd not dreamt since childhood. A boy in a little boat, a boy in a little boat on the sea, rowing round a great rock.

He was looking for something. An opening in the rock. A cave.

Then there it was. He rowed into the gaping mouth, ran his little boat up onto the sandy shore. The chest was waiting for him, humpbacked, covered with barnacle pearls.

He knelt and raised the lid. Plunged his hand into the mound of coins. *Oh joy.*

The door opened. A silhouette in the light, the stooped figure of a man, a tiny man.

Sound of whispering. "He's lying down."

He tried to raise himself, body locked, only his head went up, like a turtle's.

Someone raised a lantern. A vulture's bald head leapt to the ceiling, the lama's shadow elongated on the wall.

In the lantern light, the lama's eyes shone above him, luminous black. And he could feel his wrist being lifted, pinched between clawlike nails. The lama tilted his head, listening to the beat no one else could hear.

Then the same dry finger pressed to the base of his throat. The luminous eyes caressing him.

"You're a sick man. Must visit hospital."

He nodded. He felt comforted somehow, relieved, as though he could truly rest for the first time since the strange pain began.

Behind the lama stood Rinpoche, head bowed while his teacher chanted, barely audible, the syllables jouncing and tumbling like stones kicked down a mountain path, a barely controlled avalanche of stones.

The lama bowed, palms pressed flat together. Again the compassionate gaze swept over him. The lama retreated.

Closing the door behind him.

You walked down the fluorescent halls and you scattered om manis *like seed. Bring an end to these people's suffering, not only patients, but doctors, too. Help those doctors not to be afraid for you.*

He sat across the desk from Dr. Frankel, small, slender, compact like a rock climber, his neck a bit too thin for his button-down shirt, his freshly tied tie. A white coat hung on the back of the door, and Milarepa saw Dr. Frankel glance at it once with slight distress in his eye, as though he'd wished he'd remembered to put it on, could use that extra layer, a skin to protect himself from this patient.

Dr. Frankel gripped the edge of his desk, pulled in his rolling chair with a dig of his buttocks, then picked up the oversize manila envelope that covered the other documents on his desk.

"How are you feeling?" he asked.

He liked Dr. Frankel and pitied him. "Okay, I guess."

"Headache still there?"

He shook his head. The headache was gone, in its place a strange bunched-up feeling, bunched cloth, curtains twirled around a broomstick, swaddled and tangled, *bound.* This morning when he shaved, he'd given himself a wink that seemed more like a twitch. He'd slapped his cheeks. *No time for futzying around.* But all day as he'd gone from test to test, the bunched feeling stayed with him, the feeling his whole body hadn't shaken out quite right. A hitch in his shoulder.

"Well," said Dr. Frankel. "I have your scans here, as well as the results from your other tests. I've looked at them very carefully, as has my entire team.

"Here, I can show you —" The plastic sheets slithered out of the manila sleeve, oversize place mats the doctor suddenly didn't seem to know how to handle. The top one he placed on the lighted screen.

Weather, Milarepa thought. *Clouds on a moonlit night, storms around Jupiter.* His heart was beating quickly, the *manis* slipping rapidly across his tongue. His lips were moving but he didn't notice, as he didn't notice the sound of his beads click, clicking.

But the doctor did, glancing once at Milarepa, blinking, then going back to the head filled with bad weather, impossible storms. "You see this white mass here —" He was pointing to something that twisted and undulated, horizontal smoke trapped between sheets of black.

Milarepa nodded, trying to follow. Malignant gliomas. Frontal lobes. Increased intracranial pressure. Pressure on the spine. Could stop the respiratory system, but in his case, lucky. He was still alive. Systems and pressures. Meteorologically accurate. Systole, diastole. Yin and yang. The doctor's explanation was entirely technical, impossible to understand.

Dr. Frankel turned from the light box, swiveled back behind the desk, his butt still glued to the chair. "This all takes time to get used to, I know. But I'm going to give it to you straight: I, and the rest of the team, recommend immediate surgery."

"How immediate?"

"Tomorrow morning if we can get an operating room."

Milarepa drew a deep breath, blew it out hard. Heart Sutra suddenly droning, unbidden angel. *There is no eye, no ear, no nose, no tongue, no body, no mind.* Milarepa spread his arms. "I'm yours," he said.

Listening to his parents on the telephone, he felt like a priest might while listening to a confession, detached, compassionate, but grateful for the shield the telephone gave him, grateful he couldn't see their eyes.

On the other end of the line, his father spoke in a basso profundo businessman's voice, booming concern, firing to take charge, while his mother could not find enough wind suddenly even to speak.

They wanted to come out, but he insisted, "No. Everything's being taken care of. Everything's being done."

Forsake your family and follow me. The only way. How else could he do what he needed to do?

Everyone has the same joke or a variation, pointing to his head: "See you came prepared." And his response, always the same, rubbing his palm over his scalp, feigning ignorance or gee-whiz embarrassment, "Forgot to pick the rug up at the cleaners."

Make 'em laugh. They need it. These are the people who feel the suffering most, who are most numb to it.

Couple of orderlies, a nurse, asked about his beads, the Buddha on his bureau. And he was happy to oblige. *This little light of mine, I'm going to let it shine.* Here in the hospital he could beam the prayer of compassion, *om mani padme hung,* at all the suffering. Turn his own little laser on the place.

So he kept cheerful, giving up his arm to the needles, giving up his piss, his shit. Giving it all up in the name of Buddha, amen.

But nothing was certain, Dr. Frankel said, beagle eyes hooded, briefly, while a hand wiped his lips. There was always a possibility, good possibility, of tumors they couldn't reach, metastases too small to see.

"I wouldn't say this to most patients, but I'm going to say it to you because from what you tell me —"

(Yes, the doctor had asked one evening, slipping off his glasses after the clipboard had been read, bedside, captain's log, day 10, "So what is it you really practice? What do you believe?"

And he'd explained the notion of impermanence, the belief that everything we see is an illusion, a projection of pure mind.

"Everything?" The doctor stood holding his chin.

Milarepa nodded.

"I find it difficult to believe. Not what you're saying. Anything."

"Just breathe."

Dr. Frankel smiled. "Is that what you do?"

"Add a tune if it gets too quiet."

Dr. Frankel laughed, then fell silent, head tilted, listening it seemed with the intensity of a man sounding his own heart. "A miracle. Breath.")

Now the doctor was pinching the skin at his throat. "A year, Milarepa. Maybe two. At most. That's with a miracle — and those pills your lama sends you.

"No guarantees."

The patient's eyelids fluttered. He was picturing the rainbow. Light gleaming in a billion iridescent drops. So beautiful and empty.

"Never," Milarepa agreed.

Simple. Let go. Like John Lennon snipping the measuring tape: I now declare this bridge open.

I now declare the bridge open.

As a kid, he'd say it over and over, imitating cocky John, making his mother laugh.

Let go the idea of measuring tape, make measuring tape a bridge, cut measuring tape, wicked thrill, violate the inviolate strip of plastic-coated linen, marked with inches, quarter inches, eighths, sixteenths; decimate the useful, practical, measured tape, sacred yardstick, the hell with measurements, measure-ups, the way he was always supposed to. The hell with measuring up, John said with a snip of the scissors. Turned a measuring tape into a bridge, turned a bridge into a strip of plastic-coated linen: *I now declare this bridge open.*

Mocking the prick who held the stick, the shriveled prune of a tailor, or was it a father? A *grand*father? Couldn't remember.

Something opened in John, something opened in all who witnessed John cutting the tape. Gasps in the dark. *He cut it.* Cut one and they'd gasp too. *Who did it? Who cut one?* the kids were always saying. Embarrassed at cutting it, embarrassed and exhilarated, too.

Hey, everyone should cut one. A bridge, a piece of cloth, a fart. Once the bridge was open, anything could happen.

He closed his eyes. Prayed that all sentient beings could let go as easily as that, with a clean snip. Prayed he could see it as simply when the snip came.

Snip and his life on this planet, in this form, would be over. Snip. The bridge would be open. Snip. I now declare Milarepa open, free, cut loose to swim towards the next form or free from the wheel of birth and death forever.

There was a story going around that when the lama first saw the group of disciples lined up in the hallway, heads bowed, hands tented, he turned, delighted, to Rinpoche and said, "They must be the praying mantises I blessed on the path outside my cave. I hoped I would see them again."

Benevolent narcissism. Befitting a saint.

But the more he thought about it, the more he felt that he'd have liked to have been a praying mantis, or an ant, a fly, a mosquito. Think of it! Only a lifetime ago, he'd been an insect, and in the next he might return to winged life, and who knew how many subgenera he'd flit through before becoming a human again. *Every sentient being was once your mother.* An infinite tumbling mix-up of identities and forms, an extraordinary endless chain that had the effect, paradoxically, of making us all one. *In whatever form. I pray the end of suffering for all sentient beings.*

His head felt warm under the steady beam of the lamp someone had swung above his pillow. He smiled. In his mind's eye, sunlight streamed on his leaf green pate, his knitted legs.

Rinpoche told him, Meditate on this. Some shit who's lived a hellish life, murdered, raped, lied, thieved, a shit destined for the realm of hungry ghosts, a shit destined to spend a few million lifetimes with unquenchable thirst. This shit goes before the judge.

Then imagine the monk who's spent his life performing acts of devotion, who's dedicated every scrap of merit to all sentient beings. Who shines with the pure light of compassion. Imagine this monk before the judge.

Now imagine yourself. Imagine the judge asks you to recount every deed you've ever done, the shitty as well as the good. Where are you going, buddy?

Shit came to mind. Big acts, small ones; good, bad. Pushing a little cousin on a swing. *Whee,* she screamed. Didn't want him to stop. Like Rita fucking, the smooth suck of desire, the tears. Telling his mother and father he was splitting. Mom's shaking her head like she could never stop, Dad's thank-you. Little sister beating his chest.

Smaller acts. Dropping a loaded paintbrush. Tinging cymbals. Ladling water over the deity's head. Leaning post for Chimay fishing a stone out of her boot.

Hauling wood, hauling ass up the mountain, strumming his guitar.

Telling Grandpa, Go to hell.

Shouting from the top of a building. Hell no, we won't go.

Wiping his ass with a newspaper.

Flying down Shasta on his skateboard.

Hugging Jim.

Leaving Rita.

Letters from his father arrived every day. Handwritten, illegible, with their horizontal loops, their narrow verticals, reminding him of his own illegible script. Dragonfly shit, Rinpoche had once called it, reading a note. Pht-pht-pht, leaving a trail across the sky. *Rinpoche was completely incomprehensible sometimes, completely insane.* His father's letters brought news of the family, but mainly of his business ventures, the oil in Colombia hadn't panned out, nor had the aluminum in Utah, and so on, to chromite in Turkey, scrap metal in the Argentine. Always cheery, upbeat, yet weirdly formal, as though he'd censored himself *(but when? In his unconscious? As he wrote? Afterward?),* or as if his father thought that in his son's becoming a Buddhist he'd abandoned his native tongue. (Flash of memory, his father on the phone to a chief in Senegal, the strange baboon-like grit as he enunciated, the strain and spreading of his lips against his teeth.) In these letters he could sense his father straining in exactly that way and wished he could tell him, *Relax.*

Often he didn't finish the letters. The effort of reading between the lines was too exhausting. *"Phoebe is having a fine, if challenging time at school," "Molly is becoming quite the artist," "Mom, having changed jobs, has now found just the right firm."* He stopped, closed his eyes, begged the Buddha of compassion, Chenrezig, to ease their suffering . . . to let him off the hook.

At their conclusion, a mention of Grandpa. The true purpose of a letter always sinks to the bottom. *"I think he misses you." "He's slowing down a little." "Sharp as ever, but mellowed just a bit, if you know what I mean."*

The hints were obvious; it pained him to ignore them.

He still loved his family, of course, but it was as though they'd all shrunk down, become proportionate with the rest of the sentient world. *Every living creature was once your mother.* The fly buzzing now, high up in the corner of the room — *Hi, Mom!* — needed as much compassion as anyone else, needed just as much as anyone else to get free.

They all came to mind: Jim and Pamela and George and little sisters, and Mom and Dad and Grandpa and Grandma and Aunt B. And Uncle Robert and even those little cousins whose names he couldn't remember now, and Rita and Toby and — the list went on. He saw everyone, trying to remember what his actions towards each had been. Even when he'd exhausted a whole lineup, others came to fill their places: Pema, Karma, Chimay, Mamaki. And there were animals, too. The puppy and his sisters' kittens and a lizard he'd kept as a pet. He listed in his mind all the actions he could remember, good, bad, indifferent. Absentminded acts. Conscious acts. And new faces kept coming up, new acts.

What he saw was this: how hard it was to do something completely pure, completely kind. How confused any action he'd done had been with greed and anger and pride and regret. The bad actions poured out effortlessly, it seemed, from habit; the good actions were all stained.

There's stuff you gotta know, Rinpoche said. Stuff to get through the bardo and out the other end. Special practice. Special training.

You've got to practice being dead. Like a dog. Like how dead you'd be with the mama bear sniffing you out.

Stop it up. Stop everything.

But let the consciousness escape.

Some days he was weightless. His exhaustion so great he could practically feel himself dissolving, molecule by molecule.

Or pulled inside the black hole of himself. His being the concentrated weight of antimatter, a marble heavy enough to crush through Earth and out the other side. Those days he wanted to drop drop drop. No way to knit these molecules back together. No way to snap himself together. Head on neck, neck on shoulders. No feet, no bones.

He took a breath, fumbled the mantra on his tongue. *Om mani padme hung.* Hang on, hang on. Each syllable a handhold, the mantra belaying him. For the moment.

Course he was scared. Fuck, he was human. He wanted to live. Yes. Wanted to be loved. Wanted to learn all he could.

Shit. He'd never meant to go so fast.

Lying in his bed in his hospital room and gazing at that rectangle of perfect California sky. What was it about that shade of blue that was so true, so convincing it wiped out all other shades? A blue both deep and soaring at the same time, a blue that made you dream of flying.

He remembered being a kid on his back on a green lawn and looking up at a sky this very same shade and wondering what was it like in a spaceship when you crossed from blue to black.

A million Medicine Buddha mantras. Rinpoche's orders. Two thousand seven hundred thirty-nine a day divided by sixteen waking hours. One hundred seventy-one Amitabhas an hour. Two point eight five a minute. Mantras ticking off his last hours, minutes, seconds. Amitabhas like heartbeats, like breath.

He will die with a mantra breaking in his mouth.

In the dream, he was tumbling backwards, headfirst in the back of a station wagon, speeding down a mountain road, headfirst, the way babies are born and helpless as that, catching a glimpse of sleek black mountains racing by, tops cut off by rectangular windows.

A hand held his. Above him, the tea-stained face of the old lama, the luminous black eyes, kind, sad. The lama held his hand and the mountains whizzed by.

He wasn't scared, holding the lama's hand.

PHOEBE, 1975

When the knock comes, I turn over, hoping I can resist completely, drift back to my deep and dreamless sleep and not remember I've heard the knock at all. From the corridor outside my door, sounds of hurried footsteps, excited whispers. I open my eyes. Waking more. Always this tension, the whispers, the patter of running feet as though they're being summoned to *put out* a fire, not tend it.

I'm awake by now, listening, for what? I don't know until I hear his voice, calling to another disciple, a short, hard whisper, a little confused. I must rise.

Sometime in the true middle of the night, Rinpoche entered the temple room to start the fire ceremony. Sometimes alone, sometimes with one or two disciples, a special honor. I don't know if Ira has ever been asked. The stampede of disciples reminds me of schoolchildren, but when would they hurry like this? Frightened and excited? Not for assembly, not even for recess. So why is this moment so familiar?

Rinpoche's way ahead of them. One hundred passes over the embers before the disciples begin their flat-footed rounds. Knock number two, *he's almost finished.* Sometimes a single word whispered ferociously, sometimes, like this morning, almost shouted the way whispers sometimes flare. FORTY!

EIGHTY! This morning it's eighty. Rinpoche's making his eightieth pass. Time to get up.

Only now do I notice that my sister's pallet is empty. She's beaten me, again. I imagine her tagging at Ira's heels. Little fanatic. Well, I give up.

I don't have a cassock. Cassocks are only for the real disciples. I pull on drawstring pants instead, and the top of my long underwear, pressing my hand to my chest, hoping my nipples don't show through the heavy cotton. I don't bother with shoes though my feet are cold.

The corridor is nearly dark. Later, long patches of light will bleach the runner to an endless white train. I hear the voices in the courtyard below. I'm late. No one cares. I'm not really one of them. No one expects much from me or Molly. Yet I find myself running, eager to make a good impression. On whom? For what? Fire walking is not required, but almost everyone shows up.

At this hour, the disciples look as unfamiliar to me as if they were wearing their street clothes, their disguises. In the washed out light of dawn, they stand, half awake, necks scrawny and bare above their cassocks, summoning attentiveness, it seems, like hungover courtiers. I often wonder about their other lives: Pema's a secretary in one of those vast and towering buildings downtown; Gyalwang, a bigwig in a computer company; Vimalamitra, an engineer. What would their office mates think if they saw this scene?

The sky is the color of the ashes that fill the tin bucket hanging from Sherab's arm. Beside him stands Mamaki, Rinpoche's new consort, counting traverses on a string of beads. Wearing Rinpoche's black cassock, the sleeves rolled back, and her severe hair, loosened, ballooning at the neck, Mamaki looks surprisingly human, the scene oddly domestic.

I stand back a little, watching as the others gather around the narrow bed of coals in the center of the driveway. Rinpoche walks with short, bowlegged strides, pausing only to seek out and smash the hottest coals beneath the ball of his bare foot. He's a stocky man, thick-necked, head massive as a bull's. Even now the walkie-talkie slung across his chest emits a crackling hiss.

I'm scared of Rinpoche. Try to disappear when he appears. Sometimes I'm not fast enough, and then he clenches the top of my head in his grip and growls, mock fierce, before letting me go. Sometimes he asks, "Stay out of trouble?" And I find myself grinning giddily. "Yes."

Always he's on to urgent business, snapping orders as he goes. "Bring me the wood." "I need rose oil." "Get me three-H-O on the line." Disciples scamper to do his bidding. I scamper, too.

Ira adores this man, literally worships the ground he walks on. I think of a family joke we used to have. When you had to beg a favor, you sank to your knees and waved your arms up and down, doing a "salami." Or you ordered someone to "salami" before you'd forgive them.

I can't help it. When I look at Rinpoche, I see an imperious maharaja, swollen with power. Ever since I got here, I've been doing my salamis out of fear, fear of losing Ira's approval. And, of course, I'm jealous. Rinpoche is my brother's true love.

I kneel to roll up my pants legs, wishing Ira would show up. I feel awkward without him, a wallflower at a dance. I glance around but still don't see him, or Molly, who must be helping. They're probably in the basement, bundling prayer sticks or fetching something for Rinpoche or running the footbaths.

Now Mamaki lifts the conch to her lips and blows, bellow and moan, the birth of the world or a bull run clear through.

Ira's head pops up from the cellar door. Then Molly's. They drop their bundles of prayer sticks beside the back steps, then kneel to roll up their trouser cuffs.

Suddenly I'm mad. Why does he work so hard? Why is he happy to be their slave? How could he be my brother? My defiant, lazy brother, who grunted before washing the dishes and never once picked up his room or made his bed? How could this be Ira, the rebel? Ira, the radical? Loud, obscene, blasting, brilliant Ira?

My turn. I step quickly, letting my foot sink for a moment in the mound of coarse salt. I step past the orange embers, aiming for black. It's not a trick, Rinpoche has told us. We're not trying to prove we're Jesus walking on water. It's just to wake you up. Don't get an ego trip.

Still, I concentrate on the back of the person in front of me, trying to ignore the crunching sound like boots on frozen snow, trying not to look down.

Round and round we go. Someone keeping count. Someone banging a gong. Round and round, briskly keeping time. I glimpse the faces as they loop back: some smiling, some looking blank, some mouthing the syllables of a mantra, urgently.

It doesn't hurt. Not at all. The embers leave no blisters, only a thick layer of soot. But you must move quickly and keep your eyes focused ahead as though you were crossing a tightrope high above water.

I can't catch my brother's eye, but I hope he's watching me, hope he's proud.

Later the disciples will track black footprints down the hall that someone, probably my brother will clean.

So Ira has a path and a goal: enlightenment in this lifetime. His exact words. He has a mantra and a prayer. And a task: to write as many prayer sticks as possible, sticks that will go up in a house of flame beneath a hooded altar. He scribbles on their smooth sides, the pen point bumping over the grain, leaking inky splotches onto the tips of his fingers and down the crotch between his thumb and forefinger. He scribbles on oblivious to these stains, the words strangely legible: I pray the end of suffering for all sentient beings.

But I'm suffering and he doesn't care, I find myself thinking as I, too, scrawl the prayer onto a stick, an oversize Lincoln Log, aping my brother. A second later I hate myself for the thought, but can't ignore it. Between us is a path, a goal, something so noble, something so large, so grand, I don't have a chance, not the slightest, to merit my brother's attention.

I feel all of a sudden, what did he used to call me, our joke, a flibbertigibbet, and a *floozy.* You *floozy,* he'd say, rocking my curled body with one hand, his tickling fingers finding my armpits, the back of my neck, the arch of my soles, shrinking me from twelve to six. *Will he try there?* No, he doesn't, though it might flicker through both our minds.

My brother, seated on the edge of the bed, pretending at first not to notice me at all as I sneak attacks from behind, a pinch here, a pinch there. Each sending me into a frenzy of nervous giggle. I know he's waiting, waiting, biding his time for the counterattack. Playing dead.

Then his arm snakes back and he turns to me, his dark hair falling across his forehead. He grins evilly, his fingers tickling mercilessly as I writhe.

You asked for it! You floozy.

What's a floozy? Between gasps, between chokes and giggles.

You floozy.

WHAT'S A FLOOZY?

You.

Giggling until he stops. Suddenly. Rising as though he doesn't care. Almost as though he's angry or has more important things to do. Places to go. Ira's always going places. Is almost never home.

Where are you going?

Out.

He won't give more information. Not to anyone. Under any circumstances.

What's a floozy? I beg one last time, the words becoming a whine I suspect, though I'm not sure, is floozy-ish.

He doesn't bother to answer or perhaps didn't even hear as he disappears out the door as though obeying some silent call, an inner urgent force.

All afternoon I imagine the floozy. Blond. With hair that floats like a dandelion. A floozy . . . what? What does Ira think I am and why? Is it a compliment?

I feel now like a floozy. A fake, a fraud. I'm a good actress, I know. Sitting beside Ira, I ink my mantra, the prayer not for sentient beings but for my brother. Even as my anger grows, so does the pile of prayer sticks. In direct proportion, I pray for his health and wish him dead. My handwriting drifts, is driven to a severe slant, wheat beaten in a storm or bodies pressed unnaturally forward, elongated like the desperate sister in *Madeleine.* Faster and faster and faster.

When the surgeons operated, Ira's tumors came out one, two, three, shiny and whole as golf balls. Sometimes I imagine them lined up on a putting green, each cupped by a tree.

Ira and his friends once tried to explode a golf ball, driving a nail into one side. Ira struck the final blow. Dropping the hammer as though it were a live thing, he yelled, "Run for your life!" They ran as hard as if they'd detonated a bomb.

The doctors gave Ira one year to live. But he's surprised them, sustaining himself on a tank of faith.

Still each visit is possibly the last. A thought that jolts me into panic each time I touch it.

"Does the prayer have to be legible?" I ask. Do the gods read every word?

"Make it as neat as you can," Ira says, neutrally, without anger or even irony.

I'd like to shake him. *Where are you?*

Instead I sigh, beginning the new prayer stick in print rather than cursive: I PRAY MILAREPA HEALTH. The others use this syntax, and I imitate their strange truncated sentences, as though their first language wasn't English.

The blue words sink into the blond stick. Ballpoint seems inadequate, cheap. If I were a god, I might be offended by ballpoint, not might, *would,* I'm sure of it.

Across the table, Molly works quickly, her blond hair tucked beneath a white kerchief. She seems calm, industrious, oddly happy. An image comes to me of Molly as a little girl in a smocked nightgown rocking in her little chair. She was knitting. How old was she? Five or six. Her plump wrists cocked like a rower's. The little old lady we called her, stunned by her stiff grace, the primness of her white neck rising from eyelet ruffle. Her perfect upright posture.

Yet, one word could set her in tears. Snake. Needle. The word alone. My sister gave me the power of a magician. *Snake,* I would hiss and Molly began screaming. *Needle.* I didn't even have to make a pinch or mime the shot going in. The little old lady's peace was shattered. She dropped her knitting or her loom, ignoring the loops of the pot holder coming unhooked as it sailed through the air and she ran, screaming, down the hall . . .

I ran, too. Not because I was afraid of what our mother would do to me, but because I couldn't bear the aftermath of my teasing: the study doors miraculously flinging open, our mother poised to embrace. In seconds, Molly disappeared, her body lifted in air, her head snug in the curve of our mother's neck.

"Anyone want an apple fritter?" I ask, trying to keep the petulance out of my voice, the whine.

Ira shakes his head. Molly, too.

I don't have any magic now, no way to lift the spell that twines Ira and Molly, leaves me cold and unchanged, outside. Was it so terrible to be "Ira"? Is it such a waste to live in the real world?

The cellar door beckons, a green temptation to step back into my other life.

I shift on my stool, pick up my pen. Ira's dying. *Remember?*

Word's out. Rinpoche wants to see us. Me and Molly. In his room. After dinner. What'd we do wrong? I wonder. My stomach aches, trying to think of something. Haven't eaten meat, smoked any cigarettes. Maybe there's something he knows about me, something I don't know. Or do. Maybe he's looked into my soul and knows I'm a fraud.

His room's at the end of the hall, next door to the temple. I've only glimpsed the interior. No one's allowed to come in without an invitation, even to clean. What I remember was red, red drapes, a red curtain around the bed.

Molly and I approach quietly; she knocks on the door.

He's seated sultan-style on the low bed. I was right about the curtains, but the color's richer than I remembered, the maroon of theater cushions, the velvet snakes that keep you in line.

We bow our heads, bring our tented hands to our foreheads. He motions us to sit.

Then he smiles in that growly, joking way of his.

"Milarepa's sisters," he says. "How'd you like to be called something else?"

All my life, I've ranked people according to their spiritual acumen. There are the "light" people at the high end of the scale, the "dark" people at the low end of the scale, the "gray" people in the middle. The ranking system came to me as a way to explain the difference between me and my brother.

Ira's a "light" person, a person who can't block out suffering or hypocrisy, a person who won't become what others want him to become, a person who spends his life in search of spiritual truth.

I'm ashamed of my "grayness," my success at pleasing parents and teachers, my insatiable desire for praise. I'm constantly reeling myself in, scolding myself for my "dark," unenlightened ways. Why do I crave so much admiration? Why am I so attached to the things of this world?

Now I'm *Maitreya.* A goddess. The embodiment of loving-kindness, Rinpoche tells me. And Molly has become *Locana,* a consort, rapturously twined around her Buddha's neck.

Overnight, we have new names, special ones, names plucked from the top of the pantheon, like my brother's name, Milarepa, one of the Buddha's original disciples and founder of a lineage. The disciples smile and whisper and pat us on the shoulder. These names mean Rinpoche sees something special in us, they say. We're becoming closer to being them.

Overnight, new names. A kind of alchemy, a transformation as frightening, as mercurial as Cinderella's. Frightening to me, at least, because I know in some kernel of my self, that at midnight I'll turn back into the true lump that *is* me, that's always present, a hard black thing that wants to believe, but cannot.

I'm not sure whether or not to tell Mom and Dad my new name. At home, using Ira's spiritual name is tantamount to a political act. Everyone who's opposed to Ira's being a Buddhist (Grandpa, Grandma, Dad) calls him Ira. Molly and I call him Milarepa. Mom vacillates. When she talks to us about him or to him, he's Milarepa. When she talks to Dad or Grandpa, Ira.

But the truth is, Ira's the name I use to myself. A betrayal. Because my true preference, something I'm afraid to admit, is for the old Ira, the wild, rebellious, half-crazed brother who lived above me, smoking joints and jacking off to the tales of *Mrabet* and *Playboy* centerfolds, the Ira who ranted Ginsberg-esque poetry and plotted a revolution, who ran, carrying a red flag, into the cafeteria of my junior high, exhorting the kids, bent over their cartons of milk and squashed peanut butter and jelly sandwiches, to "Unite!" and to flee those brown-speckled halls en masse.

I sit in the kitchen, listening to Mamaki bemoan the fact that her sister's boyfriend is not a vegetarian. "He's a real good guy in other ways, but if he keeps eating meat, what's going to happen to him?"

It takes me a moment to realize she means in his *next* lifetime, that she's worried about his karma. She keeps shaking her head like she's talking about a doomed man.

This conversation frightens me. I feel doomed, too. Though I'm now a model Buddhist, reciting my mantras and checking packages for beef extract and rennet, I still feel like an impostor.

Later, I sneak into the temple room. By myself. Just to see what it looks like in ordinary light. Why do Buddhas look so mean?

Vicious, snarling even, or at least remote, frozen, stiff? How can I believe in these demon creatures with their hideous grins, their myriad fingers forming secret signs, holding secret symbols? Wisdom, grace?

I cross my legs Indian-style. My thighs ache. Pain shoots up my spine, across my shoulders. Instead of praying, I'm going to think about happiness. The goal, Ira said.

When have I ever been happy? As a little girl, sitting in a plum tree, reading a book. Playing flute. Eating banana cake.

I don't believe in happiness. That's the problem. Don't want to be calm. Don't want Ira that way, either.

Tears take me by force, bend me forward so far I rest my forehead on the carpet. Feels good sobbing brokenhearted, all out, like this. Could weep till I drowned, till I'm salt and water, dissolved.

Molly's perched on a stool at the sewing table, cutting steadily through a swath of purple cloth. Now that she's got her new name, she's making a uniform. To do this, you need permission from Rinpoche, which, apparently, she has.

Laksmancara, the best sewer in the group, is supervising her. The ashram has a few businesses, and one of them is making futon covers. All day the women sit in the basement, in this low-ceilinged room, and cut and sew. Laksmancara's confessed to me that if it wasn't for the company, she'd go crazy sewing all day.

The women sit around the huge square table, chanting long melodious prayers. I can't believe how much they've memorized. Even when they aren't chanting aloud, you can sense the syllables tumbling under their breath, quiet stones of a river, the syllables polishing smoother and smoother under their silent tongues.

My sister's concentrating on her cutting, her whole body following the motion of the scissors through the cloth the way a swimmer becomes the slice of her stroke. Her mouth bristles with pins. I want to ask her: *What's happened to Ira? Where do you think he is?*

But suddenly it strikes me: *She's one of them.* It's her turn to claim our brother.

In the old days, she was the littler sister, banished to the bottom of the stairs, not allowed to join us in Ira's lair. Once, she told on us. She was afraid we'd get cancer, she sobbed, and I believed her. That didn't keep me from twisting her wrist so hard her face squeezed into wrinkles and telling her I'd kill her if she ever tattled again.

Now I'm the banished one, I can feel it, while she sits beside Milarepa for hours, staring at the moon mandala, seeing visions, content to chant into the blue haze of afternoon.

I sit, too. But inside I'm screaming: I hate you.

Throughout the day, as the women sew, Milarepa pops in and out, bringing them supplies, cold drinks, then ferrying things upstairs. A regular Stepin Fetchit. He flirts lightly, his banter tinged with sarcasm, but always he's ready to do their bidding with an eagerness that borders on ferocity.

I've never seen anyone like my brother. He crackles with purpose and energy, yet seems as distracted as a madman. His body blossoms with lists, small scraps of paper, which he pulls almost magically from vest pockets, pants pockets, sock cuffs. His print scrawls down the margins, and even his capitals tilt off in different directions as though doing a wild dance. He squints, trying to make sense of his own writing: WOOD,

SOCKETS, LAUNDRY, SOURDOUGH. Then he's off to tackle yet another errand or chore.

Originally, my brother was apprenticed to Sherab, an electrician, who ran the ashram's construction crew. I was visiting that summer and remember it was something of an event when Milarepa left with the other men for his first day on an "outside" job.

After a few days, he was back. No one said why. Perhaps his coordination was just too poor for handling the delicate circuitry, or perhaps he was just too spaced. From time to time, he still went out with the men to swing a hammer or help with a paint job, but he insisted he was fine at home. He missed the women, he said, and they certainly missed him.

One thing is clear. Everyone loves Milarepa. Particularly the women. At least once a day, someone comes up to me and tells me that it's Milarepa's tireless devotion that inspires her. Yet none is, or has been, romantically involved with him.

In the past, I would've been jealous of my brother's girlfriend. Now I wish he had someone to take care of him, to love him. I wonder if he's lonely.

Then one morning there's a new disciple in the kitchen, the younger sister of Karma, a plump, homely, wonderfully good-natured woman who herself joined only a few months before. Norla looks nothing like her sister. She's tiny, and possesses a doll-like prettiness, milky skin and blue eyes and dark smooth hair worn in a bun at the nape of her neck. She is a perfectly proportioned little doll-woman whose head would fit snugly into my brother's armpit, I think. She's also very sweet, shy, a little lost, but smiling.

I'm not the only one who instantly sees Norla, whose name means "jewel," as the key to my brother's happiness. That afternoon, Sonam and Laksmancara and Chimay sit around the sewing table discussing the match. They're quite heady with plots of how to throw the two together.

"Let's put them in the same van when we go to the mountain," Sonam suggests.

"We could give them both brass," says Chimay.

Laksmancara looks up from her sewing. "Send them to the Laundromat — they need time alone."

Everyone giggles; it's a rare admission.

But in the midst of these schemes, I'm confused. Do they remember Milarepa's dying? *Is he?*

The course of the disease has been so strange. The first horrible announcement: one year to live, followed by the operation. Then chemo and radiation and pills from Tibet. Suddenly, another year. He's doomed and then he's not.

No one talks about Milarepa's tumors. No one mentions the word *death.* And so I'm sometimes lulled into believing his spaciness is just a whim, by-product of those hours of meditation, of recitation, his own choice to dissolve himself, to offer up his ego like silt to a rushing stream.

"Is this *reasonable?*" I ask.

The women look at me, eyes startled, yet vague, does' eyes staring into blinding light.

I want to know what to expect. I want to know how long there is, *exactly.*

No one speaks.

Once a week, Ira packs a small suitcase with prayer books, beads, bowls for his altar, as well as a few pairs of socks and underwear. Then, wrapped in his crimson robes, beret tilted jauntily on his naked head, he checks into the hospital for a few days of treatment.

Molly and I go with him on one of these visits. Perhaps in this other world, I'll find my brother.

When Ira arrives, doors open as if choreographed, candy stripers wave. I bow my head, embarrassed at being noticed at all, while envying his lack of embarrassment. He doesn't mind people *looking,* staring, actually stopping in their tracks, in their wheelchairs, to watch this swirl of cape and color stride by.

On his floor, nurses come up and hug him hello. His doctor stops en route to another patient to shake his hand. My brother introduces me and Molly, and again I stare at the floor rather than meet the doctor's eye. I'm surprised at how young he is, how cute. Later Molly and I agree that, with his rounded beak-like nose, he looks a little like Snoopy.

In his room, Ira briskly unpacks, sets up his altar, ringing for a pitcher of water to fill his bowls and pulling a box of matches from his pocket to light the candles. The deity is Padmasambhava, bodhisattva of compassion. Ira explains that Padmasambhava was enlightened as a ten-year-old boy, seated on a lotus, and this makes me think of Ira seated cross-legged on the concave surface of the coffee table. "I'm Big Buddha," he'd pronounce. "You're Little Buddha."

In the darkened living room, shadows fell on us like netting, gathered us into the experience of twilight. In front of me the air's alive, frantic with specks of light and dark like a TV screen at dawn.

Atoms? I wonder, but don't ask. I breathe carefully, blinking. Must stay quiet and good. Must prove I'm worthy of Ira's attention, his vision that penetrates the known world. The nurse is Asian and smiles when she sees the altar. Her parents are

Buddhists, she explains, but she . . . she shrugs and gives Ira a sweet smile. He smiles back. No problem, he seems to say.

Molly and I wander down to the TV room while Ira changes into his hospital clothes. There's no one watching the characters moving so assuredly in their boxed world, their voices booming with tinny confidence.

On the floor, nurses and orderlies move briskly, with purpose. I glance at Molly, who's staring out the plate-glass window, out onto the city below, and wonder if she feels as I do, more out of place here even than at the ashram.

After a long while we decide to go back to Ira's room, knocking lightly, then pushing the door open a crack. He's wearing pajamas now, seated cross-legged at the end of the bed, deep in meditation. We glide in, settle ourselves on the floor. Another memory swells. How old was I? Six? Seven? That would make him ten. At ten, he's insisting that life's an illusion, that everything I see is just a dream.

This makes me furious, outraged. "How come when I pinch myself I don't wake up?"

"Because you're even dreaming that."

I'm trapped. His logic's a full nelson I can't escape. Yet the thought springs up, a tiny flame: *You can make me say it; you can't make me believe.*

The good women of the ashram continue to scheme, throwing delicate little Norla and Ira together almost constantly. He's virtually been appointed her guardian, her tutor. He shows her how to shine altar brass (as he once showed me and Molly), which prayers to inscribe in her little black book, where to buy the group's produce and bread.

He's even given the task of teaching her guitar. I watch him bend over her shoulder, his hand resting on her fingers as she strums, and remember when Ira fell in love for the first time. It was ninth grade. Pamela Bingham. She cut his hair on the lawn of the high school. I was jealous. I could imagine the weight of his head in her lap, the sound of the scissors as she sliced through his straight, thick hair, which fell past his shoulders, which he would never let my mother cut, which he would flick away like a horse's tail if I tried to touch, which he seemed not even to trust himself to wash.

The haircut came out jagged across the bangs, scalloped around the edge. It made his neck look scrawny, revealed an alphabet of pimples across his forehead, but he didn't seem to care. He wore that haircut like a badge, like a token of her love, and seemed happier than I'd ever seen him.

I decide to sound out Ira while we're writing prayer sticks in the basement.

"What do you think of Norla?" I ask.

"Very sweet," he says, without looking up from his task.

"Don't you think she's pretty?"

"Sure."

"I mean, do you like her?" I blush at having resorted to the language of a schoolgirl.

His brow furrows. It's hard to tell whether he's concentrating on my question or on keeping the ballpoint steady.

"She seems very sincere."

My brother is seated on a stool at the table, bent over his pen as though it were a fine wire, as though the stick he is writing on were a sheet of gold.

Wake up, motherfucker, I want to scream. *Where's your passion? Your desire? What's happened to your acid tongue, your veins of bile, your transcendent rage?*

Surely the power of love should be enough to rekindle the spark, the flame that used to be Ira.

Before I left for the ashram this summer, I broke up with my boyfriend, who I know is unsuitable for my next life, my college life, which I begin in the fall. Mark's three years older than me, my brother's age, a high school dropout, like Ira. This is without a doubt what draws me to him, as well as the fact that he knew my brother long ago. This connection is something I hold like a talisman, never to explore or question fully. I simply know that when we first met, he asked, "Your brother's Ira Stein? Coolest dude I ever met."

In no other ways are Mark and I alike. He's mild-mannered, slender, a surfer reduced to skateboarding for lack of an ocean, a pothead.

Before Mark and I got together, Doris and I had long talks about whether or not to have sex. We decided we'd only sleep with someone if we were in love. Now I think that sex is just propaganda, a big scam. Before you have sex, you hear the word a thousand times a day. It drones around you like the sound of cicadas beating their wings, beating off the day. Sex buzzes at you like a taunt, something the world possesses, but you don't. Then you possess it, too, and what's so great?

When I told Mark I was breaking up with him, he fell to his knees, buried his head in my lap. He was crying so hard his beautiful blue eyes seemed to spill from their rims. He told me I was the only good thing that'd ever happened to him, that without me he was lost. He wants me to give up college, to postpone it at least, so that I can go with him to California. His dream is to ride the surf all day while I wait for him on a blanket on the beach.

I picture myself sometimes, on a sandy towel. A perfect tan, a book. Hours on hours I scan the horizon, trying to keep track of one tiny speck.

He doesn't know me at all. But it's not really his fault. I've played a part so long, so well, I don't know who I am either.

I'd like to tell Ira about him. Like to ask his advice. But I don't dare. What if he tells me I lack compassion? What if he tells me to go back?

Strange: I feel I must do whatever Ira tells me to do, that I must obey his wishes. He knows things that I don't know; he's purer than I am, he's closer to the truth.

I'm playing a part with Ira, too. Devoted sister, spiritual adept. What does he want me to do? I'm waiting for instructions. I want to know what to do.

Saturdays and Sundays are days for special outings. Fire walk on the beach, band performance in Berkeley, climbing the mountain.

This Sunday we're climbing Mount Tam to play our instruments on top. Free concert for the weary hikers.

Ira's doctor must have said something to Rinpoche, because he tells Ira he's riding to the top with the food vehicle.

I look around to see who's listening. Everyone.

Ira looks a little bummed, but he doesn't refuse.

Instantly, Chimay jumps in, says she'll ride up, too.

Chimay's Ira's special ashram friend. Nothing romantic. But they're linked somehow. Maybe because they're the youngest (though Chimay's older than Ira), maybe because they're the most devoted.

Ira told me Chimay's parents put her in a lunatic asylum 'cause she ran away from home. Everyone told her she was psychotic until she met Rinpoche.

She seems normal to me. More than most of the people.

She's very serious and kind. And she works hard. Like Ira. Often they work side by side.

The camper moves slowly through switchbacks, climbing the forested base. The windows fill with leaves and sunlight. The smell of eucalyptus is everywhere. I love that smell, this light. If I could ride like this forever, in this glorious light, this clean smell, everything would be fine.

Across from me, on a bench, Molly is chewing on sourdough and peanut butter. She and Laksmancara picked up loaves fresh from the bakery this morning, bags and bags of rolls and loaves, still warm.

Molly and I are wearing our hiking uniforms: white shirt, green fatigues, boots. The real disciples don aprons of heavy cloth over their pants to protect them when they sit on the ground.

When we get to the mountain, Rinpoche changes his mind, says Ira can walk up, too. If he has assistance.

Ira walks very slowly. Chimay on one side, me and Molly taking turns on the other. We stop a lot so he can sip from the flat, canvas-sheathed canteen on his belt. A present from Dad, I think. From his army days.

The rest of the group is far, far ahead. We can see them on the switchback, a perfectly synchronized line of white-kerchiefed heads, aproned butts.

It's Molly who hears the snake. Freezing with her nostrils flared. Exactly like a horse. I stop, too, but Ira and Chimay move on.

Then they see it, a fat rattler sitting in the path, head lifted with its chin on a breeze.

My heart's beating so fast I can't breathe.

But Ira is leaning closer, stooping a little as though he can't quite catch what the rattler wants to say.

Hey, Little Rattler, please don't hurt your son. Biting me'd be like biting your next o'kin.

In reply the snake rattles its broken chain. Then Molly gasps, darts forward with her hiking stick aimed like a spear, and the snake, unfurling like a wave, a line, disappears into the wiry grass.

She won't talk to Ira the rest of the way. Won't talk to any of us. But on the way down, in the dark of the camper, I see him put his arm around her shoulders, her head nodding suddenly. "What's the matter?" he asks. And I hear her say fiercely, against sobs, "It would have killed you."

Molly and I are cooking a special meal to welcome Ira home from the hospital. There's vegetable curry and cucumber raita, sweet-smelling rice mixed with almonds and raisins, and heaps and heaps of golden puris. Everyone pitches in, grating coconut, boiling rice, tossing salad, setting the table, which is decorated with bunches of azaleas. The idea is to get Ira to eat.

In the old days, he used to pat his stomach affectionately, listen to it speak. "Whaddya say? Ya need an apple fritter? Aw shucks." Then he'd grab whoever he could to go with him for a cup of coffee and the biggest, greasiest donut you've ever seen.

Now Ira's thin as a girl; his appetite's vanished. Occasionally, I persuade him to go to the Donut Hole with me, but it's depressing to see him pick a few flakes of sugar from the fritter's crust before pushing it aside. Then I end up eating his as well as mine. I'm growing fat for Ira, I think.

Tonight he's flushed. He looks as though he's been artificially plumped somehow, like a hothouse tomato. His skin looks boiled.

And he's spacier than usual. An entire beat behind. As though he were continually jolting awake from the vacuum of a dream.

Dinner's a bust. Ira loads his plate, but doesn't eat a single bite. Molly and I strain to hide our disappointment. Even Rinpoche's worried. He compensates by being unbearably hearty, spewing dumb jokes, bad puns, for which he's famous.

Then, after the plates are cleared, Rinpoche announces band practice. Fifteen minutes. Save the dishes for later.

Recess. Everybody running as fast as they can to get their instruments. Music is mantra, Rinpoche says. A spiritual practice.

I stay where I am. Asshole, I'm thinking. Don't you see Ira needs to rest?

In the band room, they're already beginning to tune, facing Rinpoche, who stands with his back to a wall. He props his fiddle on one fat thigh, then pauses, bending the flap of his ear to check on the others' progress. It's like a barnyard with all the chickens squawking. Four fiddles, one banjo, two guitars, three basses, one tambourine, one sitar.

I fit the joints of my flute together, glancing at Ira, who's fumbling with the snaps of his guitar case. He opens the lid and stares at the guitar inside like it's taking all his mental energy to figure out how to get it out, like the guitar's some giant body, a dead weight he doesn't quite know how to hoist.

Molly cuts me a worried look. I nod.

We both watch as he lifts the strap over his neck, settles into tuning. He's bending so close to the neck of his guitar, his ear nearly touches the strings, as though he were deaf, as though he were trying to pick up some vibration beneath the sound.

Then Rinpoche tucks his fiddle under his chin and without warning digs in his bow, his foot stomping the floor so hard it shakes.

Instantly, the band's in gear, wheezing out the first measures of "Old Joe Clark." Everyone's got the list memorized, and we simply flow from tune to tune in one long medley. "Foggy Mountain Breakdown," "Shady Grove," "Kitchen Girl."

By this time we're flying, especially Rinpoche, who stamps out a little jig as his bow saws harder and harder, sweat running down the sides of his forehead, his cheeks aflame with concentration.

I glance at Ira, who, like everyone else, is watching Rinpoche.

Something's wrong. Molly notices, too. I can tell by the way she's staring.

He's drowning, his fingers treading desperately across the strings, his left hand clenching the neck of the guitar as though to keep it from floating away.

I want to put down my flute, grab him. I want to yank the guitar from his grasp and lead him away. I want this horrible effort to end.

At that moment, Rinpoche shouts, "GET YOUR SHIT TOGETHER, MILAREPA. YOU'RE PLAYING LIKE A DYING MAN."

The words stun. I hate Rinpoche. How dare he voice such an insult? How dare he say what I can't admit to myself? I expect to see my brother crumple; I expect to see him weep as I would.

But something's happening. His chin jerks up. His spine uncramps, shoulders cracking back. His eyes focus. He's playing.

PHOEBE, 1976

Every boy I've ever been in love with has been a version of Ira: Jan's no exception. He's in my Eastern religion class, and though I've never spoken to him except to say hello, I'm certain that he, like Ira, is on his way to enlightenment.

Every single week Jan comes to class in bare feet. He fills his notebook with sketches of mandalas — careful triangles balanced by tiny Buddhas balanced by triangles. During class I find myself concentrating on his toes, each as long as a finger, gripping the floor as comfortably as if it were sand. I think of asking him if they are cold. But it's too obvious a question, and, judging from his pleasant smile as he listens to the professor, I doubt they are.

Jan's tall and blond. He wears loose alpaca sweaters and drawstring pants; his wrists are as thin as mine, covered with downy hairs. I think of Jan as some sort of lean, sinewy animal, a gazelle, but he's not restless like an animal. Quite the opposite. I've seen that kind of calm only in pictures of saints or of babies asleep at the breast. Jan doesn't look anything like Ira.

It has been a week since the news. A week since my father called to tell me that Ira has grown a new tumor. Since the doctors began their new tests. In recent conversations, Ira's assured me in his deep voice that everything's being taken care of, that Rinpoche's given him special practices, that an herbal remedy from Tibet's been sent for.

Practices for what? To get better? Or to die. Can't ask.

He's filled with confidence and there's nothing I can do.

It's late spring, the air fully leavened with the smell of moist things. Late to class, I'm walking quickly, head down. Nothing more embarrassing than a late entrance to the small conference room in which the Eastern religion class is held. Crossing a stretch of lawn behind Booth Hall (usually I'm careful not to walk on the newly seeded grass), I notice Jan sitting under a bare tree. He's on his sweater, his legs tucked in a lotus position. His eyes are closed, his heart-shaped face tipped towards the sun.

The intimacy of the moment astounds me. Don't know whether to tell him it's time for class or to join him.

To my surprise, I'm trembling, and almost at the edge of tears. Once, long ago, I thought I saw a famous writer, my favorite writer, sitting in a café. I watched the man for a long time, over an hour, wondering if I should go over to his table. What would it accomplish? I asked myself. Just read his books over again. The café was very crowded; I almost overturned a chair in trying to reach his table. Then there I was, the writer looking up at me.

Only it wasn't M. The man was a dealer of Persian rugs. He insisted on pulling out his card to prove it.

Now Jan opens his eyes. He's smiling. It's the kind of smile a saint smiles. A smile that beams kindness at you no matter what sort of fool you are making of yourself. Ira's smile.

Without thinking, I move towards him, extend my hand. "Are you enlightened?" I ask.

He grips my hand easily, and, with barely a tug, he's standing, looking down at me.

"Why did you ask that?"

Why? Because Ira's a Buddhist, because they've discovered a new tumor in his brain.

Jan listens as I tell the story, listens saying nothing, just nodding in the bright May sun. A bell rings. Students fill the walks like busy ants. We're missing class, but neither of us particularly notices.

When I'm finished, Jan says, "This is amazing. I can't believe I met you."

I look up at him, delirious with happiness. I want to grab his hands and dance him around the lawn. Instead I ask, "What are you doing this summer?"

"Hanging out until August."

"And then?"

"I'm moving to Iowa."

Iowa?

"I'm transferring to Maharishi University. I'm going to levitate."

When I think of levitation I think of a group of schoolgirls huddled over a prone body at a slumber party. One, two, three — and the body, resting ever so lightly on your fingertips, flies up like a magic carpet. But Jan's levitation, I imagine, is different, self-ignited; a purity of being, like a burning gas, buoys him up.

"Actually, it's more like hopping," Jan says. "You only levitate for a few moments at a time."

"At my brother's place, we walk on fire, hot coals."

Jan shakes his head. "Wow."

"Wood coals, not briquettes. We run across. It really doesn't hurt."

Ira's lying in a hospital bed and here I am bragging.

Jan's nodding now, smiling as if he understands. "Where you headed?" he asks.

I shrug.

"Come home with me."

"Welcome to my cave," Jan says as he opens the door to his attic room. In the dim light, I can make out cardboard boxes filled with books, a bamboo lamp with a fringed shade, an oak desk, bare except for a framed photograph of a girl about my age wearing a wide-brimmed hat.

"That's Mimi," Jan says. "She introduced me to meditation."

Where's Mimi now? I wonder, but don't ask. I don't want to seem interrogating, possessive, yet I feel, increasingly, he's mine.

Jan lights a hurricane lamp and places it on the floor next to the bed. "Want to stay?"

Something about his room reminds me of Ira's old room. His room, too, was tucked under the eaves of the house, a fortress with windows that commanded a view of the entire street.

I hardly breathe as I lie next to Jan, afraid I might roll off his bed, a narrow mat with only a single sheet for cover. The smell of kerosene fills the room, smoky, sweet, but also somehow dangerous. I'd like to turn to him, smooth his thick blond hair. I'm still wearing my sleeveless blouse, my underpants. Jan's naked. Just before he turns out the light, he leans and kisses my forehead. It's such a chaste gesture that I'm at first startled, then pleased. It's as if I've just received a blessing.

In the dark, Jan talks on and on, his voice melodic, soothing, like the drone of summer bees. He tells me I'm a beautiful person, my body and my soul are beautiful. He calls me by my Buddhist name, the name Ira calls me. The name means "lovingkindness" or "devotion." I've never told anyone at school about this name before.

When Jan talks about his meditation, he uses words like *pu-*

rity and *grace*. I'm fighting sleep, trying to figure out how to keep him in my life forever.

"God, where have you been?" Joanne looks up from packing her duffel. Her finals are done.

"Jan's house."

"Jan?"

"Guy from my Eastern religion class."

An eyebrow goes up, her left, which she once told me she trained herself to do.

"Your mother called."

"When?"

"Bunch of times."

Three little squares of notepaper on my pillow, Joanne's beautiful script.

"How'd she sound?"

Joanne shrugs. "Wanted to know where you were. I said you had finals."

I pick up the phone and Joanne tactfully leaves the room.

The number is her business telephone. Three rings and her secretary picks up. "Eileen Stein's office."

I give my name and the secretary puts me on hold. I can feel my heart beating in my throat, my underarms prickling.

"Phoebe."

"Hi."

I know that in the silence Mom's taking a breath, trying to keep herself from screaming. I know her so well.

"You've been out."

"Finals."

Another beat of silence.

When she speaks, her voice is surprisingly soft. "I forgot."

"Well," I say. Rage whips up in me as it always does when I

talk to my mother, frost blooms my cheeks. Ice person with a heart of fire. "What's happening?"

"Take it easy."

A sound comes out of my nose, a sniff, a snort.

"You're the one who disappeared," my mother says.

Yeah? Where have you been all my life?

"I want to let you know I'm going tomorrow."

"Are they going to operate?"

"They haven't decided."

"How come?"

"I don't know, Phoebe. They tell me but I can't listen."

Been breathing carefully like my heart's made of glass, now it shatters, splinters piercing here, here, here. *Can't she ever ask?* I clear my throat. "My friend Jan wants me to go to Nantucket with him."

"When?"

"In a week. After finals. It's my last chance to see him. He's leaving school."

Silence again. *Tell me no, tell me I can't go.*

"Could we get ahold of you if we had to?"

"It's not Siberia."

"Phoebe."

"What's Molly doing?"

"I guess she'll come with me."

The hate comes over me suddenly, turning my veins to ice, filling them with clear poison. I can see them ranged around Ira's hospital bed, the way it was last time. Molly on the floor; Dad in the chair in the corner; Mom comatose on the empty bed.

I'm seven years old again, the terrorist in the garden, paralyzed with hate, my heart, an icicle too large for my chest.

They don't want me.

"What would Ira think?"

"If you don't come? I don't think he'll think. He's got other things on his mind. Anyway, you can come after Nantucket."

It's hard to explain exactly why, but Molly and I, both expert readers of our mother's moods, know she's about to explode. The danger signs: her brief, unenthusiastic hug, her wanting to know almost immediately where the cafeteria is, her announcement that she's "fatigued."

On entering Ira's hospital room, she flings herself on the unoccupied bed and stares up at the ceiling. "Am I the only one who's hungry?" she asks. She's dressed all in white. White blouse, white jeans, white sneakers. Like a nurse.

Our parents arrived from New York this afternoon. The latest tests show tumors in Ira's lungs. Tomorrow the surgeons are going to operate even though they're not certain anything can be done.

"Hold off, Eileen. Let's discuss things first," Dad says.

Mom stiffens, remains silent. Is there going to be a fight? In front of Ira?

"Anyone else have an objection?" she asks in a querulous voice.

Molly and I keep quiet.

"All right then." She stands, patting her wrinkled blouse into shape. "Anyone want anything?"

Silence. The hospital door, too heavy and broad to slam, closes behind her with a hushed sound.

My mother's behavior this August afternoon has this effect on me: I am determined to hew even more closely to my brother's path. Won't tell them my doubts, my urge to rebel.

"Mind if I sit?" Dad asks, pulling the chair close to Ira's bed. He's wearing new jeans that wrinkle at the knee, a cotton

shirt, a pair of hiking boots. A California costume, a costume chosen to please Ira, I'm sure.

I sink to the floor, my back against the wall, so that I'm facing Ira.

"Mom's nervous," Dad says. "It's a lot for her."

For her? How about for us? Molly and I have been visiting for a month, then this crisis happened.

Ira nods. He's not once left off his silent recitation of mantra, a waterfall of beads spilling mechanically over his forefinger. It's a habit I have gotten used to, but I wonder how it strikes Dad. He doesn't ask Ira to stop, doesn't say with some disgust as he does when either of us girls speaks with her mouth full to keep it shut. He allows Ira to chew his mantra as placidly as a cow.

"How are you feeling?"

"Fine."

"How's Dr. Rinpoche?"

Dad always uses "Doctor." Like he can't quite bring himself to believe Rinpoche's a guru, not a physician.

"Fine."

"We'll go see him. Probably tomorrow. I'll call first, of course." Remembering an incident some years ago when he failed to call and was not seen, not granted an audience. "Grandma and Grandpa send their love, and of course Beatrice and Robert, and well, everyone, of course, sends their love."

Someone might respond politely, "How are they?" Not Ira, who's not impolite, simply absorbed by the sounds in his head like a fluid that surrounds him, protects him from us, from this world.

"We'll call Dr. Rinpoche this afternoon. He might be worried."

"Whatever, Dad."

Dad turns to me, shyly, and I look away, feeling cruel, feeling a desire to push him away, to keep Ira for myself.

"Oh ho are you popular! About a dozen boys tried to reach you in the last month, I'd say."

"Who?"

"Do you expect me to keep lists?" But he has, and even as he raises his eyebrows comically, making fun of me, he's withdrawing a paper from his wallet, so eerily like Ira that I have to blink.

Slipping on a pair of reading glasses, he says, "Let's see on 8/4 there was one Jerry and a Tom, on 8/12, Richard; on 8/14 . . . Sorry I can't make it out . . ."

I scowl but I'm excited. Has word gotten out that Mark and I have broken up?

It turns out, however, that the rest of the calls are *Mark's. He'd lost my address; he wanted to know when I'd be back, and so on. I sink back into myself. Typical Dad, I think. The tease.*

"Phoebe doesn't realize how popular she is."

I glance at Ira, but he's not listening.

"Any calls for me?" Molly asks.

"Helene. I gave her your address."

Helene's Molly's best friend.

"That's all*?"*

Dad shrugs, turns his palms up. In a second, Molly's left the room. It's not difficult to offend my sister.

"Did I say something wrong?" Dad asks.

"Duh," I say. Then, embarrassed, I glance at Ira, who isn't paying attention, who doesn't care.

Molly and Mom come back together. They don't say where they've been or if they were in the same place. We seat our-

selves on the edge of the empty bed and watch the steady parade of nurses. Occasionally, we're asked to step into the hall. There we stand, awkward, gawky tourists in this place, aimless in a world of purposeful bustle, until the door opens again and a sweet-faced nurse beckons us to enter.

Each time we go back in, I feel as though secrets have been exchanged, as though Ira were living yet another secret life we're not allowed to know about. I could ask what the nurse did, what she said. But I don't. It's all private. His own business. Like everything else.

When it's time to go, we take turns kissing Ira good-bye. Mom's first. She sits on the edge of his bed, takes his hand in her lap. She can't look at him. From the shadows, we watch her head drop and her shoulders round. Ira's patting her on the back, murmuring, "It's okay, Mom."

I freeze. The sound of my mother's crying is like a little girl's, childish, from the chest. Dad steps towards her, then stops. She is standing, her hand still linked in Ira's, her face still turned away. Then the link is broken, and she drops a swift kiss on his forehead and strides past us, strides into the hall and away.

Dad's next, saying good-bye with a quick handshake, and then Molly, whose forlorn sobs break from her as soon as she sits down.

Then it's my turn. I can't say anything, my fists balled in my lap. I want to be brave; I don't want to cry. Ira's brave. He's as calm as a god, a little baffled perhaps, a little concerned, not for himself, but for us. For Ira, the hospital, this disease, is old hat.

"See you tomorrow," he says.

From my window seat, I watch the train curve into the station, a long, silver worm flashing its dingy scales. I remind myself Jan's the one who invited me to spend the night; he's the one who invited me for the weekend.

Before I left, I called my parents at the hospital to give them the number on the Island. My father wanted to know all about Jan. I lied. We've been seeing each other for months, I said. You'd like him.

Then Ira got on the telephone. He sounded cheerful, but a little vague. I told him I was seeing a guy who followed the Maharishi, a meditator. Ira said it was a good organization. Then I said my boyfriend wanted to meet him. Even to Ira I lied.

I scan the faces on the platform as I step off the train. Will he recognize me, indistinguishable from a thousand other girls of my type: short, with curly brown hair and brown eyes? A normal nose, a wide mouth. Pretty in a way. But oddly sloppy. An oversize shirt, loose jeans, as though I'd shrunk recently and not gotten used to my size.

As it happens, I don't recognize him. His hair's been cropped to the skull, not shaven, he explains. He doesn't have to — I know a monk's head is never shaven until he's taken his vows. And Jan has not taken any vows. Not yet.

Still, the sight of his head now shiny with bristles and oddly elongated makes me want to cry. Jan takes my hand. I want to shout, "I don't know you."

In the middle of the night, there's a knock. Vimalamitra whispering, "Wake up, Rinpoche wants you in the temple room." It's cold, so I pull on a sweater, heavy socks. Did he say "you," not "us"?

"You're very lucky," he says. "Rinpoche's burning goma. *He wants you to attend."*

"I don't know what to do."

"Just keep handing him prayer sticks in bundles of twelve." Vimalamitra knocks once on the temple room door, then opens it. Rinpoche sits in front of the circular fireplace, his

face already flushed from the intensity of the fire, and, without looking at me, he pats the cushion beside him.

Next to my place are the prayer sticks already tied in neat bundles. Every night we bring up sackloads of scribbled sticks from the basement that someone, probably Ira, counts, assembles, stacks like this. Rinpoche snaps his fingers. I pick up a bundle, hand it to him. He raises it to his forehead, then kisses it. And, chanting, he drops the bundle of sticks into the already hot fire.

The wood ignites instantly, flaring yellow. Snap. Another bundle. Snap. Another. Must be twenty bundles in all. The fire roars; sweat beads on Rinpoche's forehead, squiggles down his temples. He swipes his face with his sleeve, swipes again.

I'm so hot I feel like my skin's going to burst. Like I might ignite in flames. My lungs burn. I'm calculating just how many seconds I'm going to last, but I don't move. Don't dare.

Rinpoche doesn't seem to notice. He chants as he throws handfuls of rice into the flames, then ladlefuls of oil. Sweet smell rising, then smoke.

The chanting goes on and on and we sit until the flame dies to a shimmer.

"I want to tell you some things and you can tell your sister, your parents, too, if you wish."

I draw a breath, my resistance like a cold flame, cooling me: beware.

"Milarepa did a lot of shit his last time around; he was a real bloody bastard. So this time, he's burning like a comet. He's done a lot of work on his karma. In four years, he's gotten about as far as a bastard can. He's going to be dead pretty soon, but don't worry. He's going to be fine."

The plan's to stop at Jan's mother's house because Jan's mother wants to meet me. From there, Jan's father will pick us up.

"Sound okay?" Jan asks.

"Fine." The week after school was out, he wrote to me every day in handwriting as tiny and perfect as a bird's tracings in sand. "Dear Earth Mother," "Dear Maitreya, the goddess." We've never talked about our mundane lives. Up to now, I've only known Jan's from Wilmington. And, from certain hints, that his family's rich.

He only knows my brother is dying.

"So your parents are divorced?" I ask.

"It's pretty recent." His hands tighten on the wheel, his brow sinks for a moment. "A good thing."

Jan's mother is tall and thin like Jan. She stands in the doorway to greet us, stooping to shake my hand, then holding it for a second as though she's momentarily lost her balance. I guess Jan's told her about Ira. It's the kind of gesture I'm beginning to get used to. But what else did he tell her? Did he call me his girlfriend?

"Mother meditates," Jan says.

His mother nods. "It helps my heart," she says.

Inside, Jan's mother explains that every detail in the house is from the original, prerevolutionary.

"I wish you could have met the man who restored this," Jan's mother says, pointing to the cool, dark floor. "He loved each board like a son."

I try to catch Jan's eye, but can't. How do you love a floor board as much as a son? Surely she must be joking.

Once we're seated in the living room, Jan's mother serves us iced tea the color of pomegranate seeds, then asks, "Does anyone mind if I disappear? I've got to get in my afternoon sit."

Jan consults his watch. "I should, too, before Dad comes." He turns and smiles at me beside him on the couch. "Do you mind?"

Of course I do, but I shake my head obediently.

"More tea? Soda? Water?" Jan's mother asks. When I decline, she turns to Jan. "Why don't you give Phoebe the photo album?"

"She doesn't want to look at pictures."

But I do and Jan's mother knows this. She places a leather-bound album on the coffee table. "Jan's trip to Australia last year. To visit his older brother, Mike. You probably heard about it. Mike's homesteading in the outback."

If I knew Jan better, I would arch my brows at him, make him pay for not telling me about this adventure. Instead, I shake my head again.

He smiles. "All right, Mother. If we're going to meditate." He pats the back of my head before rising. "You're sure you're okay?"

"Of course."

I hear the stairs creak, then doors clicking shut, their wrought-iron latches falling into place. *Right now they might be opening my brother's head. Why am I here?*

I open the album: photographs of a newly framed house. On every joist, it seems, a man crouched naked. And Jan's one of them, seated astride a beam, his golden hair thick about his shoulders, his long, slender legs dangling in air. And, though I don't mean to look, I can't help but notice the shy neck of his sex peeping beneath a thatch of toffee-colored hair.

A wild man. Like Ira once was. To my surprise, it gives me hope.

Jan's father's fat and bald, and doesn't look like Jan in the slightest. He drinks whiskey out of a silver flask and insists, once we pull out of sight of Jan's mother's house, that Jan chauffeur the midnight blue Mercedes.

"Love this car like an heirloom," he confides to me on the trip down. "It will be in my family after I die."

Think about what Ira's going to leave when he dies. He's taken a vow of poverty and owns nothing but a prayer book, a rosary carved from human bone. A memory comes to me, that last visit. I was going into his room for something, don't remember what. On the floor, a pair of underwear. Red, rumpled.

Ira's underwear. I began to weep.

The house stands on a promontory overlooking the sea. Downstairs there's a living room with a brick fireplace, a dining room, a kitchen, and a small bedroom tucked behind the pantry. Upstairs, a master bedroom with its own bath and another bedroom. When it comes to working out who will sleep in which bedroom, Jan's father turns very red and scuttles out of the room, saying he's certain something equitable can be arranged. Jan and I laugh at this, but we, too, are uncomfortable.

I'm hoping Jan will suggest we share a room, at least secretly. He doesn't. Instead, he says he'll take the small bedroom on the first floor and that I and his father can have the upstairs bedrooms. He's used to cubbyholes, he says.

My room has a window framed by white curtains that overlooks the dunes. In the center of the room is a large brass bed made up with a down quilt. On one wall, a pine wardrobe whose empty hangers chime as I hang up my clothes.

No books in the room, no pictures. Emptier than a motel room, I think. Motel rooms, at least, manage to celebrate your arrival with paper-wrapped glasses and fresh soaps and towels preserving the illusion you're welcome. Next door is the bathroom, and I panic for a moment, wondering just how I will use it. But something tells me I won't vomit here. I can't. I can hardly even breathe.

Right now Molly's probably settled into the room over the back stairs, our room. She's probably put on her ashram costume, the purple skirt, the white shirt. She's eating a peanut butter sandwich on sourdough bread. This morning she walked on coals, chanted prayers, headed for the hospital, a bundle of prayer sticks under her arm. *Why aren't I there?*

I lie down, close my eyes. My body feels heavy, as though little weights circled my wrists and ankles, as though I could never move again. The days I sat with Ira, we meditated straight through lunch. We would've meditated through dinner, too, if I hadn't heard the gong and woken up. Beside me, Ira was a black rock, so still I couldn't tell if he were alive or dead.

A sea breeze wafts the curtains, blows across my hot body. Ira's seated on the end of the bed. The moon mandala hangs from the closet door. Once when I was a teenager, I wrote Ira, saying, "I don't adjust to change well. Like when you left home. But I remember what you said, 'Everything changes.'" How simple those phrases. How much they hid. I was screaming, drowning, lost, afraid. What did it matter to Ira? How could he have saved me?

When I shake hands with Ira's surgeon, I feel so small, so inadequate, like I'm shaking hands with a movie star. Ira's surgeon doesn't put on airs, but it's clear he's God-chosen. Tanned, fit, schooled in the mysteries of the human body.

We cram in his office. Mom and Dad on the upholstered chairs; Molly and me standing behind them like bodyguards. Two other doctors lean against the floor-to-ceiling bookcase, their hands in their pockets. Ira's already got the news.

Dr. Frankel leans across his desk, sketching lightly on a tilted pad. The cancer's too advanced to operate on. Tumors line his lungs like silt in a river. The best they could do was in-

sert a tube so the fluid could drain from between the lungs and the chest wall. The best thing now is for the fluid to drain. The more fluid the better.

These days are like a tortuously paced movie. Nothing happens all day long. Bells ring, codes sound, an occasional phone call. Motes drift in the solid shafts of light that pierce the window. Even the light has become part of the trivia of the day. It's always sunny outside, the sky's always that soaring, faraway California blue.

Every evening, the fog rolls, or rather unrolls in, as though someone at the horizon has kicked open a roll of cotton batting. Every evening it advances on us, blankets us, seals us in. Every day we say the same predictable things: "Beautiful weather," "Fog's coming in" and so on. Every day we watch, but don't watch, the plastic pouch hooked to the side of Ira's bed, the pouch filled with liquid the color of weak tea.

Ira sits up in bed, tubes looped like antique lace across his hospital gown. Every hour or so, the nurse comes in to check the progress of the drainage, writing numbers on a form attached to a clipboard.

Once a day, the pouch is changed, carried away. The nurses are always upbeat. They congratulate Ira on the amount of liquid in the pouch as though he were somehow responsible, the way babies are congratulated for eating and shitting.

Every day Dr. Frankel comes in to look at the pouch, squashing it a little from the bottom, rubbing his chin. He doesn't give compliments as freely as the nurses. He's not complimenting much at all, I notice.

At night, Mom and Dad drop us at the ashram before heading to Berkeley, where they're staying with friends from the old neighborhood. So far they haven't stopped in. Dad always says the same thing, "Give our best to Dr. Rinpoche. Tell him we'd like to see him sometime, but not tonight."

Flicker of irritation on my part. Dad's assumption that Rinpoche's dying to see him.

Much as I hate to admit it, like my mother, I'm in a rage all the time. I'd like to fling myself down and weep. I can't. I have my pride. And no one would care or notice. There's no energy left. None. Except the energy it takes to show up at the hospital every day to wait.

Feels like some kind of torture on Ira's part. Something he's inflicting on me, as though these were the old days when he used to pin me to the ground, force me to say "uncle" before he'd let me up for air. Uncle, uncle, uncle. There. I've said it. Let me up for air before I die.

Jan's father insists on taking us to a fancy restaurant: crystal chandeliers, white linen tablecloths and napkins, real silver. I'm wearing my nice dress. But even the nice dress doesn't seem nice enough for this elegant dining room. Jan and his father are wearing identical dinner jackets, maroon with a gold crest on the pocket. I wonder if it's their family crest, but I'm too shy to ask.

Before we left, Jan's father insisted that Jan call the restaurant to make sure that the chef wouldn't be offended by our ordering vegetarian plates.

After the waiter pours the wine, Jan's father lifts his glass. "A toast," he says. "Your food bills will be cheap, but I don't know what you're doing to your bones."

I glance at Jan, who raises his glass without touching it to his father's and without drinking from it. He's blushing up to his ears, and I have the feeling that I'm the very first girl he's ever introduced to his father. Should be happy, instead I feel uneasy.

Jan's so awkward with his father, filled with grimaces and tight smiles, embarrassed at what his Dad might say or do. But for some reason I like Jan's father, his bizarre attempts at telling Jan he loves him.

Tonight he drinks glass after glass of red wine and teases Jan about how much a particular waitress misses him at the country club. "She's always asking after you, Jan," he says.

"But, Dad, I was only six years old."

Jan's father turns and winks at me. "See how long he's been breaking hearts? Just like his mother."

There's silence after this and Jan's father summons the waiter and orders another bottle of wine.

"Did your mother tell you that I bumped into her last week at the A & P?"

Jan shakes her head.

"Damnedest thing. I'm wheeling my cart past the produce, thinking about I don't know what, the price of broccoli, I suppose, when crash bang, our carts hit head-on, and lock together like braces in a kiss. No matter how hard we tugged we couldn't get them apart." Jan's father pauses to mash an invisible pea in the center of his plate. "It scared her, I think."

On the way home, Jan's father falls asleep in the backseat. He's curled on one side, snoring gently, his maroon jacket scrunched into a pillow. I'd like to say something to Jan. So you have a mother, a father, a brother. What are they like? Why are you leaving them?

I can see only the blade of Jan's cheekbone illuminated from time to time by the streetlights of the villages we pass through.

"You're so different from him," I say at last, glancing back at his father.

An eyebrow lifts, a faint smile.

"I was born to this family," he says. "I don't know why."

It's like I'm traveling in time, traveling backwards. Jan's Ira, of course. Ira in larval stage. I'm here to examine the chrysalis, to record the exact moment of emergence, to observe the transformation to wings. How do they do it, these "light" people, these butterfly sons, how do they leave their families behind?

The floor is smooth, almost slippery beneath my bare feet as I feel my way along the hall. I don't dare turn on a light for fear of waking Jan's father. The staircase is circular with a thin metal banister for support. Toe down, step, toe down, step, I make my way carefully. There's no moon tonight, but after a few minutes my eyes adjust slightly to the variations in blackness. I'd be good at being blind.

Jan's door is slightly ajar and to my surprise there's a wash of electric light from the dials of the washer and dryer in the pantry. Jan's sleeping, curled in a mound of covers. I'll just slip in, tuck myself into his curves, and be safe.

Gently, I sit on the edge of the bed. He looks so young with his short, short hair, every lump of his skull exposed, and his soft cheek, I don't think he could even grow a beard.

I kiss his forehead, and Jan starts awake with a cry.

"It's only me," I say.

From the way he clutches the covers, I know that he's naked underneath. He blinks twice. "Poor little one," he murmurs.

Taking this as a signal, I lie down beside him on top of the covers. I'm wearing a thin nightshirt. It's cold. This is only a pose. I'm waiting for an arm, an invitation, the blankets thrown back, ushering me into their warm tent.

"May I come in?"

Jan's silent. He raises himself on his elbow. Now he's looking down on me. I have his attention.

"I want to tell you something," Jan says. He traces his finger back and forth across my forehead as though he wants to engrave something on it.

My heart is thudding. *Just kiss me.*

"I've taken a vow. Not *to* anyone. Not like your brother. To myself. I want to be pure."

My body is suddenly chilled and twanging like struck glass. "Then why did you invite me?"

Outside the surf roars like a jet. *Why did I come?*

"I liked you," he says. "You seemed so alone."

Trying to understand what's happening as the days go on. But it's impossible. I see the family spindling, the nucleus disappearing, poles forming. The cell of our family dividing along its truest lines. At one pole, Dad and Ira. Ancient enemies have become twins. Same tilt of head, same gestures, same tone of voice, same utter calm, same cheerfulness in the face of utterly disastrous news. At the other pole: Molly and Mom, passing out, bingeing, staggering, weeping.

I'm in the middle, this middle place, weightless, alone. Riding the elevator, I shuttle between two worlds, the hospital room and the cafeteria, between two camps. In the hospital room, Dad and Ira are inking prayer sticks. Dad, of all people. Dad, the irreligious one, sits, scribbling thoughtfully, silently, proud of his ever-growing pile of supplications.

In the cafeteria, Mom and Molly have staked out the wall end of a long table. Around them, fluttery stacks of paper plates, greasy cardboard, empty cartons, wrappers. I don't know how they feed themselves. I can't eat anything at all. I don't know what they talk about all day or if they talk at all. Still they seem to need each other, joined head to toe.

I need no one.

Not true.

I am a needy child. A greedy child. A child with an un-

quenchable thirst for love. I'm the middle child. Middle, a kind of hole I was dropped into against my will.

I am screaming, Help me. Hold me. Don't let me go.

But he has.

Ira suffers us gently, patiently. Tolerates our bungling presence in the way the teacher endures his disciples. With compassion.

I can't stand it. I've got to escape.

In the morning, Jan and I stroll down to the beach. We've already discovered that the water's too cold to swim in. Overnight, I've become as silent as Jan. I've found that I can lose him for hours at a time. Mostly I think of Ira.

An image floats through my mind as I look out at the flat ocean, of playing marbles on the smooth, hot tar of the playground of my elementary school. Ira taught me to play. Sitting on the floor of his room, he untwists the neck of the woolen ski sock, peers inside, judging which marbles he can spare. "You're only getting cheap ones. Maybe a couple of others."

I don't mind. I listen to the watery click of marbles dropping into my pouch. Ira's giving me a present, can't remember this ever happening before.

"Here's one purie," he says. "Don't lose it." He holds the marble to the light, and I gasp as a deep blue pool opens on the floor in front of me.

"Worth ten cat's-eyes," he warns. "Don't bet anything less."

Then he shows me how to balance the big fat mama on the crook of my index finger, and how to flick it away with the edge of my thumb so that it shoots along a perfect beeline towards its target, an unassuming little cat's-eye suddenly sent spinning clear out of the circle.

Since I've been here, no word from the hospital.

"I'd like to take your picture," Jan says.

I nod, ashamed of the little flame of desire that instantly licks my collarbone. *Is he interested?*

He poses me sitting cross-legged in a stand of reeds beside the marsh. Then he gets down on his belly in the white sand and pokes the nose of the camera upward. Cattails stripe my face like the bars of a cage. I want to make a face, to spit. I hope that I look like a wild animal, camouflaged, about to attack.

"Tilt your head a little. Smile!"

It comes back to me. A trip to the shore with Ira and Molly and our parents. He was fifteen; I, twelve. In a year, he'd run away from home, for good. All of a sudden, Ira, who'd been sullen all day, tossing his long hair away from his pimpled forehead and kicking sand, perked up.

"Cool," he said. He was pointing to a row of plywood figures on the boardwalk. Cowboys, ballerinas, fat ladies, a policeman.

When I caught up to Ira, he grabbed my hand, bent me back in his arms. I held still there, peering through the eyeholes of the woman with a rose in her teeth. "Darling," Ira crooned, "my little Rosalita."

The camera clicks. I blink away tears. Jan's staring at me quizzically. His strange prickly head, his gangly frame. I turn away. You cannot have your brother; you cannot be a girl with a rose in your bandito brother's arms.

"Do you miss your brother?" I ask.

Jan smiles in that sad way of his, shakes his head. "I love my brother and all. He's a good person, he has a good life. But I'm not devoted the way you are. What you have is rare. Your love for your brother. It's something I've never felt."

"For your brother?"

Jan shrugs. "For anyone, I guess. I have problems with my heart."

* * *

Driving across the Bay Bridge, I'm overcome with a delirious sense of freedom. I whoop into the air, reach to turn the volume on the radio full blast. On either side of the railing stretches the sea, vast, churning with a superb energy of its own. I'm light, freed for the first time in weeks from the fog of guilt and rage.

Here I am. Driving across the bridge, by myself, *to Berkeley, the childhood paradise. Here I am. Returning. As to the long lost lover, the bosom friend.*

Yet three quarters of the way across the bridge, stuck suddenly in a traffic jam that seems to have materialized from nowhere, I find myself thinking of Ira, wondering how he's doing, if he misses me or feels abandoned.

When I left the hospital, he was asleep, rare, and I whispered the fact of my departure to my exhausted family as they themselves were preparing to disperse, taking advantage of this lull to go their separate ways. Will anyone be in the room when he wakes up? Is the drainage okay today? (I forgot to ask.) Did I write enough prayer sticks?

The traffic breaks up and car engines rev all around me, having been given their heads. I step on the gas pedal and push forward with them.

The exit shunts me onto a wide boulevard lined with shops, motels, supermarkets. Not particularly beautiful in any way, but suddenly I remember and can barely keep my eyes on the traffic. I know suddenly, with certainty, that if I just keep on straight, then bear left, this boulevard will lift me into the old neighborhood, that I'll soon pass the ice cream parlor, the courtyard in which we ate pizza on summer nights, followed by a long dazzling stretch up into the hills. Then, bearing right, I'll pass my old school, the stucco building, faintly pink in the afternoon light. But if, on the other hand, I decide to continue straight, I'll reach the park we used to stroll to on summer afternoons, a basin of roses, tiered in a majestic, yet slightly frightening display. And if I park and walk back a little ways, I'll find the wide, concrete stairway that leads up to the sidewalk that faces our house.

I point the car uphill and begin to ascend the steep, snaking roads. This is where our lives were perfect, in these hills, in this light, in this air so pure it almost breathes for you. These are the smells I remember: eucalyptus, rose, cedar, earth. These are the views I remember of water, of space, of the shimmering horizon. These are the heaving paths, the sidewalk squares thrusting up and down, tilting this way and that as idiosyncratic as a mouth full of crooked teeth, and these are the hidden paths, alleyways arched with twisting vines, tunnels as mysterious as the passages in fairy tales.

I park the car and get out. Our house rises from the hillside, a dark majestic house, the same deep color as the earth, that follows the curve of this steep, curving road, and the curving thick hedge that shields it from view. You could easily miss the house altogether as you concentrate on the steepness of this hill, as you plod one foot in front of the other as I am doing now.

I ache, not for the house itself, or even for the jewel I know it embraces, the terraced gardens, the fruit trees, the rose garden, the garden of wild quince. I ache for the sense I once had that all this beauty, all this light belonged to me, was my own precious gift, my entitlement, that the whole precious world was created just for me.

The gap in the fence isn't hard to find, a space where the cedar boards don't quite meet the pine slats of the neighbor's fence. I'm in the back of the garden, in the uppermost corner, that once contained row on row of staked rosebushes, climbers snaking up freestanding trellises. It was in fact my least fa-

vorite part of the garden because it was the tamest, the most cultivated, the gardener's special project. We never cut these roses, merely observed them as though they were elaborate ball gowns hung on mannequins in a store window. Beautiful, but somehow always remote.

I preferred the snapdragons with their working jaws, the lilies, the woozy delphiniums, flowers that waved on their stems in what seemed a kind of greeting as I brushed by.

The rectangular bed's now a patch of dried canes, the upper lawn, deeply torn. For what? A vegetable garden? I move quickly along the back wall, past an overturned wheelbarrow, a pair of worn gloves resting by the half-sunken tire. I'm listening for the sound of a dog, for people. If they ask, I'll tell the truth, I lived here a long time ago.

Another shock awaits. The wild garden, the corner that used to erupt in quince and eucalyptus and grape, has been mowed under and paved for a tennis court. A limp net sags between two flaking posts. Other than that no sign at all of play.

I venture closer to the house, down the stone path (these stones, lumpy as unpunched dough, familiar as old friends, are what bring tears to my eyes), past the stone wall, to where the path meets a flagstone tier above the courtyard. There I crouch behind a hedge.

As a child, I thought it was possible I lived in a fairy tale. Wasn't our house with its ivy-covered balconies, its spiraling staircase, its diamond-shaped windowpanes, a castle? Wasn't our brimming garden a place where fairies would like to live?

The curved wall of the house, vulnerable as a cat's belly, rises before me, its windows glazed a dull red, as though each contains a dying fire. As far as I can tell, the place is deserted.

I sit, legs sprawled on the cool flagstone, and images emerge. Hours spent wandering the maze of the Oriental rug outside my mother's study, waiting for the majestic doors to part, for her response to my picture slipped under her door. A blue-orange-red drawing of a girl wearing a pineapple on her head. "Look, it's me, Phoebe!"

And my father stopping me unexpectedly one afternoon in the dining room. He grips me quite firmly by the shoulders and says in the most solemn voice imaginable, "The most important thing in life is happiness, Phoebe. I don't want you to forget that."

Instinctively, I shake loose of his grasp. "No," I say angrily. "I don't want to be happy." I'm seven years old. I want something more than happiness. What?

No one questions where I've been. No one cares. It's a little past eight. Visiting hours are almost over. Seated on the empty bed, my mother hunches over the remains of Ira's dinner, spooning up cubes of green Jell-O doused in milk. My mother's always liked mushy dishes, milky puddles of oatmeal, bread steeped in milk until the pores bloat and disintegrate, rice pudding drenched in milk. She feeds ravenously, barely swallowing, not bothering to look up.

On the other side of the room, Dad and Molly and Ira are scribbling prayer sticks. The burlap bag is nearly filled; the fluid pouch nearly empty.

Dad's the only one to notice me. "Did the car behave?" he asks in a cheery voice.

It did, I tell him.

"I meant to tell you about the rearview mirror. It wobbles a bit."

A bit? It's dangling from one end, I tell him. "And you didn't exactly mention the seat doesn't move."

"Don't snap at your father," Mom says.

"It's all right, dear. Phoebe's right. I should have fixed these things before letting her drive the car."

Behind me my mother lets her spoon bang on the rim of the bowl.

"It was really peaceful here before you came back. Perhaps you'd like to take a hike somewhere."

"Eileen."

I head for the door. Behind me I hear my father, "Now see what you've done . . ."

But I'm not feeling what he thinks I am. I feel a strange sense of victory, a bitter elation. I've always held this peculiar notion that it's good *for the family to be angry with me. Something I'm good at. I draw trouble to me. On purpose, to distract them, to save them, from their own unbearable pain.*

In the dark, I listen to the heavy whisper of Molly's breathing, trying to figure out if she's really sleeping. Except at the ashram, we haven't slept in the same room since we were five and six, and I kicked her out for breathing too loudly. Even now I can remember my rage at being reminded of her presence. Her every inhale seemed to suck the air from my room, her every exhale to pollute it.

I shake her arm lightly. "Molly?"

"What?"

"Talk to me. What did the doctors say? Was there a lot of fluid?"

In the silence, I think she's gone back to sleep, so I'm taken aback by the fury of her reply.

"How come you left me alone with them! Where were *you!" Molly's pallet's only a few feet away. I stretch my arm, trying to reach her, but she has turned on her side, facing away from me, curled tight as a poked spider.*

I move to the edge of her mattress and, kneeling, grasp her shoulder, rocking her towards me.

"Go away," she says gruffly, but I ignore her, thinking, we

were never in our entire childhoods united. Rivals unto the death, each with her own arsenal: Molly's sore throats; my moods. Competing for Mom's attention, unobtainable prize.

"Molly," I murmur. "I'm sorry."

I feel a sob move through her. One electric jolt. She is opening, opening to my embrace, clinging so tightly I can feel her forehead burning on my shoulder.

"Don't leave me again," she says. "Promise."

"I can't."

"What do you mean?"

"I can't stand it any longer. I'm going home."

"Leave him?"

"Yes." I didn't know I was going to say this, but all of a sudden it's clear. "I have to. I'm going crazy." Any minute might start screaming at Ira, might start cursing him for growing those goddamn tumors, might start beating him with my fists.

"Me, too," she says.

"Come with me."

"I can't."

"Why not?"

She shakes her head violently, blond strands working themselves free of the kerchief she wears, even to bed. "I have to take care of Milarepa."

"He doesn't need us, not really." I feel Molly pulling away, letting the night air fill the space between us. Her arms drop.

"They won't let you go."

"They will. They'll be glad."

I'm right. My parents receive the news calmly.

"You've been out here for a long time," Dad says. "Of course you need a break."

This irritates me a little, but I don't say anything.

Mom nods. "There's a lot to do before college. I'd lost track of that."

That leaves Ira, who looks up distractedly (I'm not even sure he heard me). "Oh sure. Whatever you need to do."

We return flushed and thirsty to the house. Jan empties an ice tray into two large glasses and fills them with mineral water. From where we stand in the kitchen, we can see Jan's father reading the newspaper on the deck. Every morning he dresses in blinding green trunks, pale pink shirt and white floppy hat.

Now he folds the paper and slides open the screen door. "Sun's passed the meridian. Time for a Scotch." He says this with the urgency of a man who's been sitting on the deck all morning to gauge the movement of the sun. For his efforts, he has developed a deep burn on his kneecaps and shins.

On our way back to the house, Jan told me that when his parents first split, his father used to haunt the old neighborhood in the blue Mercedes. Round and round the block to settle finally at the end of the driveway. He sat there until Jan's mother came out to invite him in. "Like one of those turtles who'd crawl a hundred miles to get back to home."

"What are you two drinking?"

"Water," Jan says. "Want some?"

Jan's father waves his hand in dismissal and reaches for the bottle of Scotch in the cupboard. "What do you kids think about supper in town tonight? Lobster or an old-fashioned clambake?" Silence, and he looks around. "Don't you eat fish?"

It feels like the question's directed to me, so I shake my head slowly, hoping not to seem rude. "I don't."

"Neither do I," says Jan. "What if we make dinner tonight?"

I smile, but Jan's father looks skeptical. "You cook?"

"I make a great soufflé."

"That sounds wonderful," I say.

"How about you, Dad?"

Jan's father stares at us. "I had my heart set on lobster."

"You'll like this, I know you will."

"Do you have the ingredients?"

"If we don't have something, I'll pick it up."

Jan's father moves an ice cube around with his index finger, then takes a sip of his drink, testing the flavor. I've got the feeling that he's savoring this pause, a brief moment of power. But, raising his glass, he says, "Outnumbered."

Jan waits until he hears the click of the screen door before he turns to me. "Hallelujah!"

The triumph binds us for the rest of the afternoon and we're suddenly happy: mixing, chopping, sautéing. Jan cooks as though he were conducting a ritual, as though the utensils were sacred objects. A whisk becomes the diamond scepter that cuts through illusions. A tablespoon spills scented water over the deity's head.

Jan teaches me how to make a cheese soufflé. First, he sprinkles flour into melted butter. The mixture's called a *roux,* he explains. It's very temperamental. Burns easily, forms lumps. At Jan's signal, I dribble milk into the roux, then egg yolks, then cheese. I'm the magician's assistant, his acolyte.

"Think about it, soufflé's the ultimate spiritual dish," Jan says. "It's all about impermanence and *souffle — breath."* As Jan speaks, he's beating the egg whites into beautiful soft mountains that remind me of clouds. "Now I'm going to fold some of this into the batter to lighten it before adding the rest."

"You mean *en*-lighten," I say. Jan laughs, pleased at my cleverness, at me, it seems.

The soufflé's delicious. Jan's father has three servings. He beams at his son, as pleased as though he'd made it himself. After dinner, Jan suggests we play poker. Jan's father is delighted. So am I, though I've never liked poker before. We decide on five-card stud. Jan's father supplies pistachio nuts as ante.

Jan, it turns out, is an old shark, a family legend. He wins most of the hands. "Bluffs like an angel," his father says. But neither I nor Jan's father minds. It's the first time all weekend we've felt comfortable with each other. We crack silly jokes, talk slyly of acing the next round. I wonder if Jan's truly celibate.

The phone rings around midnight, startling us. There haven't been any calls since we arrived. Jan's father picks up the phone. The call is for me. It's my father.

This is the moment I've been waiting for, yet now that it's here I feel I'd like to plant myself like a stubborn child and refuse to speak.

"Take it in my room," Jan says. "You'll have more privacy."

I manage a prim turn, a straight back. Father and son are watching me.

Carefully, I shut the door. Inside, the room is cool and dark, scented with beach plum and salt air from the open window. This is it, I think. If Ira's dead, my life will never be the same.

The day before I leave San Francisco, I need to ask Ira questions. Are you scared? Are you going to miss me? Will you still love me if I don't become a Buddhist? What do you expect of me?

This morning his doctors released him from the hospital. They've drained all the fluid they can. Now it's just a matter of, of what? No one will finish that sentence. Just a matter. Of time.

I've managed to wangle a private audience, feel guilty for taking up his precious time. We're walking to the flower shop to pick up flowers for the altars. Now or never, I tell myself. "I have my own path," I begin. "My own path," words chosen for his sake, a special language, not my own. I'm always watching what I say, choosing words like plums, testing for bruises, for ripeness, for impurities of any kind.

Ira's brows are knit in concentration, his head's bowed. What an effort it takes for him to listen, to pull himself from the current of his mantra or the drone of his headache.

"That's good," he says.

It is? Do you understand what I'm saying? My own path. Maybe not a Buddhist one. "I don't quite know what it is yet, though. I still have to find it."

He's nodding, lips moving, beads swinging. When he looks up, it's to gauge the distance to the shop, an unconscious summoning of energy, mental and physical, to make it to his destination.

People flow around us, elderly women and stylish young men, women with children and white-aproned shopkeepers. In Ira's neighborhood no one even glances at his bald head, his flowing crimson robes. I feel as though we're invisible, interlopers in this world of solid things. Ira's moving slowly, but with great force, like an athletic man dragging ball and chain. His expression's concentrated, not fierce. He seems unaware of the brilliant sky, the sharp clear air I want to inhale in gulps. So intent on his mission. The altar flowers.

Don't think he's got a clue what I'm talking about. Doesn't know I'm plotting a rebellion.

"Something with music, I think. Maybe even biology." Hastening to add, "I know that's egotistical, I mean, maybe there's a way I could play for all sentient beings." So false, so strained.

He stops, and looks at me, and I feel myself begin to shake.

What if he says no, what if he says there's no better life than following Dharma?

"Don't sweat the small stuff, Maitreya. It's only a refuge. Put it on the shelf, take it off. Don't worry."

I smile as if I'm relieved, I'm not. Maitreya. That's not my real name.

On the nightstand next to the telephone is an empty glass, and a magazine lying facedown.

The telephone waits coiled, ready. Like the snake Ira moved towards that day on the mountain.

All these years I've been running from this moment, from this exact moment. This one.

I pick up the telephone. My father speaks. He doesn't have to. I already know.

ABBEY, 1976

Abbey and Ellen are lying on their backs in their separate, but abutted beds. If the room were larger, they might have separated them; they were not trying to create an illusion of intimacy, there simply was no choice. The lights are out and their sleeping masks of black silk are slipped in place so that viewed from above they look rather like twin raccoons or elderly bandits or like children on their backs playing blindman's bluff. It is nearly midnight; an alarm clock ticks heavily on Abbey's side table, as familiar to the listeners as the thudding of their own hearts.

"You have to go," Ellen says aloud into the silky dark (without her hearing aid she cannot tell that she is shouting). "You won't able to live with yourself if you don't."

How does she know he is awake? he wonders. "What makes you think so?"

He hears her groan and mutter to "wait a minute" while she fumbles for her aid.

"You're his *grandfather,* for God's sake. You must go."

"Murry's coming next week."

"Murry's a stuffed shirt."

"He's an intelligent fellow."

Ellen snorts. "When he has something genuine to discuss he's intelligent. It's been years since that was true."

She is right of course. Murry's an ass, but he does not see why she should be allowed this judgment. Murray's *his* colleague, after all.

"I'll make a reservation for Friday."

"So soon?"

"Yes."

He rolls on his side away from her, rolls from darkness into darkness, glad for his mask. He doesn't want Ellen to know how much she affects him. It is not a good idea. But she does. She has her weight.

A week ago, Michael called to tell them Ira's cancer had taken a turn for the worse. New tests revealed tumors in his lungs, tumors that were probably there all along too small to detect. Now the dormant seeds have come to life and they are sapping Ira bit by bit. *If you want to say good-bye to him, the time is now,* Michael said.

If you want to say good-bye. But does he?

The last time he'd seen or spoken to the boy, Thanksgiving, six years ago, they had argued fiercely over whether or not there was a need to study mathematics, which the boy, fifteen, was failing along with every other subject.

The great scientific discoveries of the world: that the Earth moves around the Sun, that gravity is a force, that light is both wave and particle — none of these would be valid without their mathematical proofs, he found himself screaming at the boy.

There was silence in the room, Eileen and Michael looking on, along with Ellen and his younger daughter, Beatrice, and her husband, Robert. The boy stared at him. His face was blotched with sore spots, some picked at, some shiny, hard hills of pain. His glasses tilted on the bridge of his nose, held in place by a single earpiece. Greasy dark hair to the shoulders, a wispy hint of mustache.

"Why should I listen to you more than to any other old man?" he'd asked.

The boy had poured himself a drink sometime in the afternoon, which no one had objected to, a whiskey on the rocks, which he sipped, without wavering, fitting the rim of the heavy glass between his lips, more experienced than any of them had imagined.

"Why? Because I'm your *grandfather,*" he had shouted. "A hell of a lot smarter than you." The tip of his cane came down on the boy's glass, shattering it.

No one moved; no one spoke. The boy sat, his hand still frozen around the phantom glass, but he was squinting at Abbey through those cockeyed glasses, and nodding ever so slightly, as though what had transpired only confirmed something he knew. *He hates me,* Abbey thought. *He hates me as I hate him.*

Abbey punches the soft pillow beneath his cheek, yawns. Thinking of the boy exhausts him, like contemplating an unsolvable equation. Not unsolvable so much as inelegant, one of those theorems that must be manipulated, a little hocus-pocus here and there to yield results; sure there is an answer, his parents did this, his parents did that, a bad school, an insensitive teacher. But there are loopholes in any theory of how Ira became who he is, and none explains why the boy is dying at the age of twenty-one.

He wakes in the dark, breathing hard. A sharp pinch in his left breast as though a crab had his heart in its claw. On the side table, Ellen has set out a pitcher of tepid water, a glass on a napkin. He should take a nitro, but he doesn't dare take the time.

He needs a pencil, paper. He has to capture the symbols as fast as he can; he will write blind if he has to. He doesn't dare turn on the light; he is still seeing the afterglow of the equation behind his eyeballs, like the afterimage of a bright flash.

"Ellen," he cries. "Paper!"

Her figure, humped on its side, does not stir.

He shoves her, not caring if it hurts. "Wake up."

She shifts slightly, a whooshing noise issuing from her mouth. She cannot hear him or see him or even sense his presence. *What good is she,* he thinks. *I could die and she wouldn't notice.*

On her desk is a little pad, a slender gold pencil that feels as though it might snap in his hand. He touches the strand of lead to the paper and closes his eyes. In the dream, the equation poured out across a field of black, glowing symbols written in his own hand, a glowing white noodle of thought, breaking here and there, the symbols shaping and reshaping themselves as he hovered like a moth before the flame of his creation. He thought: *I must remember this when I wake up.* Simultaneously, he cursed himself: *Do not think.* His hand moved on, a maestro's shaping hand as he stroked the heads of the lions roaring in his ears, the dream chalk stroking, stroking without a bobble.

In that slippery dark, that silky dark, Abbey had an equation boomeranged at him as if by God. It was more than the equation of a lifetime. It was the equation of a thousand lifetimes or more. It was the equation that unified everything, the bush in flames. Now you see it, now you don't.

At breakfast, he distracts himself with the opening of his soft-boiled egg. Using the slender back of his penknife, he taps lightly around the dome, then flips the blade neatly to slice across his battered line of demarcation. Then he raises a tiny, silver spoon, a child's spoon, and scoops the sloppy yolk in its rubbery cup. It is a perfect egg, three minutes and change. Without speaking, he reaches for the toast, Ellen's homemade white, the pot of orange marmalade, also Ellen's. His newspaper is folded to the left of the linen napkin.

Ellen, at her end, breaks into her biscuit of shredded wheat. The grapefruit halves, their sections loosened in their sockets, remain on the lazy Susan.

"I had a remarkable night," Abbey says.

Ellen looks up. "You don't have to shout. My aid's on."

"You're the one shouting." Why does he bother?

"Why 'remarkable'?"

"I dreamt an equation."

She leans forward. She has always been loyal, he will say that. Always his genius was the thing.

"What sort of equation?" she asks.

"Something important. Perhaps the most important idea I have had in my life."

She nods. His mind is extraordinary, she believes. He sees what she has never seen, never imagined. She does not need to understand.

Abbey pauses to scrape the last bit of clinging white from the basin of the shell. "It was a symphony — Beethoven's Ninth at the very least."

She turns the lazy Susan so that the grapefruits will face him. "Take one. You need your vitamin C."

He obliges, placing the egg cup on its small plate, then onto the Susan, then sliding the new plate in front of him. "Do you understand what I'm telling you?" It comes out fiercely.

"Don't threaten me," she says. "I'm not impressed."

"I don't expect you to be."

He watches her spoon a grapefruit wedge into her mouth, the

movement of her cheek as a pit emerges; she spits it carefully into her napkin.

"The reservation is made. You're leaving from Kennedy, seven P.M.; arriving at nine."

"Who will meet me?"

"What do you want?"

"I'll make my way to the hotel alone, I suppose?"

"You could take Beatrice. She would help with bags and such. She wants to go."

He presses the napkin to his lips. "She'd be a nuisance."

"What do you mean? She's very capable."

"She likes to boss me."

"No one can boss you."

Abbey smiles.

"I suppose *I* could come, but I've said good-bye. And I thought you might want to see him alone. It's up to you. You don't have to take my advice."

"Thank you, madam."

"Lunch in or out?"

"Out. With Michael. He's in the city on business."

"Are you coming back with him?"

"If there's time." He moves his chair back, preparing to stand up, and finds himself transfixed by the milky surface of the plate under his egg cup, like a piece of photographic paper shining in its bath. Fermi sometimes drew diagrams on a napkin, the images seeming to rise from some property of the tissue to meet his pen. Abbey blinks. Not a single line of the theorem comes to mind.

"Seriously now, Abbey, should I make a reservation for Beatrice?"

"No," he says.

* * *

His daily walk is down the block and up the hill to the university. His daily attire, a dark suit, the fish-eye rosette, the Légion d'Honneur, poking through the slit in the lapel, a tan raincoat, raglan cut, a navy beret (looked down on now by the Parisians he was amused to find on his last trip; it marked you, his host said, urging him politely to take it off; he did not) and the plain rust red cane that folded like magic on a core of elastic strings.

At the bottom of the hill, Abbey breathes in deeply, exhales, humming as the throws himself against the force of gravity, enjoying each defiant step. *Cut me down now, heart.*

He carries his briefcase snug against his chest, a schoolboy's leather satchel stuffed with papers his colleagues have asked him to read, reams of insights into the physical world, still in draft for his approval. The great gift of his life, he has always thought, is that he has been able to do science at the highest level.

At the top of the hill, he pauses, resting the satchel on the pavement. From here, he can see out across the park and across the river and, on a clear day like today, to the cliffs of the Palisades. From this point, the city feels like the island it is, receptive to strong breezes and briny air.

He has lived here his entire life. Eighty years in one city. Yet he has never felt so in love with his city as today, so in debt to it, as though he owes something to the life throb of these streets, the ocean sting of this air, a brew that has nourished him and given him the strength to see visions at his age.

"Thanks for coming," his son-in-law is saying as he rises from the diner booth to shake Abbey's hand.

Don't smile so much, Abbey thinks.

Michael is wearing a businessman's well-cut pinstripe; a long coat hangs from the hook beside their booth, a deflated camel. Ellen complains that Michael loves clothes too much, spends too much money on them. Eyeing the soft coat, Abbey thinks perhaps this is true.

"I want to give you a picture of what's happening with Ira."

"Which is what?" Abbey asks, leaning in, preparing to be briefed.

Now Michael's head comes down, his knees part and his hands fondle an invisible ball between them.

Abbey is alarmed. *Is Michael going to cry?* The boy's father is known to be an optimist, a man who never fails to pull sweet-smelling roses from his hat.

"Ira sent me a letter last week to the effect that — " Michael grins for a second, dropping his hands to the edge of the table, fingers crimped as though to play a tune. "He doesn't consider me his father anymore."

Michael releases the edge of the table, throwing his back against the pale vinyl cushion as though he has stepped off a cliff. "I'm only telling you, Abbey. I wanted you to know."

Abbey nods. As early as he could remember, he had dismissed his father as a good but weak man, an ignorant man to be treated lightly.

"Who's replaced you?"

"Ira's leader. Rinpoche he's called. A sort of madman. With some redeeming qualities. He cares for Ira."

Abbey contemplates his son-in-law, head thrust forward, revealing one ruddy fold from chin to neck. "Given what you've told me, perhaps I shouldn't visit."

"I didn't mean that. You must talk to Ira."

To remind the boy before he dies that he has a family, I suppose. Abbey closes his eyes, tents his fingers. What he sees is a piece of the equation, hard and bright as a limb of bric-a-brac, tangible enough to be plucked. He fumbles for the silver pen in his jacket pocket, then grabs the white rectangle of napkin, pressing it open against its crease, and starts to scribble, blind, consulting only the field behind his eyeballs.

"Abbey? Can I help you?"

"Shush!" he barks, squeezing his eyes tighter as his mind gives chase to the fleeing symbols. Yet already the fluorescent light pries at the seams of his eyelids, then pours in, washing away his vision. Peeping down at what he has written, he sees that it is unintelligible, mutilated hieroglyphics in fuzzy ballpoint.

"Idiot! I was thinking!"

Michael pinches his nostrils, stares down at the napkin, which floats in the middle of the table like a raft set adrift.

"I dreamt an equation last night. A true vision." *Why tell him?* "Now it's gone."

Abbey twists out of the booth to hail the waiter, a man in a soiled tuxedo, who has already passed them twice without taking their order in his dash around the narrow restaurant.

"You're in business today?"

The waiter glares at Abbey as though he would like to spit. "What do you want?"

Abbey orders, then Michael. The waiter jams his pen point against his pad, scrawls something in one jagged motion, the soiled buttons on his chest rising almost to his chin.

"Did you notice the hands?" Abbey asks. "Filthy."

"If I could do it again —" Michael says.

His fathering or his interruption?

"I wouldn't have moved the family."

"Hindsight. I don't believe in it."

"But you're a student of history?"

"History of an entirely different scale. I guess I'm lucky. I've lived as I wanted to. I don't understand men with regrets."

⁂

The designer of this hotel room has striven to make it feel like a room in a palace. Louis Quartorze copies, a lowboy with drawer pulls shaped like crowns, a television hidden in the mahogany girth of the armoire, the gilt mirrors with panes of impeccably pure glass. Abbey catches a glimpse of himself as he passes. At home the only mirror is above the bathroom sink; one never catches oneself unawares. But in this room, it feels to him as though he is being shadowed. A couple of times he has had to jerk his neck — "Hello" — to confront his own image. "Oh you," he says and smiles at the joke on himself.

He has a secret, one no one knows except Ellen. There has been a tragedy in his life already. The woman sailing the bay alone off Truro, swept into the sea one brilliant August day.

That he had a mistress is not a secret from Ellen. She discovered them five years into their affair. A clumsy mistake on his part. Like a careless spy, he'd left Diana's letter in his jacket pocket; and Ellen, caressing the garment as she always did before sending it to the cleaners, picking its pockets for scraps of paper and other debris, withdrew the envelope.

"You can leave me," she told him that evening when he returned, "but I won't be cheap."

Ellen had read the obituary. He was certain. He had watched her turn back the page of the newspaper, sit for a moment, then turn the page again, saying nothing. No hint of pity or glee. She turned the page and folded the paper and set it on the table beside her chair and heaved herself up and said, "I must be starting supper." She had read the obituary. Yet she had said nothing, noted nothing, comforted perhaps by the thought that she had vanquished her rival years ago.

And he, as usual, as though it were any day of the week, had taken up his briefcase and set out for his office. He had waved at John, old John the doorman, in his usual way. As usual John had waved back, a single upswept motion, almost a salute. The hand never fell until Abbey had passed.

I must do the little things, he remembers thinking. At the end of the block, he had dropped his correspondence in the mailbox, had paused to listen to the door clanging shut. Then headed uphill. Steeply. Usually he enjoyed his struggle against the force of gravity, that magnificent force. That day he had thought he might give in, go tumbling backward into the avenue below.

It had been a strange feat to mourn in private, to grieve entirely by himself. It had been as though he had imagined her, or murdered her. There had been no one to whom he could confess.

At the closet he remembers he waved off the valet the night before who offered to unpack his clothes, to smooth them and brush them like a woman's hair. At that moment it had seemed unbearable to have another human being in the room for even a second, so he'd tipped the man and sent him on his way.

Now he regrets it. Usually Ellen was there to unpack his clothes, to organize them, so that the right shirt hangs beside its jacket and tie. She even laid out his socks and his shoes, so that he did not have to think about his attire, did not have to waste precious time making these choices. Every moment in his life has been reserved for thought, his time served to him like nectar.

Abbey unzips the hanging bag, waves a hand over the sleeves, across the curtain of ties. Choosing seems impossible, so he puts on the same jacket he wore the day before. Same tie, same socks. A different shirt. Certainly no one will notice.

On the telephone this morning, the boy sounds harried. Not impolite but in the middle of things. He sounds like Michael, breathless, churned by too many places to put his attention. As they speak, Abbey has an image of the boy at an editor's desk, many phones ringing. In the background, he hears others talking to the boy, male and female; a child yells something enthusiastically; a radio crackles.

He offers to meet the boy somewhere else, a private place where they can talk. But the boy does not seem to hear him. He repeats the address, says Rinpoche will be home by noon. The boy sounds robust. So it seems beside the point to ask him how he feels, is there anything he needs?

The house is larger than he expected, a Victorian painted a flat gray with maroon trim, prim as a Quaker lady. Abbey takes a moment, looking for a bell, then notices the old-fashioned key in the center of the door.

A young woman opens the door, her head wrapped in a plain cotton scarf. A serious face, lightly scowling. He is taken aback, not expecting a woman so serious, clearly with so much on her mind.

"Yes?"

"Ira's grandfather."

She frowns, her skin wrinkling. He imagines a layer as thin as fish skin. "Ira?"

"He has another name." He can't for the life of him think of it. "Come on. The sick one. I'm his grandfather."

She straightens, giving him a positively evil look. Can she be working towards enlightenment?

"Milarepa. Of course."

He nods. "He's expecting me."

She bows abruptly, somewhat satirically, he suspects. "You never know. The other day, a man in camouflage, boots, helmet, everything came looking for Rinpoche. I thought we were going to end up page one of the *Chronicle.*"

"I'm not here to do combat, just to say hello."

The light in the hallway comes from a single pane above the front door, washing only a few feet down the narrow corridor.

The young woman sails ahead, calling the boy's new name as though he might be anywhere at all.

Abbey suspects a trick. Is the boy really dying? He expected a cot, a corpse. Taking a limp hand in his, he might have given his blessing. *What is this?*

There, at the end of the corridor, a figure framed by the open doorway, a figure moving towards him, straining forward as though against a current.

"Grandpa."

How he says it. Like a young boy.

"Ira."

In the shadow he can make out only a bald head, a slight barrel-chested boy.

"I should have met you at the airport."

"Nonsense."

"We would have carried your bags."

"I found someone."

"I confused the times. When I spoke to Grandma I heard ten not eight." In his hand, a profusion of notes written on slips of paper. "I wrote it down, and forgot."

"It wouldn't have mattered. You had the time wrong anyway."

The boy nods. Not offended.

The child prodigy? The teenage assassin? Perhaps we've been fooled all along.

"Shall we just stand here?"

"Come on in the kitchen. Everyone wants to meet you."

"You're up to this?"

"I'm fine."

As they talk, they are moving down the corridor. The boy again giving the impression that it takes all his concentration to keep forward motion, as though there is some force at all times countering him midchest. His breathing is heavy. The only other sign.

Seated around the butcher-block table: two older women, wearing the same garb: white kerchief and long maroon robes; a plump woman with an oddly narrow, horsey face; a giant of a man who ducks his head as though apologizing for the space he inhabits; a tall, thin man wearing wire-rimmed glasses who strikes Abbey as being reasonable.

One of the older women gazes at Abbey with slanting eyes and smiles. "Milarepa's grandfather, how now."

The others look up from their sandwiches as they're introduced. No one offers a hand, though the slant-eyed woman rises gracefully, insists on his taking her chair.

"Hungry?" she asks.

Me or the boy?

"We're trying to get Milarepa to eat. Used to be he was a cherub, now he's a toothpick," the large man says.

The boy smiles. "I was fond of the donuts once. Check this out." He saws on the tongue of his belt, taking it in another notch, and the women hoot.

"You've made me hungry," Abbey says. "Perhaps I should set an example. Can I take you somewhere?"

The boy refuses. "Come," he says. "I want to show you the temple."

Abbey follows Ira back along the corridor, down the faded carpet, past rows of doors — *what goes on here?* — up the front staircase, which itself is concealed behind a door.

"This used to be an infirmary," Ira says.

"Whose?"

"Sisters of Mercy, I think."

"I was quarantined once. In college. There was whooping cough."

In the bed beside his, a boy coughed and coughed, spewing gobs of thick mucus, fat, gelatinous bombs, which landed on the cuff of Abbey's sheet, on his throat, his cheek, igniting these words in his feverish brain: Get out.

Lucky: a first-floor room, the window, tall as a door, left open to the night air. Abbey dove.

Within a week, that boy and all the others in that room were dead.

"Where do you sleep?" Abbey asks.

"In the dining room."

"Not enough beds?"

"Rinpoche wants me there."

In the center of things, so he won't get lost?

Across the landing, Ira presses his ear to the center line of a set of double doors, listens a moment, then draws them open, revealing to Abbey a room hung in red and yellow silks, a bordello's flaming parlor, smelling of woodsmoke and myrrh.

Swiftly the boy touches his pressed hands to his forehead, his throat, his chest, then collapses facedown on the floor.

Seated above tiers of flickering candles, a brass Buddha, cheeks bursting in petals of flame, smiles down on him.

Abbey starts. *Should I call someone?* But, shortly, with a small grunt, Ira is heaving himself up again and, unaware of his grandfather's panic, repeats the gestures, prostrating himself before the Buddha. And again.

Something rises in Abbey's stomach, a creature suddenly lifted that has been reposing in the mud, and, controlling an urge to vomit, he steps back into the hall. An image came to mind as he watched the boy. His father dropping, facedown, to the wooden floor of the *shul* as though God had chopped him between the shoulder blades. When his father rose, stripes of dust floated across his chest like bars.

The boy's hand touches his arm. "Are you all right, Grandpa?"

"Why do you do that?"

"Do what?"

"Why do you bow down to idols?"

"Not idols. Chenrezig, Buddha of Compassion."

"You haven't answered my question."

"I'm the wicked son."

"The golden calf fooled a lot of people."

"I'm bowing to the embodiment of compassion."

"Yes? Then do your grandfather a favor — cut it out."

The boy cocks his head, concentrating it seems on placing an unfamiliar sound, an unfamiliar language. A look of concern as his fingers grope the string of dark beads across his palm.

"I'd like to take a walk around the block," Abbey says. "Get a breath of fresh air."

The boy consults his watch, gold, overlarge on a flex band of peeling metal. "You want to do that while I finish some work? Then Rinpoche will be home. I'd like you to meet him."

"Work?"

The boy pulls a small notepad from his back pocket, flips open the cover, prepares to read from his list.

Abbey waves his hand, dismisses the notepad, the boy. "Another day. I think I'll return to my hotel."

Climbing into the taxi, which the boy has called for, Abbey watches a pickup swing into Ira's driveway. At the wheel, a thick-necked man wearing a crimson beret, walkie-talkie at his lips.

Their eyes meet.

"Wait!" the man barks. Leaping from his truck, he puts up his hand to halt Abbey's taxi.

The lunatic in camouflage or the Rinpoche? Abbey leans forward, touches the partition. "Ignore," he says.

* * *

"Where we going?" the cabdriver asks.

Was going to name his hotel, but another thought comes to mind. "The bridge. Golden Gate."

"You a jumper?"

A what? Oh. The man's curiosity's genuine, no alarm. "A professor."

The driver nods. "Lawyer, professor. That's what I figured. The hat, the tie. A little well-dressed for a professor."

As though his identity was still up for speculation.

"What d'ya teach?"

"Physics."

The driver shrugs, locks his gaze on the bumper ahead. "You're going to blow us all up, aren't you? Why can't you guys relax?"

Abbey feels his cheeks tighten, his forehead. *This is what it's come to. Before the war, no critics. Except God.* "Imagine playing a role in the discovery of the world, imagine spending your life tracing God's design."

The cabdriver's eyes in the rearview mirror are all pupil, fiercely bright. "That's your mistake," he says. "God didn't tell you to make the A-bomb."

Ahead the bridge's towers rise, shouldering their heavy cables, and Abbey feels a pinch in his chest, as though someone has grabbed the skin from inside. He pauses. *Wrong side.* He takes a few cautious steps, as if the walkway was made of shells. *Okay.*

The bridge is not golden, of course, but the deep-hued orange of a harvest moon. As Abbey walks, he can feel the wind, a solid presence at the small of his back as though someone were continually trying to propel him forwards.

The boy invited him back to the house for dinner, but Abbey

did not commit himself. It seems to Abbey that he and the boy have nothing to talk about, that it was in fact a mistake to have come. Either the boy has become a sort of moron thanks to his treatment and his mindless chanting or he was always a moron. A distinct possibility. It is a tragedy beyond his comprehension, and somehow a failure. Who knows what the boy would have become if everyone had behaved differently all those years ago. Who knows what the boy would become if he lived.

A gust knocks Abbey's hat from his head, sails it up and over the railing, out across the bay. Abbey watches the gray circle wobble, spin, flop this way and that, caught in a vortex of air. Above, a pack of gulls caws savagely yet cannot seem to organize to dive after the whirling hat.

Suddenly Abbey laughs. What a marvelous joke to have your hat knocked from your head, to have your hat cast for you into the San Francisco Bay. At this instant, some blunt-nosed shark might be looking up at the dull sinking object and thinking of it as dinner.

The cold air burns his cheeks, his earlobes. *I'll make it to the first tower,* he thinks. Years ago he walked across the bridge. He'd been recruiting for the lab in the desert, selling in secret the importance of the war work being done. A young scientist suggested the walk as a cover. Even if they were followed they couldn't be overheard. An earnest fellow. Quite brilliant, actually. The sort of young man he liked to encourage, to include in whatever research he was doing. Hence, a few months later, the invitation to cocktails on a summer's evening: "Come partake in the demon rum. Bring spouse or other." She came, a spouse, a slender blonde in a white silk dress. Diana. Everyone stared, and Ellen murmured, "Real class." With sincerity.

He pretended to take no notice. His mind was on the war. He

moved to shake the young man's hand, noticing his rather coarse fingers, the bony knuckles that had something in common with knees. She stood back, smiling at her husband, almost maternal, as though she had launched this man, not he her. Then their fingers touched, skin like plump petals, cloaking bone. She shook first his hand, then Ellen's, and smiled, the goddess overtaking the mother; she shone.

A week later he heard the news, the young man, Edmund, had signed up, frustrated by the oblique angle at which he contributed to the war effort. The others made jokes, were not kind. This sort of defection was not good for morale. Was he some sort of romantic? Abbey wondered. *Did she push him?* He never thought to ask.

The bridge railing is surprisingly low, shoulder high on Abbey. Easy for suicides to negotiate apparently, for the night before on the news he'd heard that a man had leapt. Now as he walks, head bowed, he looks up, half-expecting, since the thought has occurred to him, to see the bright orange police ribbons, the chalked footprints.

Ahead a woman leans out against the railing, a slight figure in a parka, the hood drawn tight around her ears. The ends of a red scarf fly out behind her, pulled by the wind like reins. And as he draws closer, he notes a tiny tube of a skirt, black stockings, hiking boots. *The suicide's wife? His girlfriend? His sister?*

"Hello," he calls out as he passes, cringing at the falseness of his cheer. But she does not respond. Perhaps she didn't hear him, and Abbey walks on, forcing a hum. Something to keep the courage up. He remembers that afternoon when he walked with Edmund, the wind so strong around the pilings they were able to sink back on it without falling. How delightful the sensation had been to rest on nothingness, cradled by the force of the wind.

Below the bay seems deserted; the sailboats and sailboards have vacated, making way for the giant steamers, the rust red and blackened tankers. It is impossible not to feel the pull of the water, to feel the lightness of the fall: one irrevocable step, one shove and you are free. Instantly Abbey calculates the velocity at which his one-hundred-and-thirty-pound body would fall. *If they could perform this calculation, they wouldn't jump. A reason to study mathematics.* They see themselves drifting like feathers or diving headfirst, executing a graceful arc. They don't understand that the body might twist and spin, that they might hit face first, facedown, slap against the hard water. They don't understand that the wave will become solid, can't imagine the flat rejection of the concrete wall. Or do they care?

That morning in a rented cottage outside Wellfleet the breeze had blown the curtains high the way a girl's skirt lifts from the backs of her thighs as she spins. He had spun Diana once in a bar in Germany, delighted to find she knew his dances. *White gloves and patent leather shoes every Wednesday afternoon.* Pearls, too, he had imagined and her mother's Chanel on her throat.

That morning Diana had propped herself on a slender elbow, observed the gently wafting curtain and said, "I'll go for a sail."

"Alone?" Only after they'd resumed their affair, after they'd become truly clandestine had he begun to feel protective as though she were his wife.

She laughed, lit her cigarette. That he could not spend the day with her was already understood. He had meetings, important consultations. "If you marry me, I won't have to sail alone."

Instead of attending his meeting that afternoon, he struck off down the beach, walking briskly, close to the water's edge, smoking his Camel, ignoring the clusters of bathers, the children tipping sand from their buckets. *If you marry me.* They hadn't discussed marriage before — before Ellen's discovering them, before her ultimatum.

Gulls cruised overhead, screaming as they dropped like girls on a roller coaster, all for show. His pants legs were rolled carefully to the ankle; he never wore a bathing suit, even on the hottest of days. His shirt, open at the collar, was his concession to the brightness of the day. The surf surrounded his feet and he thought of Prufrock. Would he ever hear the mermaids? Was he hearing one?

In the distance stood Marconi's famous tower. Strange to think of this shore as an outpost; a moment of history taking place there on the cliff as the President's greeting, buoyed by electromagnetic waves, flew across the Atlantic. Was his own personal moment of history about to take place? He had promised Ellen, but the promise did not take.

The wind was strong in his ears, making them ache even on that warm day. Somewhere his beautiful Diana held the sheet taut, the boat heeling beneath her, a wooden wave raging to break beneath the fulcrum of her slender body. Special straps held her feet so that she could lean farther and farther out, so that she could feel the whole boat against her and with her at the same time.

Where the antennae had stood, nothing was left but crumbled bits of concrete, fragments of rusted iron, a plaque that sketched the arc of Marconi's achievements. The ocean had swallowed nearly all the land on which the station had been built. He stooped to pocket a shard, all the while scolding himself: It was meaningless, this artifact.

Still, he found himself fingering the prickly lump on the way back to the cottage, and by the time he arrived, he had made up his mind to marry her.

He had waited into the evening, his mind playing a million

tricks. Why of course she hadn't gone sailing, just as he had not attended his meetings. But whom could she be meeting? And where? He had always been impatient for answers. He had always liked his scientific results by the end of the day. It was that impatience that had provoked so many brilliant solutions, so many dazzling intuitions. But he could not intuit anything that night.

At the pier, the last of the rakers were unloading the day's harvest. The men worked quickly, shoveling mussels into barrels as though stoking a fire. It was cold and the wind had picked up. Abbey went from man to man. No one had seen a woman sailing alone. He stood at the end of the pier, scanned the horizon. A band of orange bled into the night. Above it, the moon hung, a bright hook.

Glancing back, Abbey notes the woman still at the railing, still leaning heavily as though she were a trapeze artist contemplating a somersault. Should he turn around? Her tears might be caused by the wind. His own eyes are watering now. Should he stop her? Offer words of comfort? Offer to pay her cab fare? He turns, contemplating the heave of her back (is she rocking or is that the wind billowing an overlarge parka?).

Even as he approaches, he tells himself she seems too sensibly dressed for a suicide. The parka, the scarf, the sturdy boots. More sensibly dressed than he, who has lost his hat. Except (he is close enough to spot them now) for the stockings, sheer, with ladders down both calves. She must have ripped them plodding in those thick-soled boots, hiking boots (brand-new, he can see now), laced sturdily to the ankle.

Boots heavy enough to sink a small body.

Beside her at the railing, he follows her gaze downward to the sea, the color of lead. The surface, hacked and splintery. She does not seem to notice him.

"Hello there," Abbey says.

Ignoring him, she rises on her toes as though to get a closer look at something or perhaps to turn her somersault, then sinks again on her heels.

Abbey clears his throat. "Sprechen zie Deutsch?" He could move on. He could leave this woman to her fate. He has no business standing here.

The sleeve of her parka compresses almost to nothing beneath his touch, a forearm as slender as a stick. He feels a compulsion to tug as though he were a child. "Could you help an old man?"

The hood turns. He had the impression in passing her the first time that she was dark, but this woman is fair and so pale he can see inky bruises beneath her eyes, veins running down her cheeks.

"Sorry, what? I didn't hear you."

It is a voice dredged up against the speaker's will; polite, accentless, remote.

"I wondered if I might take your arm. Ferocious wind." He has to shout the last part of his speech to be heard over a gust.

She stares at him, trying to decide, he supposes, if he is angel or devil.

"It's not far, but I'm afraid of blowing over."

A glint of light in her eye as though she understands now, is willing to share the joke.

"Sure," she says. "Hold my arm."

She is a few inches taller than he, and he can feel her adjusting herself, careful not to lean as she shortens her stride to match his. Still she walks a little faster than he would like, as though to dispatch her duty as quickly as possible.

Above them, the clouds have thickened into a mass of blackened ticking, and a few long globules of rain burst on the pavement, on their cheeks.

"All hell's going to break loose," Abbey says. He is feeling remarkably cheerful. "At least you have a hood."

The woman says nothing. The fur edge of her hood prevents him from seeing her profile, from telling whether she is smiling or grimacing. Yet beneath his hand rises the heat of the living.

At the bus stop, he releases her arm, mumbles his thanks. If this were his city, he would hail her a cab in manly fashion, seat her inside, slipping a twenty to the driver. "Take her wherever she wants to go." He might invite her for a drink at his club.

A bus lumbers towards them, the bright banner across its brow proclaiming its route. He has already decided to board any bus that will take him to civilization.

"You know where you're going?" she asks.

He names his hotel, but she registers no admiration, no surprise.

"Take this to Marina, get a transfer, then change to the thirty."

He nods. He has an urge to give her something, his cane, his wallet. The line of passengers is moving, feeding into the lighted hull of the bus.

"Aren't you coming?" Abbey asks.

The woman smiles, not answering, and as Abbey is jostled forward, she pivots, striding quickly back in the direction from which they came, back across the bridge.

The apologies are made quickly, easily. The boy has no expectations of him, it seems. Is content whatever Abbey does. It is impossible to locate this boy. Like trying to pinpoint an electron.

They agree to meet tomorrow. Ira would like to show him the little shop the group runs, perhaps visit the ocean.

"Fine, fine," Abbey says. He does not talk to the boy as though he is dying. It is nearing six o'clock and Abbey is impatient to learn the worst.

He fumbles with a key in the armoire. Miraculously, the doors open, like the wings of a great bird taking off. Abbey reaches into the refrigerator beneath the TV, chooses a Scotch, but doesn't bother to pour it into a glass. He sips, his eyes on the fair-haired anchor, his moving lips. News of war, news of the shivering Earth, news of strikes and other complaints. *No news is good news.* Surely, her leap would have made it on the air. But perhaps not. Perhaps she hasn't been discovered. Perhaps no one knows. He finishes his tiny bottle, his mouth and throat warmed by the whiskey, but the rest of him still chilled. To the bone.

He sits on the edge of the bed, removes first his jacket, then his tie. Even as a boy he wore proper clothes. A fresh collar. Shoes, not boots. A tie and jacket though he was still in knickers. He made certain his clothes, not just his mind, set him apart. He is unaware that his knees are trembling until he steps out of his trousers. Stop, he wills them, holding his thighs. *Whose are these? Not his.* The caps protruding, pushing up freckled skin, the caving sides; bony knees, skinny, shaking knees. No, these knees do not belong to him, nor do the slender, spotted calves, the veined feet with their buckled toes and curving nails. *Thank God for my mind,* he thinks.

Abbey gets beneath the covers, pulling the extra pillows over his stomach, his knees, until it feels like another body atop his, pressing him down. He won't see his equation tonight. He knows this.

Still, he reaches out a hand, fumbling along the glossy surface of the side table until he finds his mask, jumbled like a girl's panties against the base of the lamp. He slips it over his eyes, sinks back, embracing those pillows. In the dark her pale face rises above his, her thin mouth and those eyes leaking dark ink trapped beneath shiny skin. She is stroking him, his forehead, his cheeks, pressing a cool palm there and there as though he were a child, as though she were remembering the boy behind this face, the boy she loved. Through her touch she is telling him something he knows he cannot grasp.

The noise is incredible, the roar of a giant vacuum cleaner punctuated by the staccato whistles of a warning signal. He throws back the covers, stumbles to the window. From above, he can see men circling an enormous machine as though it were a randy elephant.

"How long is *this* going to go on?" he says aloud, as though the figures below could hear. Somehow this is all Ellen's fault. If she had booked him in the usual place, if she had come along, if she hadn't persuaded him to make the trip. He thinks of calling to tell her this right now. It is three o'clock in the morning in the East. A chance she'll be awake. But as he is about to dial, a voice reminds him that he chose to come alone, insisted on it.

"There's a racket outside," Abbey says to the hotel operator. And he adds, because it seems as though she may not be listening, that he has an important meeting in the morning. The lie surprises him for only a moment. It is not quite a lie.

"Tried earplugs?"

"Got any?"

"You're not the first request."

But he hasn't requested, she offered. "Tell them to knock it off."

The operator hesitates, not certain whether or not he is joking. "We have no control over the situation."

"Should I eat something? Read?" He means to put the telephone down; out of sheer habit he consults her.

"I count sheep," she says.

It seems impossible from her throaty voice that she ever has trouble sleeping. Still he finds himself taking her advice, getting back into bed, giving sleep another chance. He pulls the blankets to his chin, props the pillow behind his head, turns off the light, but does not put on the mask.

On the side table is a small notebook and a silver pen. In case. Should he try again? He closes his eyes, hugs the pillow up around his ears. A trick of the mind can make that roar the ocean, but, hard as he tries, he cannot squeeze the swimming dots of light, those minnows of light, into the glowing symbols of his equation.

What comes to him, oddly, is the memory of a fight with Diana. He'd sent her the press release of his obituary, one of the alternates. *Dateline: Alamogordo, July 16, ". . . strange deaths of many famous scientists, victims of an accidental explosion in New Mexico."*

A joke.

No excuse, she told him. She was moving around her flat, shutting things, not slamming, shutting, with a deliberateness that frightened him: the window above the radiator, the lid of her jewelry box, a drawer, the mirrored wings of her vanity, the closet door. He had never seen her angrier.

You don't trust me.

It was a joke.

A test.

I'm an ass, he said. She had no idea of what he'd witnessed, why the release he'd sent was in some part true.

Do you peep in my windows, too?

Whenever I get the chance.

He wishes he could talk to her now, wishes he could tell her what he'd wanted to tell her then: that the trees stood out with such clarity, every branch, every needle, every crenellation of rock, of bark, that he had seen a light that made you see things as God had seen them when he created the heaven and earth.

And then the wind came. And the cloud rose.

He wishes he could tell her that all he had hoped for in his lifetime was to help bring an end to war, but that it now seemed more likely he and the others had sped up the end of civilization.

He wakes to the ringing telephone and reaches for the receiver. The young woman at the ashram. He recognizes the voice. Yes, he tells her. This is Milarepa's grandfather.

The girl hesitates, muffles the phone with her palm.

Still he can hear voices in the background that make it sound as though there is a large gathering in the room, a party.

"Rinpoche's going to speak to you," she says.

He has an impulse to protest, but why? Of course he will speak to Rinpoche.

"Something wrong?"

The noise at the end of the line is like the wind in a shell. It could be the ocean.

"Hello. Who's this?"

He hadn't expected a Brit. The man's enunciation as clipped as though each word has been bitten off. "Abbey. Milarepa's grandfather. Who's this?"

He can hear the man take in the information with an inhalation of breath.

"Listen, our boy took sick in the night, so we packed him off to hospital. His white blood count's sky high, but what's new, he's got cancer, hasn't he? He's conscious. They're doing tests."

Abbey feels a thudding inside his right temple. What did he expect from the guru? Soothing words? Words of wisdom? "What's going on?"

"Hard to get a straight story out of these wonkers. Two years ago they tell us Milarepa will be dead in one year. A little Tibetan magic changed that."

Insufferable man, Abbey thinks. "What do the doctors actually *say?*"

"Not rosy."

"What are your plans?"

"Don't follow."

"Your plans for Ira. You direct his life, his spiritual life. What happens next?"

"Milarepa is prepared for death."

Bastard. "The boy should come home. He has a family. He should be with them."

"Milarepa loves you, Professor. He's told me this. But Milarepa is no longer your 'boy.' He'll die where he likes."

The ward is nearly empty, the double dutch doors latched top and bottom. A television is on in the lounge, but mercifully the sound is off. Abbey shivers and pulls a small knife from his breast pocket. The knife has a graceful blade half the length of his pinkie, which he edges in and out the corners of his nails. He curls his fingers and brings them close to his face for inspection. Perfect nails, scrupulously clean, pink. Diana used to say he had a woman's hands, so slender.

He folds the blade into its silver sheath. What could you say to a dying man? If Ira were a philosopher, they could converse like Socrates to the very end.

A year ago, he'd visited a dying colleague who'd had his best idea in many years, a book on the fragility of civilization. Henri, a historian, had conversed brilliantly, as though the whole essence of his being had become focused on this important vision. *Look at McCarthy,* he'd said. *One man had the whole country terrified from the president on down. Not from facts. But psychology. Pure psychology.* On the breakfast tray sat an egg in a cup, untouched. Henri picked up his spoon and started bashing the egg on its head, its sides, reducing the shell to a cloak of sagging tiles, a buckled mosaic. *There goes civilization,* he said. *Without rational thought, we're just a mob.*

The cleanliness and light of the room blinds him at first so that he is guided by the voice, deeper and more resonant than the voice he expected. A man's voice, not a boy's, singing a chant to the empty room.

The boy is propped upright, his legs crossed on top of the covers. A bulbous mask covers his nose and mouth, linked by a plastic tube to an oxygen tank, which stands, an upended missile, on the far side of the bed.

"Hi," Abbey says. For some reason he is whispering.

The boy reaches for the crimson beret on his lap, covers his stippled scalp.

"Better," Abbey says, attempting by his tone to turn his revulsion into a joke. *How did he know?* "You want a knife?" The knife, a tiny silver fish, gleams on his open palm.

The boy waves it away. "You gave me one." The words are slightly muffled, spoken now into the misty cavity of an oxygen mask.

"Did I?"

The boy looks smaller than Abbey remembers, thinner even than the girl on the bridge. You can practically see the shapes of his bones beneath the hospital gown, the light arch of his rib cage, the peaks of his hipbones and knees.

"Ellen sends her love."

The boy nods. Polite interest. Nothing more. He is fingering a necklace of wooden beads, his lips moving slightly, and Abbey realizes with a flicker of irritation that the boy probably never stops chanting, even when he speaks.

Abbey settles in the chair beside the bed, gripping the ends of the arms as though he might decide to get up at any point. On top of the bureau, amidst a jumble of tissues and rubber gloves, sits a small figurine of a Buddha with slender arms and hands resting palms upward in the hollow of his lap.

"I feel I should tell you something about my life, but I don't know what. You don't know me."

The boy looks at him so calmly. Does he hear him?

"Are you always chanting something?"

The boy doesn't answer.

"Is it important to you to know something about your grandfather?" Which direction should he have turned that morning in Truro? Toward her waiting arms? Or the way he turned, showing her his short, freckled back, his plump buttocks, which she refused that morning to stroke?

"If my father had stayed in Poland, I'd have been a tailor." *If he'd stayed, I'd be dead. Shoved in a cold shower to drink gas, openmouthed as though it were water. Or shot, a simple lout, against a wall.* His grandfather had died in his sleep before the war, but the others, whom his father never talked about, never wept over, never mentioned, except as he inscribed their names in Hebrew in a branching chart inside the front cover of his prayer book, had perished.

"Did I ever tell you? I looked up my father's village after the war. A nice Catholic town with a big church, a neat square, an enormous cemetery covered with white marble crosses.

"So where's the Jewish ceremony? I asked. We got into the car and drove along a road to the far edge of town. There was a beautiful field, a valley that seemed to go on forever, bright bright green. It was spring.

"Stop here, I said, and I stepped out of the car, into the field. Cold morning, but clear. I began to walk, and as I did, occasionally my toe would strike something in the grass, the edge of a something poking through the grass.

"I went back to the car, and asked my driver if the cemetery had been as big as the one in town. He looked at me, surprised. 'Oh!' he said, and he gestured with hands. '*Much* much bigger.'

"Do you understand what I'm telling you? A whole history of ancestors wiped off the the Earth.

"No matter what you call yourself, you're a Jew."

The boy coughs into a fist, coughs again. A protracted wheeze.

"Water? A nurse?"

Ira points to a drawer in the side table. "Medicine," he whispers.

Abbey turns to the table behind him. The drawer rattles and sticks as though something is caught.

"This?" Abbey asks, holding up a round tin of pastilles decorated with a picture of snowcapped mountains.

Ira nods, the cough overtaking him again, filling the mask with droplets. He twists off the lid, and Abbey glimpses not bonbons but small dark pellets, the exact size and shape of rabbit turds.

Ira slips one into his mouth, then reaches for his water bottle.

"What are those?" Abbey asks.

"Herbs. From Tibet. Want one?"

"Your doctors know you're taking this stuff?"

"Yes."

Abbey watches the boy settle back on the pillows, resume his beads. The coughing has stopped.

"Perhaps I'm tiring you."

"Not really."

"I should probably go." But he does not, taking in the room again, a bland little cell, save for the Buddha with the mischievous smile.

"You can't imagine what it was like to grow up as I did. With God a continual presence. A sort of patriarch or patron who must always be appeased.

"Why does the sun come up in one place and set in another? God's will, of course. Why do the stars change position in the sky? Same answer.

"Then I read Copernicus and my life changed. No hocus-pocus there. No mystery. No shroud.

"A system of the universe that didn't require divine intervention. A system that could be *proved.*

"I ran home, enlightened, and said to my father, 'Who needs God? It's already perfect!'"

The boy's lips part beneath the mask. "How did your father take it?"

"Badly. But I could outtalk him, you see."

"He was angry?"

"Frightened. Hurt." *He didn't understand: I bore good tidings, I would free them all from fear.*

"I'm not a complete skeptic, however. You can't imagine how much I wanted to believe in nuclear spin. It sounded so right and explained so much. For me it would almost prove there was God.

"But I knew from the history of physics that something could sound right and be completely wrong.

"Then one day I was walking up the hill at 116th — you know, very steep — and suddenly, I was a molecular beam, streaming through a vacuum chamber. I was clinging to an electron of a sodium atom, then to its nucleus. I was spinning." *More like flopping.* "And I can feel the beam split as we hit the magnetic field and I know I have the answer: If I can figure out a way to isolate those beamlets, to measure the deflection of that nucleus, then I can prove there's spin.

"The experiment I devised was beautiful: it satisfied everything I wanted to see. Analyze these atoms in one field, then another field, turn your focus back, and there they are: Count them! Four peaks. Wonderful.

"I ran into the hallway. I wanted to grab someone. I wanted to shout: 'The spin of nuclear sodium is 3/2!' I was the only person in the world who knew this." *The only person except God.*

Abbey plucks open the little knife in his hand, presses his forefinger against the sharp edge. "I had a dream the other night. An equation that has eluded me my entire life. And on waking — poof. Nothing. And now I don't know whether to believe or not. Is your grandfather a genius or a fool?"

He means this to be a joke and means to grin, but even as he says it he looks over at the boy, whose eyes have closed, who with the strange mask over his face resembles an astronaut, sleeping, weightless, in his chamber. *What am I babbling about? The boy is going to die.*

Milarepa is breathing, his mind filled with nothing but the endless breath, the eternal spinning of breath as though he were breathing an endless satin ribbon unspooling from a wheel, a wheel of breath turning and he turns with it, carried on that wheel. Phat! *he exhales, shattering it all.*

He opens his eyes and there is an old man seated beside his bed, a navy beret turning beneath his fingers like a wheel.

The old man nods. "Hello."

Grandpa.

"I'm ashamed."

Why?

"It shouldn't be you."

He would like to tell the old man that it didn't matter now. He would like to tell the old man that what he spoke of was like the white fringe of foam at the lip of a wave. He, Milarepa, was trying to navigate along the bottom of the sea. The foam welled up and broke on the shore and disappeared into the sand, but he was going to swim on and on through a thousand lifetimes or more, this was what Rinpoche said and this is what he believed.

Already sound was transformed and he was listening for echoes, for shrieks coming back to him in the dark, steering him along his path. He could not pretend to listen to the old man, he could not pretend anymore, so he struggled to tell the old man what he knew, watching the silvery bubbles floating upward, hoping they carried light.

"Grandpa, I'm not afraid. I've taken a vow. To be reborn until the end of suffering."

What can Abbey say? Though he has seen things that others have not seen, has intuited the strange workings of the nucleus, he does not know how the spirit works. He cannot lecture his grandson on this. He opens his mouth — *pink radiant shell* — and closes it, closes the old shell of flesh and bone, closes the old cavity. He swallows. Perhaps his grandson knows something. He cannot say. Perhaps. He is the dying man today. He seems to know something.

Light pours into the room from one square window, bleaching the bedsheets, the boy, forcing Abbey to squint. In his mind's eye Diana is laughing in that cello way of hers, a bow bouncing and stroking low across the strings.

What is it that amuses her? Does she know that, though he has spurned her, she will always be his? Or has she discovered true joy in being free?

She doesn't know what's coming, doesn't sense movement, doesn't panic at all as the wind changes and a heavy wing unfolds, sweeping her in its path.

No time for thought or prayer.

Like his father, who, alone in his store one winter's morning, fell to his knees, touched his forehead to the floor. Almighty God.

Abbey reaches for Ira's hand. He wants to shake hands. Man to man. But when his fingers reach Ira's, something happens. Abbey's two hands hold Ira's fingers. Abbey is kissing those fingers. He can feel their roughness on his lips.

Ridiculous, Abbey thinks.

He lets go of the hand, backs away, wiping his eyes. *I'm drunk,* he thinks, but he takes his grandson's handkerchief, nodding curtly, blowing sharply, as he turns for the door.

Abbey stands in the shade beneath the hospital canopy, hesitating before he steps into the brilliant sunshine. His head feels wobbly, as though his neck has turned to string, and he leans his weight on his cane.

Delirious cries of a clarinet blast from a set of loudspeakers atop an RV, mix with the shouts of gulls, and Abbey spots, too late, a young man, all in black, black fedora, black coat, black trousers, black shoes, striding towards him.

Lubavitcher? Here?

He steps back instinctively, steps out of the young man's path, but already the young man is before him, a pale hand outstretched.

"Are you a Jew?"

Abbey taps his cane on the pavement, ignoring the proffered hand. "I am."

"May I ask if you've put on *tefillin* this morning?"

"I've been in the hospital. A visitor."

"Sorry."

A young man his grandson's age, but in place of his grandson's smooth chin an untidy beard, dense at its center, teased red cilia at the ends, a cheap fake pasted on the chin and up the sideburns as though it is held in place with a strand of elastic running behind the ears. At any point, the wearer might pull it off to reveal his true identity.

"Why does a young man turn to religion in this day and age?"

The boy stares at Abbey, dark eyes bright behind thick lenses. "The Rebbe says each time you put on *tefillin*"— he's not going to lose an opportunity, Abbey thinks — "you make the Earth a more hospitable place for the Messiah."

"What do you expect when *He* arrives?"

The boy pushes up the brim of his heavy fedora. Pimples glisten like rubies across his forehead. "The end of suffering."

"How long will it take?"

"Messiah?"

"Tefillin."

"Not long. I'll show you."

Inside the camper, the young man moves swiftly, handing him a small kit, and a card with a prayer. Then he is removing from a bag the *tefillin,* two sets of leather thongs wrapped around small leather boxes. He begins to explain.

"No need," Abbey says, but he watches the boy roll up his sleeve, place the leather strap with its boxed prayer on his left bicep — *the weak hand, the hand closest to your heart* — tugging the thong until it grips his flesh. At once the boy is in rhythm with his task, his actions fluid, sure. He is filled with confidence, with purpose, his belief as seamless as the wrapping and unwrapping of his arm, his wrist.

Abbey feels clumsy though the young man is not watching. The flesh-colored foyer smells of sweat, acid and curdled, a smell you can taste in your mouth. Someone tugs the shade cord and the blinds clatter down. *Here I am like my father, binding myself to air.* There are ten men in this room; were

Abbey to leave, the prayer would have to stop. He can feel the door handle pressed in the small of his back. He has only to reach around and let himself out.

"Don't forget your head," the boy whispers, touching his *bayit* strapped like a miner's lamp to his forehead.

Abbey nods. His heart feels hot, heavy, a vessel about to crack. *Why a young boy, O God? Why an innocent woman knocked into the sea?*

Abbey raises the circlet of leather in both hands, lowers it onto his head, a crown.

Out of the near dark, damp fingers at his nape, at his temples, as the boy divines for the spot on Abbey's forehead where the brain pulses, a naked heart, on which to place the sign of God.

This is because of what Yahweh did for me when I came out of Egypt.

Abbey fumbles for the straps at the back of his neck, tugs on them, hard, as he brings them over his shoulders. Sadness burns in his chest. In his arms and legs, a liquid fire.

Shema, Israel, Adonai eloheynu, Adonai Ehad.

He bows, first left, then right, then left again. Abbey joins the humbled, fervent men, bowing and bowing. The King of Kings is everywhere.